SAVANNAH JUSTICE

VIGILANTES FOR JUSTICE BOOK THREE

ALAN CHAPUT

Library of Congress Control Number: 2019918478

ISBN: 978-1-947295-04-9

Savannah Sleuth (Book One): Patricia's darling mother, a prominent philanthropist, drops dead, and the police are baffled by her untimely death. Patricia recruits her three friends to help her investigate what she believes is murder.

Savannah Secrets (Book Two): When Patricia Falcon's husband Trey is kidnapped, she is plunged into a complex race that crosses continents and decades and pushes her to her emotional and mental limits. Patricia's investigative talents are further challenged because her husband's ransom isn't money. Desperate to ensure the safe return of Trey, Patricia reaches out to a Catholic bishop, a local witch doctor, and two secret organizations hoping to piece together the clues she needs to find and deliver what the kidnappers want before it's too late.

AUTHOR NOTE

While I have frequently used actual Savannah places in this story, Falcon Square and Saint Gregory's Cathedral are entirely fictional places.

CHAPTER 1

It was late afternoon when the bridge club ladies and their guests wrapped up their activities and began filing out of Meredith Stanwick's restored antebellum home. Patricia Falcon lingered behind to help Meredith, her best friend for as long as Patricia had been in Savannah. But Meredith and her caterers had everything under control.

"It was a lovely party," Patricia said to Meredith.

"Thank you, it was wasn't it?" Meredith blinked her brown eyes. "I'm glad it's over for another year though."

"It's a lot of work," Patricia agreed, eyeing the state of the kitchen.

Hannah Hunter, a legacy member of the club who traced her ancestry to one of the club founders, approached with stress etched on her delicate face and dark circles under her eyes. "Pardon me, Meredith. Do you mind if I borrow Patricia?"

Patricia frowned in concern.

"Not at all. We were just finishing up." Meredith brushed a strand of black hair from her face and stepped away to another group of women hovering in the foyer.

"Patricia." Hannah gestured toward the back of the house. "Could we speak? It's a matter of urgency."

Hannah's expression and tone caused Patricia to nod and follow Hannah outside into the stifling humidity on Meredith's back patio.

A light breeze ruffled Hannah's shoulder-length blonde hair and her floral cocktail dress. They crossed the manicured lawn and sat next to each other on a teak bench in the gazebo. The sweet, jasmine-like smell of tea olives filled the air.

Hannah stared blankly at the back of Meredith's sprawling house and fidgeted with her emerald ring.

Patricia hadn't seen Hannah much since the memorial for her husband the previous fall. "How have you been holding up, Hannah?"

Hannah settled her hands in her lap and fixed her pale blue eyes on Patricia. "Cletus always took care of our finances. He had trusted advisors and invested conservatively. After he died unexpectedly, I took over managing the investments." Hannah sighed. "I think I may have made a terrible financial mistake."

"I'm sorry to hear that. What happened?"

"Right after Cletus's death, I put some money into Jackson Capital, a local private investment fund. The returns were exceptional, much better than any of my other assets. So, each quarter I added to my investment there, until now I have nearly everything I own in the fund. And the returns have continued to be exceptional. But last week, when I tried to make a substantial withdrawal, I was told my account was currently fully invested and didn't have free cash for withdrawal." Hannah paused and spun the wedding ring she still wore around and around on her finger. "I think I may have been swindled. And if so, all my savings are gone. I'm devastated."

"Are you sure? Perhaps your account really is fully invested. What was in your portfolio? What exactly were you investing in?"

"It had something to do with old automobiles. I'm ashamed to admit it, but the returns were so good I didn't ask many questions."

"You think it could be some kind of Ponzi scheme?"

"I don't know. I'm scared it is. I have no resources to investigate them, but I thought perhaps you…"

"Me?" Patricia bowed her head and looked out of the tops of her eyes in disbelief.

Hannah took a deep breath and let it out slowly. "Rumor has it you're a PI."

Patricia laughed. "That's absurd."

"Please, Patricia. Can't you do anything?"

"I'm not a PI."

A knowing smile formed on Hannah's pale face, deepening her dimples. "From what I've heard, you're a brilliant sleuth."

Which was exactly what Patricia was afraid of. You don't shoot the wife of everyone's cardiologist without gaining some notoriety in Savannah circles. Even if it was in self-defense.

Hannah's eyes turned pleading. "You've taken on murder and kidnapping. Why not this?"

Patricia shook her head. "I'm sorry, Hannah. You should go to the police with your concern."

"I went to the police. Two days later, they said they looked into it and found no evidence of a crime. They won't help me. No one will. You're my only hope." Hannah took Patricia's hand. "I'm desperate, Patricia."

Patricia looked away from Hannah's pleading gaze. It was probably nothing. Perhaps she could have a look into it and ease poor Hannah's mind. But after murder and then kidnapping, Trey and Patricia had both decided perhaps Patricia's work with the women's shelter was enough excitement in their lives. Should she really jump into something so soon if she didn't have to?

"I made a good profit on my investment," Hannah pressed on. "Help me get my money out, and I'll contribute half the profit to the charity of your choice. We're talking hundreds of thousands."

Patricia glanced down at the burn scars on her arms and thought of the burn unit currently being built. And there was the shelter her mama used to support. They could use a renovated play yard for the children, maybe even a better kitchen to serve the meals. Patricia eased her head back and exhaled. She supposed she could run this investment problem by Meredith.

"Do you have records? Statements?"

Hannah handed Patricia a manila folder. "Everything's in there. Right from the beginning."

Patricia scanned the contents. "Looks like Jackson Capital got just under five million from you."

"Unfortunately." Hannah's eyes moistened. "Please. I need a miracle."

Patricia chewed on her lower lip for a moment. "Okay. As I said, I'm not a PI, but I have some connections. I'll look into it."

THAT EVENING, PATRICIA AND TREY DINED IN THE FRONT salon of The Olde Pink House restaurant. Antique portraits gave the room a gentle grace. They both ordered scored flounder, a house specialty.

Patricia nibbled on a cheese straw while they waited for their meals. She hadn't had a chance to look more closely through Hannah's folder yet, but she'd bet Trey knew a thing or two about Jackson Capital.

"How was your bridge party?" Trey asked.

"Unusually interesting." She raised an eyebrow. "Have you heard of Jackson Capital?"

"I have. In fact, we're investors. Great returns. Why?"

Patricia straightened. "We invest there? So does Hannah Hunter. She told me she couldn't make a withdrawal."

"I'm not surprised. It's not intended to be a liquid investment." Trey picked up his wineglass and took a sip. "I like this wine. I'm glad we took a chance on it."

Patricia swirled the sauvignon blanc in her glass and took a taste. "Yes. It's very smooth." She relaxed back in her chair. "So, why isn't Jackson Capital liquid?"

"The fund invests in rare automobiles. Maywood Jackson, the fund manager, has acquired quite a distinguished portfolio of collectible vehicles. If I recall correctly, they've appreciated just over fifteen percent per year for the past decade, far outpacing any other investment asset. These are long-term investments, so they discourage client cash outs."

"Doesn't that worry you?"

"Not at all. The Jackson family is well-established here and absolutely reliable. I went to Country Day with Maywood," he said, referring to elite private prep school Savannah Country Day School, which had served the wealthy families of Savannah for decades. "We've done business together for years."

Servers brought their entrees and the waiter replenished their wine.

Patricia picked up her fish knife and separated a section of flounder. "So, how does Hannah get her money out of the fund?"

"She doesn't."

"Nothing?"

"There's a small cash distribution at the end of each year."

Patricia frowned. "There's got to be a way to cash out."

"As I said, it's a long-term investment. Buy and hold. Hannah's investment is safe, but if she wants to liquidate, she can sell her participation units to another investor. In fact, I wouldn't mind putting more money in Jackson Capital."

"Does that mean you'd give her the current value of her investment?" Patricia asked.

"Yes," Trey said. "But if Hannah wants to retain the investment and just needs cash, she can take out a bank loan and use her Jackson Capital participation certificates as collateral. Loan rates would be well below the rate of return on her participation units."

"That's good to hear." She couldn't wait to tell Hannah.

Trey checked his cellphone, returned it to the tabletop, then raised his wineglass. "To swift resolution of problems big and small."

"Speaking of which," Patricia said. "Did you notice the square-chinned guy in the corner has been taking a great interest in us?"

Trey winked. "I'm running his photo through our facial recognition program as we speak."

Coming into the kitchen the following morning, Patricia inhaled the enticing aroma of the coffee Trey had brewed for her before he left for work. She poured black coffee into a mug and headed to the kitchen table.

Just as she passed the back door, a fluffy gray and white cat bolted from the edge of the patio.

Patricia gasped. Heart pounding from the surprise, she went outside, then stooped and peered more closely at the dense azalea bush the cat had disappeared into but couldn't see the feline. Movement on her left caught her eye, but it was the sweet hummingbird that often visited her tea olive blossoms. She hoped the cat hadn't been after the humming-bird. Where did the cat come from? She wondered if it belonged to one of her neighbors, but she didn't recall seeing a collar. Anyway, the feline was long gone. Or was it? There hadn't been rain for days. She worried the poor thing might be thirsty.

Patricia returned to the kitchen, drew some water and left a water bowl on the patio.

As Patricia straightened, she admired the shimmering

sunbeams that had penetrated the tree canopy and now danced over the backyard. Jasmine scented the warm air.

Around nine, Patricia called Meredith. "What do you know about Jackson Capital?"

"An excellent investment. Maywood Jackson, the fund manager, is a financial wizard and very selective about who he allows to participate. If you get invited, jump on it."

"I know it's probably nothing, but Hannah Hunter is having second thoughts about investing there. She asked me for help. I know you think it's a good investment. So does Trey. But I thought it wouldn't hurt if we take a quick look and confirm the money is in safe hands. It'll be a quick easy job. You game?"

"Sure."

After talking with Meredith, Patricia drove to Isabel Alton's law office to sign the final papers on the recently approved Snyder Burn Center, which was funded by Patricia's mother's estate and named after her.

Isabel, dressed in a black suit, her gray hair pulled back, came around the desk her esteemed father and Patricia's revered friend had once occupied. After greeting Patricia with cheek kisses made awkward by Isabel's height, Isabel gestured for Patricia to be seated in one of the two guest chairs positioned in front of an antique, black marble fireplace.

"Coffee?" Isabel asked.

"Yes, please." Patricia sat on the soft leather chair with Isabel facing her. "How's your father doing?"

"He's taking it easy." Isabel poured coffee for both of them and placed the china cups on the thick glass table between them, then sat. "He's as mentally sharp as ever, though the chemo and radiation are hard on him. He's tired all the time. I consult with him on legal matters and Coalition business to keep him mentally involved, but his body isn't what it used to be." Isabel paused and looked around.

Patricia reached for her coffee.

"You know, Patricia, I feel like a fraud using his office, but he insists our clients need to see me in here now that I'm the managing partner. Personally, I don't see that it matters."

"I'm sure he appreciates you following his advice." Patricia took a sip of coffee.

"I know it makes him happy and that's what's important at this point. I'm even using his heirloom coffee service and china."

Patricia looked at the china cup in front of her and nodded. "Very thoughtful of you."

"Thank you." Isabel beamed. "I have papers for you to sign."

"Is everything in order?"

"Yes." Isabel opened a burgundy leather portfolio. "Everything seems to be as we requested. You'll finance the construction, then once a certificate of occupancy is issued, Falcon Memorial will take title of the Henrietta Snyder Burn Center and be responsible for all operational costs. All we need is your signature." Isabel passed the open portfolio and a pen to Patricia. "This is a much-needed facility for Savannah. It's a wonderful thing you're doing."

A feeling of pride swelled as Patricia signed the documents. "It's a big step for the community," Patricia said.

"And a lovely tribute to your mother." Isabel notarized the signature.

. . .

As they walked back to the lobby, Patricia paused and turned to Isabel. "Have you heard of Jackson Capital?"

"Sure. It's an extraordinarily innovative concept-fractionalizing rare automobiles. Outstanding rates of return."

"So, you wouldn't hesitate to invest in it?"

"Already have. Quite some time ago."

"Have you ever tried to get your money out?"

"I keep a small cash balance," Isabel replied. "But I've never tapped it. Why?"

"Just curious."

Once home, Patricia scoured the investment records Hannah had provided. They included a glossy prospectus for Jackson Capital, with what appeared to be full and highly detailed disclosure, photos of several vintage automobiles, and an annual report listing assets and the appraised value of each of the 130 vehicles owned by the master fund. There was also a copy of Hannah's initial investment contract covering a pool of seven automobiles, monthly statements that documented Hannah's additional investments, and the monthly capital appreciation credited to her account. Everything was there, and it all seemed to add up.

Patricia set aside the records and powered up her laptop. A general search on Jackson Capital provided nothing but positive articles lauding the innovative fund and its brilliant manager. A search of local criminal records only yielded a couple of traffic tickets for Maywood over the past ten years. She checked the County Auditor's online file for possible judgments or defaults, finding none. When she visited the Georgia Secretary of State's website and did an investment adviser search, she found no disciplinary action involving Maywood Jackson or his fund. She had similar results when she checked the federal SEC website.

Patricia sat back and racked her brain. What had she missed? Of course. She hadn't checked personal and business credit ratings. Using Trey's business account, she checked Maywood's credit report and found it to be outstanding, as was the business credit report for Jackson Capital LLC.

She had to face it; Jackson Capital appeared completely legitimate. When she had time, she'd verify the assets. She texted Hannah.

PF: Lunch tomorrow at Cohen's?

HH: Sure. Any news on Jackson Capital?

PF: We'll talk tomorrow

HH: Bad news?

PF: Good news. Sleep well.

HH: So you found a way for me to get my money out?

Patricia chewed her bottom lip, hoping Hannah would be willing to wait six more months to do that.

CHAPTER 3

The following morning, Patricia sat cross-legged at the kitchen table dressed in comfortable pink sweats, once again combing over the information on Jackson Capital.

Patricia looked up and smiled as Trey strode into the kitchen. He looked sexy in his trim black suit.

He returned the smile, then came over to the table, leaned down and kissed her on the forehead. The touch of his soft lips sent a pleasant shiver through her.

"Thank you," she said, looking into his eyes.

Trey winked.

Midmorning, Patricia, now wearing a cantaloupe Lilly Pulitzer shift, met with the architects designing the Snyder Burn Center to review their preliminary plans. She had nothing to contribute to the medical details, but wanted to confirm there were adequate onsite facilities for families of patients to stay at the hospital with their loved ones. Because of her own experience, she also wanted at least one high-security patient room.

The architects led her through the patient experience from admissions, to treatment, to recovery and discharge. At each stage, the architects had designed a facility that assured exceptional patient comfort without compromising patient care.

They then led her through the relatives' experience as well as the medical providers' routine, from arrival, to treatment, to the end of day. Again per her wishes, the designers had sought to maximize caregiver comfort.

She left the meeting satisfied the architects had met her wishes.

Patricia arrived at Cohen's Retreat on time for her lunch meeting. Hannah, wearing a lemon floral shirt dress, arrived moments later. The sparkle in her pale blue eyes matched the smile that deepened her dimples.

The greeter showed them to a corner table in the main dining room. They ordered beverages and salads.

After their drinks arrived, an expectant look crossed Hannah's pixie face. "You said you had good news?"

"As far as I can tell, Jackson Capital is legitimate. There's no apparent fraud."

"Then I can get my money?"

"I'm afraid it's not that kind of investment."

Hannah fixed eyes on Patricia. "That's not good news."

"Your investment bought a portion of a fleet of rare automobiles. Until one of those automobiles is sold, you have no free cash in your account. Your investment contract specifies one car will be sold at the end of each year, and your share of the cash proceeds will be credited to your account. It's summer so you still have six months to go. The good news is Jackson Capital is so well regarded you can probably sell your participation certificate to another investor. In fact,

Trey said he might be interested. But if you don't want to sell to another investor, you can use your investment certificate as collateral for a personal bank loan, one that will cost you much less than you'd lose if you withdrew your investment."

The server brought their salads.

"So, thanks to that scoundrel Maywood, I have to take out a bank loan to meet my expenses?" Hannah asked in a crisp voice.

"Did you know this fund was designed to be a long-term investment?"

Hannah nodded.

Patricia stared at Hannah, then looked down and took a bite from her Caesar salad. After her mouth cleared, Patricia asked, "What's wrong with a bank loan?"

"Nothing. Except I wish I had realized this before I invested. The loan interest will cut into my profit. But I guess I will have to do that immediately. I have no choice."

"Then why are you so upset?"

"Because Jackson Capital won't give me *my* money. That's just plain wrong."

"In what way is it wrong?"

Hannah's cheeks flushed. "It's my money."

"You gave them your money to invest in rare automobiles, which is precisely what they did. Your money is no longer money. It's now a piece of a rare car."

"I'm sorry if I sound dense. I guess I misunderstood what this investment was. I was too focused on that big rate of return."

"Well, because of that big rate of return over the past year, you can borrow a lot more money than you could have borrowed with any other investment."

"I know, Patricia. I really do." Hannah scrunched her eyes. "But it seems fundamentally wrong to have so much money in my account and not be able to put my hands on it."

"It's not money until one of the automobiles is sold, Hannah. Right now, it's the book value of an asset. It's like buying a home. If your home goes up in value, you can't realize that appreciation until you sell the house or borrow money on an increased valued asset."

"So, you're not going to do anything?"

"Is everything all right, Hannah? Why do you need access to so much capital right now? Are you in trouble?"

Hannah cast her eyes down.

"You can tell me. Are you all right?"

"No. Yes. Well, I have debts that need to be paid right now."

"What kind of debts?"

Hannah's eyes darted around the restaurant before her chin tucked down. "A gambling debt," she muttered so quietly Patricia almost didn't hear it.

Patricia inhaled in surprise, but quickly covered it. "A five-million-dollar debt?"

"Gosh no." Hannah grimaced. "But big enough to be trouble. *Big* trouble if I don't pay it right now."

They sat in silence for a moment, then Hannah leaned forward. "I bet Maywood pays salaries to himself and his staff. Where does that money come from? And why can't I have some of it?"

"I don't know."

"Well, maybe you should. Maybe *we* should."

"Maywood Jackson is an upstanding citizen. I can't cast aspersions on him by investigating him when he's done nothing wrong. I'm afraid I'm not going any further on this."

"Well, I am."

Patricia straightened. "What does that mean?"

"It means I'm going to the newspapers with this story. Maybe they can talk some sense into Maywood."

Patricia clenched her jaw. "Look, Hannah. Any journalist

worth his or her salt is going to research everything I did and conclusively find it's a reputable investment. If there's no story, there's no story. Also, you'd be shooting yourself in the foot."

"How so?"

"Well, firstly, the fact a Savannah socialite has a gambling debt she can't pay seems to be the bigger story." Patricia winced apologetically at having to be so candid. "But more than that, if the investors get shaky and lose confidence, then the perceived value of the automobiles will go down and none of you will get your returns. Is that what you're willing to risk?"

"Then help me."

"How?"

"Find something. Anything I can use to persuade Maywood to get my cash out. Everyone else can stay in. I don't care. But I want out."

Patricia took a breath, held it for a moment trying to calm, then slowly exhaled. "There's nothing to help with."

"Final word?"

"Final."

Hannah threw her napkin on the table and shot up. "Maywood is going to pay. One way or the other, he's going to pay. Big time." She turned and stormed out of the restaurant.

As soon as Hannah was out of sight, Patricia texted Trey.

PF: Hannah definitely wants out. Why don't you contact Maywood about buying Hannah's certificates?

CHAPTER 4

Salon Li, Savannah's most exclusive hair salon, was discretely located in a corner suite on the sixth floor of the Hyatt Regency. Facing westward, the suite commanded an unobstructed view of the sunset over the Savannah River.

Though the salon had a number of talented stylists, Ken Li, the owner, only took one appointment a day, and it was always exactly timed to take full advantage of the setting sun's glow on the Savannah River.

Patricia arrived at the hotel at eight-thirty, a bit late in the day, but anticipating yet another spectacular view while Ken coiffed her hair. As the elevator rose to the sixth floor, she fondly recalled his assent from new immigrant to tycoon and mulled why a man of his wealth and influence continued to style hair.

Over the years, his back had curved and his fingers had swollen with arthritis. "Why do you still do hair?" she'd asked him just last month.

He'd smiled and said, "Sophia Loren said, 'Nothing makes a woman more beautiful than the belief that she is beautiful.'"

Ken gestured to her. "Helping women believe they are beautiful is my life's work."

Ken had been doing her hair for more than twenty years, and she was positive she was the one getting the greater measure of joy.

Exiting the elevator, she walked to the end of the hall. As usual, the red door was open. She stepped into the softly lit, sandalwood-scented lobby. The teak walls, columned counter, red silk upholstered sofas, floral arrangements, and soft Chinese classical music all made Patricia feel as though she was in an Asian temple.

A woman she recognized but couldn't place was at the reception desk, checking out.

Patricia settled on a sofa and picked up a copy of *Garden & Gun* magazine.

"What do you mean my card didn't go through?" the woman said to the receptionist in a nervous tone. She took the rejected card, rummaged in her oversized purse, then pulled out another credit card and offered it. "This is so odd. There must be a mix-up at the bank. Can you try this one?"

Lily, the receptionist, took the card, and bit her lip as she tried the card again and again. Red splotches formed on Lily's cheeks. Eventually she returned the woman's card. "I'm sorry. This one didn't go through either."

"Try again. This is ridiculous," the woman grumbled, and looked around.

Patricia ducked behind her magazine.

"I'm so sorry." Lily's voice warbled like she was on the verge of tears. "Do you want me to bill you?"

"Do whatever you want," the woman snapped. She took the card and tossed it into her purse. "And cancel my next appointment. I'm through with you, your employer, and … I'm just through, period."

Dumbfounded, Patricia watched as the customer stormed

out, leaving poor Lily in tears. As soon as the woman was gone, Lily turned to Patricia. "I'll let Mr. Li know you're here." Lily dabbed her eyes, then stood. "Would you care for a beverage?"

As a long-term client, Patricia understood that beverage included champagne, but after the rude display of staff mistreatment she just witnessed, Patricia didn't feel like celebrating. "I'll pass but thank you."

"I'll go tell Mr. Li you're here and get the washbasin ready." Lily left.

Moments later, Ken Li, a diminutive man, entered and bowed.

Patricia acknowledged his courtesy.

"I'm so sorry you had to endure that unpleasantry. Shall we?" Li gestured to the corner where his wash station was. Lily stood ready to wash Patricia's hair with the special shampoo Ken Li imported from China. A secret formula of soaps originally concocted for the Empress Dowager Cixi.

After the wash, Patricia settled into Ken Li's styling chair. The sky had just enough clouds to promise a magnificent sunset, and the sun was just over the Talmadge Bridge.

"Your previous client. I know her face, but I can't place her."

"That was Abigail Jackson."

Patricia bolted upright. *Maywood's wife.*

CHAPTER 5

*P*atricia immediately texted Trey.

PF: Don't invest any more in Jackson Capital.

TF: Why?

PF: I'll explain over dinner.

They met at Garibaldi's for a late dinner, where they were seated at a leather sectional in the dining area of the bar, an elegant room of mahogany and mirrors. A massive crystal chandelier provided light. Trey ordered salmon with asiago sauce. Patricia selected seared scallops with country ham risotto.

After the waiter left, Trey leaned forward. "That was a provoking text on Jackson Capital. What's going on?"

"How much do we have invested in Jackson Capital?" she asked.

Trey looked up at the ornate tin ceiling as he thought for a moment. "I think we put in a hundred thousand." He rubbed his forehead. "Though it might be two hundred." He shook his head. "I don't really recall. Why?"

"Two of Maywood's wife's credit cards failed at Ken Li's salon today."

"I know Hannah's situation is troubling you, but I hardly think Abigail's credit card problems are a reflection of the health of Jackson Capital." Trey took a sip of his chardonnay. "Jackson Capital's financials are based on hard assets. As for Abigail, she could have maxed out her cards. I don't know about her spending habits, but Maywood is well-known as a lavish spender," he added thoughtfully.

"You've seen Jackson Capital's fleet of rare automobiles?"

"Yes."

"Recently?"

"Not in the last year."

"Well, until we know more, I don't think we should increase our investment in Jackson Capital."

"Agreed."

Their entrees arrived and talk drifted to their daughter, Hayley.

"Considering my kidnapping experience last year," Trey said, "I think we should accelerate Hayley's threat training later this summer when she gets back home from forensic training."

"What exactly do you have in mind?"

"Advanced awareness training would be a good start."

Patricia nodded. "Good idea. It's long overdue."

"I agree, especially after your Paris incident with your mother's killer and my being held hostage. I think she has a good idea of the magnitude of the threats our family face and her vulnerability."

"Are you going to use Simon for the training?"

"I'll give him the lead, but I think we all should participate."

"I'm game."

As soon as Patricia came into the kitchen the following morning, she noticed two cats sleeping on the back patio. Beautiful cats. Fluffy, long-haired felines that looked like Himalayans. One looked like the cat she'd seen a couple of days before.

They seemed well fed. Pets? More likely they were feral. Wild cats accustomed to going wherever they wanted. Today it was Patricia's patio. She didn't mind them being there. She'd heard outdoor cats kept snakes away. Patricia poured coffee, opened her laptop and read email.

Promptly at eight, Sheila, wearing her signature long blue shirt, hair in a bun and rosy cheeked, arrived at Patricia's front door with the weekly floral arrangement for the foyer, a lavish bouquet of pale-yellow Fuji mums and asparagus ferns.

"Are you busy today?" Patricia asked as Sheila fluffed out the flowers.

"Normally I would be, but at the last minute the Jacksons cancelled on me. Now I'm stuck with several bouquets."

"Stuck?"

"They cancelled. I'm stuck."

"How rude of them not to offer compensation." Patricia picked up the foyer phone and punched in Marcy's number. "I'll check with Falcon Memorial to see if they can use them. How many bouquets?"

"Four big ones. If they want them, I can give the hospital a very attractive price."

"Hello, Marcy. My florist got stuck with some floral arrangements that would look great in the hospital lobby and waiting rooms. I told her you might be willing to take them off her hands. Is it okay if I send her over in half an hour?"

"Sure," Marcy said. "Just make sure she asks for me."

"Thank you."

After Patricia hung up, she wrote Marcy's name and department on one of her calling cards and handed it to Sheila. "Marcy will take care of everything. And bill the hospital your regular price."

"Thank you." Sheila put the card in her pocket. "This means a lot to me."

"So, what happened with the Jacksons? Did they find another florist?"

Sheila's eyes moistened. "I don't know. I've provided them flowers for years. I'd hate to lose their business."

"I'm so sorry. I'll check with Marcy later and see if she can give you a standing order."

Sheila beamed. "That would be very nice."

Once Sheila had left, Patricia called Meredith. "Do you have any open time on your schedule today?"

"How much do you need?"

"A half hour."

"How about ten?"

Before Patricia left for her appointment, she took another

look at Jackson Capital's AAA credit report. Not a single blemish. Same with Maywood's personal credit report. Abigail's report was another story. Late payments. High balances. And some recently cancelled credit cards. Why Abigail and not Maywood?

Patricia got to Meredith's bank a few minutes early.

"Good morning, Mrs. Falcon," the reed-thin receptionist said. "I'll let Ms. Stanwick know you've arrived."

Moments later, Meredith, dressed in a navy shift, came into the lobby. "Good morning, Patricia."

They embraced, then walked to Meredith's office, where they sat across from each other in an ensemble of leather chairs.

"I think the Jacksons may be having some financial troubles," Patricia said.

Meredith's dark eyebrows rose. "The Maywood Jacksons?"

"Yes."

Meredith rubbed her square chin. "Come to think of it, he's always loved throwing a party, but lately his parties have gotten more extravagant."

"Oh really? How so?"

"He flies entertainers in from Vegas on his private jet. That's got to cost a fortune."

"Where does he get the money from?"

"Until Jackson Capital took off, his father supported his lifestyle. Now, I suppose Jackson Capital does."

"If Maywood can support an outrageous lifestyle with cash from Jackson Capital, why can't Hannah take some of her money out?"

"He's entitled to a salary, however outrageous."

"Good and true, if he's outrageously profitable. If not, where does that kind of money come from?"

Meredith stared into space for a moment. "Put in that light, it's a good question."

"And why are Abigail's credit cards being cancelled?"

Meredith straightened. "Really?"

"Really. And they just cancelled a standing order for weekly floral deliveries."

"I see what you mean about financial trouble. Since so many of us are investors, it wouldn't hurt to take a closer look at the Jacksons' cash flow."

Patricia smiled. "Like you always say, 'Follow the money.'"

"I didn't originate the expression, but it's darn good advice."

"So, what do we do?"

"*You* don't do anything for now. Let me get the investigation ball rolling. I'll dig deeper into their monthly spending and try to trace where their funding comes from. I'll also look into any bank accounts Jackson Capital maintains. I wish I could audit Jackson Capital's books, but short of that, I'll try to identify who does their accounting and taxes. With any luck, it'll be an outside firm."

"I wish I could help."

"Laying this financial groundwork is just a start. Once we see what the public financial records show, we'll need to find out what's really going on inside Jackson Capital. And that's when you come in."

"How?"

"We'll figure it out when we get there." Meredith paused. "But it wouldn't hurt if you got to know Maywood socially right now. He's having a garden party on Saturday afternoon."

"We regretted the invite, citing a prior commitment, but I think perhaps we may attend."

"I agree." Meredith looked at her phone. "I'd love to

continue this discussion, but I need to get ready for my eleven o'clock meeting."

Meredith and Patricia stood, and walked to the lobby.

"You know this is going to take time," Meredith said.

"Yes. And if there is crime involved, it could become dangerous."

Meredith patted her head where she'd been shot. "We've never let a little bit of danger deter us."

CHAPTER 7

As soon as Patricia got home, she sent Hannah a text telling her they were starting an in-depth investigation and to not do anything rash until Patricia had a chance to meet with her again.

Since Patricia was going to meet Maywood on Saturday, she went back to all the web information she'd first found on him, and this time she gleaned as much personal information as she could.

His father owned a major auto franchise in Chatham Country and had prospered. Maywood was an only child and had attended Savannah Country Day School. He majored in Automotive Marketing and Management at Northwood University in Michigan before joining his father's business. Maywood's marriage to Abigail was a high society event.

The formation and astonishing growth of Jackson Capital was well documented. All in all, the public information was entirely flattering. So flattering, Patricia was suspicious. Everyone had skeletons. If Maywood had ever made any mistakes, and everybody does, his had never once appeared in the press.

Patricia's accountant Sonny Carothers stopped by midafternoon to discuss the tax aspects of the funding of the burn center. Patricia considered asking him about Jackson Capital but decided to wait until Meredith completed her forensic accounting of the firm.

Trey was home by five and over a glass of wine, she brought him up to date on her conversations with Sheila and Meredith.

"I hope it's nothing," he said. "But if there's a problem, there are no two people better suited to ferret it out than you and Meredith."

And Trey, who rarely attended parties, seemed quite open to going to Maywood's garden party.

"I'll let the Jacksons know we'd like to attend," Patricia told Trey, who was seated in his favorite chair nursing a glass of port.

"Wonderful."

Patricia took a chair next to him and settled back. "You went to school with Maywood?"

"Yes."

"What was he like back then?"

"Brilliant. Quiet." Trey took a sip of port, then returned the goblet to the leather coaster on the end table between them. "He always seemed to be trying to get out from under his overbearing father. I think that's why he went to college in Michigan."

"But he came back to Savannah and went to work for his father," Patricia said, noticing how perfectly the Baccarat crystal table lamp illuminated Trey's strong jaw, Roman nose and tapered cheeks.

"Probably an economic necessity for Maywood. But he was always looking to be his own boss, and Jackson Capital gave him that opportunity."

Trey and Patricia spent the rest of the evening in the

family room. Trey read through a legal deposition. Patricia combed through the information Hannah had provided, looking for more tantalizing tidbits on Maywood and wondering what had put a financially secure man on the path to possible fraud. In her experience, motive was a big clue. And, sometimes, motive was the key to finding irrefutable evidence.

Meredith had said Maywood was known for lavish parties. Patricia wondered what the garden party on Saturday would be like if the Jacksons were really having money problems.

CHAPTER 8

When Patricia went to the kitchen first thing Saturday morning, two bicolored cat heads peered in the lower panes of the mullioned back door. Alert eyes. Clean, fluffy fur. Patricia stepped closer to the door, slowly so as not to startle the felines.

Both cats held their positions. No fear of humans. Probably socialized at some point.

Patricia knelt, her knees cracking.

The black and white cat backed off a few inches, but his gray and white companion stayed glued to the glass. Clean eyes, ears and mouth. Alert.

Patricia tapped on the windowpane. Though both sets of ears perked up, neither cat moved. They seemed healthy. Well-fed. Probably someone had been feeding them. If so, why were they at her back door?

Patricia said a prayer for the cats, stood, then went to the coffee maker and started a new brew cycle.

Once the coffee was finished, Patricia poured a cup, sat at the kitchen table and scoured social media for posts and photos of Maywood Jackson. Neither Maywood nor Abigail had social media profiles that Patricia could find, but Maywood had plenty of admirers who'd posted selfies with him. She made a list of those names. The elaborate Jackson Capital website had scant information about Maywood.

A check of Ancestry data provided reliable birth and marriage dates, as well as lineage. Like Trey, Maywood's family had deep roots in Savannah. And roots like that meant connections. And connections often meant trust.

Patricia thought about creating a relationship map on Maywood, but decided that as a son of a local auto dealer and social icon he probably had too many contacts to make the map useful. She needed to dig deeper and discover who his closest associates were.

After lunch with Trey-crawfish *étouffée* delivered from Huey's-Patricia showered and changed into her newest Lilly Pulitzer shift, a sleeveless hot pink number that would be perfect for Maywood's garden party. She added a citrine ring that matched the flowers in the print and a rose gold Rolex previously owned by her dear mother.

On her way out the door with Trey, Patricia checked herself in the foyer mirror and, when she saw the floral arrangement, chided herself for not getting back to Marcy about placing a standing order with Sheila. A quick text message to herself assured she'd get to the matter on Monday.

Maywood's estate covered an entire city block. The antebellum home was impressive, and the expansive backyard was skirted by tall, ivy-covered brick walls. Positioned on the walls were security cameras cleverly disguised as antique gas lamps. Two men dressed in black prowled the second-floor balcony overlooking the yard.

In one corner of the yard, a string quartet performed classical music. In another corner, *Cirque du Soleil* aerialists performed. So the lavishness continued, Patricia noted.

While servers circulated with *hors d'oeuvres* and beverages, Savannah's social icons roamed the backyard like a muster of peacocks. The ladies were in an array of colorful florals and Savannah men had never been afraid of some bright bursts of pink and green here and there.

Trey led them to a large white tent spotted with high-top tables and fans that provided much needed cooled shade. Patricia took an iced tea when offered and scanned the crowd, noticing Meredith, Bishop Reilly, and Preston Somerset, as well as several other close friends.

Trey spun off to speak with a state supreme court judge he went to school with and hadn't seen for some time.

Patricia made her way through the crowd to Meredith, who was standing, thankfully, in the dense shade of a moss-draped oak and well away from the security cameras.

"So, what's the occasion?" Patricia asked Meredith.

"I don't know." Meredith took a dainty sip of champagne. "Though I doubt Maywood needs an occasion. Have you met him yet?"

"I haven't seen him in years. I'm sure he wouldn't remember me. Perhaps you could reintroduce us."

"Certainly." Meredith looked around. "I don't see him. Maybe he's inside." Meredith put her nearly full glass on an empty tray and headed for the back of the house with Patricia right behind.

The window wall panels to the great room were slid to either side, providing easy access. Like the yard, the great room was packed with guests. And, like the yard, the room had security cameras.

"There he is." Meredith nodded toward the huge built-in bar on the side of the room.

Patricia recognized Maywood from his photos. His prominent cheekbones and hollow cheeks were distinctive, as were his thin lips. Though he looked bigger and more imposing in real life. And he didn't appear to have personal security hovering close to him.

As they approached Maywood, he turned from the older man he was with, and a broad smile filled his tanned, tapered face. "Hello, Meredith. I'm so glad you could stop by." He extended his hand and they shook. "And who is this charming lady you're with?"

"Patricia, this is Maywood Jackson. Maywood, please meet Patricia Falcon."

Maywood extended his hand and Patricia took it. "Pleased to see you, Patricia. Your husband and I went to Country Day together."

"My pleasure."

"Could I interest you ladies in a drink?"

"A little champagne would be lovely," Meredith said.

Maywood turned to Patricia with an expectant look in his brown eyes.

"Champagne for me too, please," she said.

"Is Dom okay?" He snapped his fingers at the bartender, who immediately responded.

"Of course," Meredith said.

"Dom for my two friends."

The bartender removed a fresh champagne bottle and two etched crystal coupes from a chiller, placed the glasses on a silver tray and filled them.

Maywood handed one to Meredith and the other to Patricia, then toasted them with his whiskey glass. "Only the finest for my guests."

"Thank you so much." Meredith took a sip. "Outstanding."

"Pierre," he said to the bartender, "only these ladies drink from that bottle."

"Yes, sir." Pierre smiled at them and returned the capped bottle to the chiller.

"Patricia is interested in Jackson Capital," Meredith said.

"I believe your husband is already an investor."

"He is. A happy one. My mother recently passed, so I'm looking to place my inheritance. Trey mentioned Jackson Capital."

"Smart man." Maywood elevated his glass. "How can I help you?"

"Tell me about your firm."

Maywood's eyes widened. "Here? Now?"

"I could make an appointment, if you wish."

"No. That's not necessary." Maywood put his glass on the bar.

Pierre rushed to replenish it.

"No more," Maywood said to him.

Pierre returned the corked bourbon bottle to the top shelf.

"Let's discuss this in my office." Maywood gestured to the back of the room. "Would you care to join us, Meredith?"

"No, thank you. I've heard it all before. Keep your hand on your purse, Patricia." Meredith smiled, causing Maywood to guffaw, before she headed toward the backyard, champagne in hand.

As Patricia followed Maywood, she noticed a familiar face at the other end of the bar but couldn't place him.

Maywood went through one ornately decorated room after another. Security cameras monitored each room. Vaguely familiar classic oil paintings hung on the walls. Finally, he paused at a carved teak door and punched in a code Patricia immediately memorized. As Maywood gestured Patricia inside, she mentally thanked her father for developing her memory.

Just inside the room, Patricia pulled her phone from her purse. "It's Trey." She texted herself Maywood's passcode and returned the phone to her purse.

Patricia scanned the room. She'd seen a lot of offices, but

this one took the prize. Gilded walls. Gilded ceiling. Gold everywhere. A massive crystal chandelier. Maroon leather chairs. An oversized, carved mahogany desk.

Then it struck her. The familiar face at Maywood's bar was the same person who had been watching her and Trey at The Olde Pink House. Trey had run his photo through facial recognition and came up empty, but it was clearly the same person. Coincidence? Possibly, but she'd check with Trey just in case it wasn't.

Maywood pulled a high-back chair from the conference table and waited for her to sit, then sat opposite her and opened a red leather portfolio to an automotive photo. "Years ago, I noticed how stable the long-term prices were for rare automobiles."

He turned the page to show a chart of investment yields for various classes over the past fifty years. "Unlike stocks, land, and precious metals, collectible automobiles always went up. Never down. Of course, there were price swings, but they tended to correct quickly. I investigated and discovered the reason for the long-term trend was simple. Fixed supply."

He turned to a photo of a rusty sports car. "No one can make more of the old automobiles, though occasionally one might be discovered tucked away in a long-forgotten barn."

The next photo was the same car restored. "And these collectable automobiles are not only beautiful and eminently nostalgic, they are also easily recognizable symbols of great wealth. Which means if you are proud of your success, you want one or more of them. Of course, not all wealthy people are ostentatious, but enough of them are to keep demand high for the most collectable automobiles, and that keeps the prices stable and growing."

Patricia gestured toward the portfolio. "People drive those?"

"No. But many collectors keep them handy in specially built garages."

"Here in Savannah?"

"In every community where there's wealth."

Patricia surveyed the office and didn't see any cameras. She guessed they were there, just extremely well hidden. "So, how does this become an investment?"

"I bought my first classic car twenty years ago, intending to flip it once it had appreciated sufficiently."

"Like speculators do with homes."

"Exactly. The problem was the darn thing kept appreciating, and I finally realized there was no point in selling it."

"Buy and hold. Like investing in good stocks for retirement."

"Definitely buy and hold." Maywood flipped the page to a graph. "Here's a chart of the yearly Hagerty value on that first car. Also, a report by Marcel Massini, the world's leading collectable-Ferrari expert. And finally, a copy of the *Ferrari Market Letter* that confirms the data. Note that the market value growth was hardly affected by the great recession."

"Impressive."

"That was my reaction when I finally figured this all out. So, I told a few of my friends, including Trey. Of course, they didn't know the automobile business like I did, and most didn't want to spring for the full amount of a rare car. They run a million dollars or more. That was when I came up with the idea of fractionalizing the automobiles."

"How does fractionalizing work?"

"I pool investor money until I have enough to buy the next car."

"You run everything?"

"Not alone. I have a team of advisors, appraisers and accountants."

"Full time?"

"Yes."

"What kind of advisors?"

"Perhaps you've heard of Doctor Zeitfeldt? He's a noted economist and a former director of the Federal Reserve Bank in Atlanta. And there's former State Supreme Court Judge Adam Wainright. Bernie Stellman was formerly a vice president with PricewaterhouseCoopers."

She'd use those names for a relationship map. "Impressive talent. So, what exactly would I be buying?"

"You would buy participation units, which represent a factionalized piece of several automobiles."

"And if I should have need for some reason, how would I get my money out?"

Maywood winced slightly, but enough for Patricia to notice. He steepled his fingers, then threaded his fingers together into a clasp and leaned forward. "Well, it's a buy and hold investment, so your account has an asset value, but no cash value until a car is sold and the proceeds distributed to investors."

"Thank you for explaining that." Patricia swiped a loose tendril from her face, only to have it fall back. She let out a sigh and tucked the errant hair behind her ear. "When do you sell automobiles?"

"We're contractually obligated to sell one car a year. The car we sell is usually one that is"-he waved a dismissive hand in the air, as if he couldn't fathom such a thing-"*under-performing* the overall growth in value of your fleet." Maywood thumbed through the portfolio, stopping at another graph. He let out a pained sigh. "Here's a car we sold last year. You can see we made a huge profit on it. Not a bad return for an *under-performer*."

Patricia memorized the vehicle's serial number at the top of the graph. "So, over time investors will get a substantial amount of cash."

"Theoretically yes. In practice, most investors choose to immediately reinvest the cash credited to their account."

"How do you get paid?"

Maywood shot her a dirty look. "I take a one percent annual management fee from each account. Since the fleet appreciates approximately sixteen percent a year, the fee has little effect on investor returns."

He's living well beyond that. "There are a lot of automobiles in that book."

"One-hundred-thirty at last count."

"Total value?"

"You ask a lot of questions."

"I have a lot of money to invest."

"The last valuation was just over 350 million."

Huh. So, Maywood was making 3.5 million a year. From what she understood of his overhead, that probably just covered his costs. He had to be getting additional money from somewhere. "Where is this fleet?"

Maywood smirked and plucked a cigar from a humidor at the edge of his desk. He proceeded to sniff it, sliding it across his upper lip in an exaggerated manner. "In a secure warehouse."

"Can I see it?"

"I'm sure you understand, we *must* keep the location secret."

"Trey saw the fleet." She tried to play up the left-out spouse, complete with a small pout. Her high school theater teacher would have been proud.

He inspected her for a moment. "Once a year, we have an investor party at the warehouse."

"So, investors know where the warehouse is?"

"We bus them to the party in vans with the windows blacked out."

Patricia feigned shocked and impressed surprise. "Major security."

"Yes, indeed." Maywood leaned back. "Any more questions?"

"No. I think I have a much better picture."

"Would you like me to send you a prospectus?"

"Thank you." Patricia smiled the most grateful and simpering smile she could muster. "I'd like that."

When Patricia returned to the party, Meredith scurried to her. "How'd it go?"

"He answered every question," Patricia said, leading Meredith away from the crowd and far from the cameras.

Meredith stepped closer. "What do you think?"

"Just a minute." Patricia removed her phone and texted herself the vehicle identification number and the names of the three advisors. "Okay."

"So, what do you think?"

"He's very convincing." Patricia looked around to make sure no one was listening to them. "But the math doesn't come out right. His management fee will total 3.5 million this year, which I figure just covers his costs. Considering his lifestyle, something is fishy. I wish I could actually see those automobiles."

"Any idea how?"

Patricia thought for a moment. "He's got to carry insurance on them. I would imagine his insurance records would list the location. Plus, he said it was a secure warehouse, which means a security firm would be monitoring the place."

"I can check his bank records. With any luck, I'll be able to see who he's paying for insurance and security."

Patricia smiled. "It's a plan then. How are you doing digging into the Jacksons' cash flow?"

"I'm still pulling data, but on the surface it appears his personal funding is currently coming from offshore accounts. And most of those banks hate to share information."

"Maywood takes a one percent annual maintenance fee on a current assumed asset base of 350 million," Patricia said.

"He told you that?"

Patricia nodded.

"Good work. I should be able to get you Maywood's insurance and security company information tomorrow."

"That's Sunday."

"Data doesn't take the weekend off." Meredith gestured toward a sparkling fountain and small, rock-rimmed pond where a man sat perched on a stone bench. "That's Maywood's father."

Even from afar, Patricia recognized his weathered face and signature red bowtie from decades of television commercials.

"Would you like to meet him?"

"Sure."

As they approached, the elderly gentleman slowly stood and graciously tucked his cigar behind his back. "Good afternoon, Meredith. What a delight." He extended his hand and they shook.

"Andrew, I'd like you to meet Patricia Falcon. Patricia, this is Andrew Jackson."

Patricia shook his hand. "After all those television ads, I feel like I already know you."

"I get that a lot."

"Are you enjoying the party?" Patricia asked.

"Can't say that I am."

Meredith tilted her head. "Are you feeling okay, Andy?"

"I'm feeling fine. It's just that I'm a simple person and all this"-he gestured toward the crowd-"this, I don't know what to call it, is wasteful. A disgrace. In my time, we saved for a rainy day. The new generation spends like there's no tomorrow. I keep telling Woody to slow down, take his foot off the accelerator."

"Woody?" Patricia asked.

"Maywood," Meredith added.

"I raised him to be a good Catholic boy. Sent him to the best schools. He doesn't even go to Mass anymore. And those models he flies in..." Andrew gestured dismissively. "Disgusting."

Patricia and Meredith exchanged a look.

"He's doing well though," Meredith said. "Surely, you must be proud of him."

Andrew shook his head. "Success isn't measured by the size of your wallet, but rather by the size of your heart. And by that measure, he's a total failure. He wants to live with freedom, but he abuses the incredible freedoms he's been given." Andrew let out a long breath. "I tell you this, he's a big embarrassment to me. That boy's coming up for a fall. I guarantee it."

Silence hung too long.

Meredith fanned herself. "Gosh, all this humidity and talk of hubris have gotten me melting. Can we entice you indoors for some air conditioning?"

He waved them off. "Nah. I'm just fine right here."

"Pleased to have seen you." Patricia backed away.

Andrew brought the unlit cigar out from behind his back to his mouth and sat, muttering to himself.

"You know anything about Maywood and models?" Patricia asked once they were away from the pond.

Meredith shook her head. "I'd say we've got some work to do."

. . .

THAT EVENING, PATRICIA AND TREY SETTLED IN THE QUIET OF their great room. Patricia told Trey about seeing the man from The Pink House at Maywood's party and what Meredith was doing. Trey acknowledged the information, then returned to reading, while Patricia pondered the Jackson Capital organization. If something illegitimate was going on in a company of that size, Maywood wouldn't be able to do it by himself. Should Jackson Capital be a charade, there would be too many moving parts for one person to control. He'd need at least a bookkeeper or CPA to keep the illegitimate financial balls in the air. And probably a lawyer to stay ahead of regulations and examiners. He'd pay them well and keep them close. Were his accomplices the three advisors he'd mentioned? Or were those three just window dressing, and the real day-to-day managers of the fraud buried with mediocre titles and off-book compensation?

Patricia's phone chimed an incoming text from Meredith.

MS: I think we need to put a CPA on this.

PF: Why?

MS: Too many accounts. Very complicated. Above my head.

PF: Sonny Carrothers?

MS: Excellent.

PF: I'll contact him tomorrow.

MS: It's Sunday.

PF: Sonny's always available for an adventure.

CHAPTER 9

*P*atricia arrived at Goose Feathers at nine for a meet up with Sonny. He'd suggested the early time to beat the Sunday morning church rush. She looked around. He was nowhere to be seen. She got a cup of coffee and found a table.

Five minutes later, Sonny, a thin, short, stick of a man, strolled into the restaurant like he owned the place. He grabbed a pastry and a cup of coffee, crossed the room and sat across from her. "What's up, Miss Patricia?"

Patricia waited for Sonny to settle. "Meredith and I have a job for you."

"And what might that be?" Sonny's thick eyebrows arched.

"Have you heard of Jackson Capital?"

"Hasn't everyone?"

"Do you have any professional relationship with them?"

He pushed black hair from his broad brow and cocked his head. "No. Why?"

Patricia lowered her voice. "We're interested in finding out if they're legitimate."

He scooted forward on his chair. "Have you found a problem?"

"Their numbers don't add up."

His brown eyes widened. "Which numbers?"

"On the surface, their income seems to just cover their expenses."

"Could be good tax accounting." He shrugged. "Anyway, why do you care?"

"We're investors in the fund."

"Then it's a little late to be raising questions." Sonny slurped some coffee.

"Better late than never."

Sonny slathered his cinnamon roll with butter. "Okay. Where do we start?"

"From what Maywood Jackson tells me, there are a lot of assets involved in the fund. More than three hundred million worth. I thought you might know or easily locate who does their accounting. Check on professional scuttlebutt about the health of the fund. Find out what the accounting pros have to say about the risks there. That kind of stuff." Patricia signaled the waiter for more coffee. "Also, Meredith has unearthed a large number of personal accounts used by Maywood. You can pick up her information at the bank tomorrow. We want you to see if you can figure out where his income comes from and see if the numbers add up."

"Do you want me to look into Maywood's cash flow or Jackson Capital's?" Sonny took a bit of his cinnamon roll, sending a trickle of melted butter down his chin.

"Both. We suspect Maywood may be using Jackson Capital as his own piggy bank."

"That's quite an accusation." Sonny wiped his dimpled chin with a napkin. "Okay. Anything else?"

"As a matter of fact there is. Jackson Capital's business is buying and selling rare automobiles. Could you find a way to verify Jackson Capital's assets and to document those trans-actions independent of Jackson Capital?"

Sonny gazed into space for a moment, then focused on Patricia. "I think I might be able to. What's the timing on this?"

"A week or two."

Sonny nodded his curly-haired head.

Patricia consulted her phone and wrote down the serial number of the car Maywood said he had recently sold. She handed the note to Sonny. "This is the serial number of a car Jackson Capital claims to have recently sold. You can start there."

Sonny shoved the note into his shirt pocket, right behind the pocket protector. "Let's hope he and the prior owners registered their automobiles."

SHORTLY AFTER LUNCH, MEREDITH STOPPED BY PATRICIA'S home to drop off the names and addresses of a local insur-ance company and a security firm. They sat at the kitchen table over coffee and cheesecake Patricia had brought home from Goose Feathers.

"Jackson Capital has been sending monthly checks to both for years," Meredith said.

"I'll check them out tomorrow."

"How'd it go with Sonny?" Meredith forked a sliver of cheesecake.

"He's on board. Told him he could pick up the Jackson account info from you tomorrow. I gave him a week or two to pull everything together."

Meredith nodded. "Did you make any progress on Maywood's models?"

"I haven't started yet." Patricia paused for a moment. "How do you investigate something like that?"

Meredith shrugged. "I don't know. You're the sleuth."

Patricia gave Meredith a wink. "Maybe Abigail knows something about his proclivities, but I wouldn't know how to broach the subject."

"Speaking of which," Meredith said. "I didn't see Abigail at the party."

"My instinct tells me they're having marital problems. If so, she might open up about him. Do you know anything about her socially?"

Meredith shook her head. "As far as I know she keeps to herself. We could see if she's interested in coming to next month's bridge social."

"We don't even know if she plays."

"I'll check on it." Meredith fingered her hair. "Come to think of it, she's quite active in philanthropy. Maybe you could discuss the new burn center with her."

"Her credit cards just bounced. I doubt she's up to passing out money."

Meredith stared at her plate, then looked up. "I've heard she's active at St. Gregory's in the children's ministry and that she conducts a Bible study. Maybe we could reach her through one of those avenues."

Patricia tapped the table. "That's it. Bible study. I'll see if I can get on her calendar tomorrow."

Sonny called late in the afternoon. "I have an appointment with one of the principals in the CPA firm that does Jackson Capital's books."

"Someone you know?"

"Cotton McNaly. We were best friends at Benedictine Military School. He'll share whatever he knows."

CHAPTER 10

As soon as Patricia came into the kitchen Monday morning, she went to the back door to greet the cats.

On seeing her, the cats scampered in tight circles on the patio, then nudged each other with their heads. Had they spent all night in her backyard? She hoped they got everything they needed outside. They looked healthy.

Trey came into the kitchen dressed for work and gave her a morning kiss.

"The cats are back on the patio," Patricia told him.

"How about giving them some of that leftover shrimp," Trey suggested.

"I don't want them to become dependent on us for food."

"One time won't matter." He poured coffee and sat at the kitchen table. "Go ahead. Make their day."

Patricia ran water into a salad bowl, then removed some leftover grilled shrimp from the fridge, chopped them into bite-sized pieces and placed them into a bowl.

When she opened the door to put the water and food out, the cats scooted off a safe distance and stayed there until

Patricia returned to the kitchen and closed the door. Then they pounced on the bowl of shrimp bits.

She watched while they ate, bringing back childhood memories of the Maine Coon cat her family had when she was young. Good memories, tainted by the early death of her beloved pet and a lifelong desire to avoid repeating that agony.

After Trey left for work, she made afternoon appointments to speak with a partner at the local insurance company retained by Jackson Capital, and with the owner of the security firm Jackson Capital used. After several tries, she managed to get through to Abigail Jackson and arranged to take Abigail out to lunch at Gryphon at noon.

Sonny called around ten. "I just left my meeting with Jackson Capital's accounting firm."

"How'd it go?"

"When I told my friend Cotton McNaly I was interested in investing in Jackson Capital, he told me to invest somewhere else."

A shiver went through Patricia. "Did he say why?"

"He wouldn't go into details. He was being helpful, but not a snitch. My conclusion is it's likely there's something fishy at Jackson Capital."

"Good work. Anything else?"

"No, that's it for now. I just wanted to keep you up-to-date," Sonny said.

"Much appreciated," Patricia said as she ended the call.

DRESSED IN A PALE-BLUE, FLORAL SHIFT, PATRICIA ARRIVED AT Gryphon fifteen minutes early and found Abigail nursing a martini. Abigail's prominent cheeks were slightly flushed nearly matching the color of her pink sundress.

After greeting Abigail, Patricia sat. "I can't believe we

haven't met. Though, I believe we use the same hair salon, Salon Li."

"Yes. I thought you looked familiar." Abigail sipped her martini. "I'm sure you saw that ridiculous mistake with my credit cards. So embarrassing. Maywood forgot to pay them. It's all taken care of now." Abigail exhaled. "So, what can I do for you?"

"I understand you're active at Saint Gregory's."

"I've taught Bible study there for several years." Abigail popped the last olive from her drink into her mouth.

The waiter arrived to take Patricia's beverage order. She ordered tea, Abigail requested another martini.

"What's your class studying right now?"

"Hebrews. We've just started."

"I don't know much about Hebrews."

Abigail smiled. "Then why don't you join us? We meet at my house at ten on Wednesdays."

"You don't mind?"

"Oh no. Not at all. It's summer, so there's just a handful coming to class. Would you be interested?"

"I'll be there Wednesday morning. Thank you."

"Give me your email, and I'll send you the class schedule."

Patricia handed Abigail a calling card. "My email is on the card."

The waiter returned with their beverages and took their orders.

"Should I bring anything on Wednesday?"

Abigail brushed a strand of brown hair from her face. "Just your Bible."

"I really appreciate this, Abigail." Patricia took a sip of tea.

Abigail started on her second martini.

"I was at your lovely home on Saturday afternoon," Patricia said. "I'm sorry we didn't meet then."

"Oh. You mean Maywood's latest extravaganza for his whales."

"Whales?"

"His biggest investors." Abigail took another drink. "I don't attend those events. It's all people I don't know."

"I met your father-in-law."

"I'm sure he gave you an earful."

Their salads arrived and Abigail ordered a third martini.

"What did you think of Andy?"

"Not at all like his television persona. He seemed lonely. He was sitting by himself."

"I'm surprised he went. He hates Maywood almost as much as I do."

Patricia tried to hide her embarrassment that Abigail was discussing this in public. How bad did it have to be to have Abigail say this so freely to a stranger? She had to be deeply wounded. Hurting. So sad. "He did seem to disapprove of the party."

"That's the skimpy Scot in him. I swear, I think he still has the first dime he made."

Patricia took a bite of salad to provide an excuse for not answering.

"You know," Abigail said, "I think things might have been different between Maywood and I if someone else had been his father."

"How's that?"

Abigail averted her hazel eyes. "Let's just say Maywood has serious *Daddy* issues."

"I'm sorry to hear that."

"It's impossible to live with a man who is totally obsessed with outdoing his father."

Patricia shook her head. "I can't imagine."

"And his father brutally berates him at every opportunity, which drives Maywood to more and more excess.

And I'm in the middle of all this." Abigail took another gulp of her drink. "I tell you, Patricia, I'm not a happy woman."

Such a heartbreaking situation. "Is there anything I can do?"

"Yeah. You can find me another husband." With that, Abigail broke out in laughter, then covered her mouth. "Oh my. I've forgotten my manners."

The next time the waiter stopped by, Abigail ordered a triple espresso, which was promptly delivered.

AFTER LUNCH, PATRICIA MET WITH MAXWELL STERN, managing partner for Peterson Financial, the insurance company retained by Jackson Capital.

"What can I do for you, Mrs. Falcon?"

He certainly didn't waste time on chitchat.

"I'm interested in securing construction insurance for a burn center to be built at Falcon Memorial."

Maxwell, a smile on his face, leaned forward over the mahogany conference table. "We can definitely handle that."

Patricia could practically see the dollar signs spinning before his eyes. "I'm talking to several agencies."

"I can assure you, you won't find a more suitable insurer than us."

"Do you have references? Big clients I can talk to?"

"We haven't handled any hospitals. We focus our offering primarily on financial institutions."

"Are there any I could talk to?"

"River Street Bank comes to mind, and Jackson Capital. They are our two largest. I could arrange for you to speak to them about our service."

"What kind of insurance do you provide for River Street?"

"Primarily deposit insurance and theft insurance, but also key officer liability insurance."

"And Jackson Capital?"

"Property insurance."

"Just real estate?"

"And business assets," Maxwell added.

"No liability insurance?"

"No."

"Okay. Thank you for your time. I'll get back to you."

On Patricia's way to the security firm, Meredith texted.

MS: I've been going through Jackson Capital's corporate checking account. Their insurance spending doesn't add up.

PF: How?

MS: Maywood said the cars are worth 350 million?

PF: Yes.

MS: Jackson Capital isn't paying anywhere near the going insurance rate on those cars.

PF: Different agency?

MS: Probably … or no insurance. Give me a call.

Thankful for Meredith's thoroughness, Patricia punched her friend's speed dial.

"What's going on with the insurance?" Patricia asked.

"The only obvious insurance company getting checks from Jackson Capital is Peterson Financial," Meredith said. "But the checks are too small for a 350-million-dollar asset. If Peterson Financial isn't handing the insurance of the automobiles, perhaps Maywood's using a company that's not an obvious insurer. Can you scout out companies specializing in insuring rare automobiles? I'll check the names you come up with against Jackson Capital's bank records."

"Will do immediately. Anything else, Meredith?"

"No."

"Okay. I had productive meetings with Abigail and

Peterson Financial. I'm on my way to the security firm. I'll fill you in on everything after my last meeting."

"Good luck."

PATRICIA MET WITH KEN CRAIG, THE PRESIDENT OF THE security company presumably protecting Jackson Capital's property.

"I'm looking for construction security while a burn center is being built at Falcon Memorial."

"The general contractor usually handles those arrangements," Ken said, picking up his ballpoint pen. "Which contractor are you using?"

"Since I'm paying for the construction, I told them I wanted to be involved." She'd always been able to think fast when things didn't go as planned.

"Oh, pardon me, Mrs. Falcon."

"Can you handle that kind of security?"

He smiled. "Yes."

"Do you have references?"

"As many as you want."

"Who are your largest clients?"

When Ken rattled off several names, Jackson Capital wasn't among them. And based on the size of some of the companies Ken mentioned, Jackson Capital's auto warehouse would have been much larger.

"I've heard you also provide security for Jackson Capital."

Ken keyed his computer. "Yes, we do. Central monitoring for an office. Not at all the magnitude you're talking."

Well, that was interesting. "Okay. Thanks so much for your time. Please send me a quote. I'll get back to you after I review your proposal."

. . .

Shortly after Patricia returned home, Sonny called. "I've spoken to several major car collectors, and none has sold or bought a rare car from Maywood or Jackson Capital. I'm told it's a tight-knit society, and Maywood isn't a player."

Oh my goodness. "Wait. Maywood isn't a player, but he says he has 130 automobiles."

"Maybe he does, maybe he doesn't. But you know that serial number you gave me? It matches up with a registered car, but neither Maywood nor Jackson Capital have ever owned it. In fact, it's been with the same owner for the past thirty years."

Things were looking shadier by the minute. Trey needed to get out of this investment right away. "Are you sure?"

"I've seen the registration record. Some guy in Switzerland owns the car."

"Hold on for a moment. I need to get something." She put the phone down, retrieved Hannah's paperwork from the desk and shuffled through the sheets until she came to Hannah's purchase contract that listed the seven cars she'd bought an interest in. With each description were chassis/engine serial numbers. She picked up the phone. "You still there, Sonny?"

"Yeah."

"As soon as I hang up, I'm going to fax you serial numbers for seven more automobiles. Track them down as fast as you can and let me know if Maywood ever owed any of them."

"You think he's selling interests in phantom automobiles?"

"He might be."

"Then what's in his warehouse?"

"I think it's time I see those automobiles."

. . .

WHILE PATRICIA AND TREY WERE CLEANING UP THE KITCHEN after dinner that evening, Patricia brought up her concern.

"Trey, honey, we need to talk about Jackson Capital."

"Your investigation?" Trey turned on the water, rinsed a plate and put it in the dishwasher.

"No. Our investment." Patricia twisted her wedding rings. "I don't know how to tell you this." She let out a long breath. "At my request, Sonny Carothers spoke with a partner at Jackson Capital's CPA. A guy called Cotton McNaly."

"I know of him. He's reliable." Trey put another plate under the water.

"Seems Cotton went to school with Sonny. They're still close. He told Sonny to invest somewhere else."

Trey dropped the plate in the sink.

"You okay?"

He nodded, picked up the plate and placed it in the washer. "That spells trouble. If there's a problem with Jackson Capital, a lot of Savannah families could come tumbling down." Trey closed the door and turned the washer on. "I never much liked what Maywood became after the success of Jackson Capital. Too ostentatious for my taste. But when it came to rare automobiles, he seemed to know what he was doing. If there's something shady going on, a lot of people, including many of our friends, are going to take a beating."

She debated telling Trey about the car Sonny told her about, but it could have been an anomaly. She'd wait until Sonny had traced the other serial numbers.

"All I have are suspicion and hearsay. I don't know what his scheme is or who's involved in it. And I certainly don't have sufficient evidence to prove criminal activity." Patricia paused. "Do you know anything about his organization?"

Trey massaged his neck. "I've always dealt with Maywood. No one else."

"He told me he has three full-time advisors on his payroll." She checked her phone notes. "Zeitfeld, Wainright and Stellman. Do you know anything about them?"

Trey nodded. "Three of the best in their respective fields. The only one I know personally is Adam Wainright, a retired State Supreme Court judge. I spent a fair amount of time with him at the party on Saturday."

Finally, an insider who might shed light on Jackson Capital. "Do you know him well enough to probe what he knows about the inner workings of Jackson Capital?"

Trey paced the kitchen. "I can't imagine him being involved in any kind of criminal activity."

"That's not what I'm talking about. We haven't identified a crime, but if those three advisors are just window dressing, Judge Wainright is going to be relatively ignorant of the inner workings of Maywood's scheme. But he may have—"

Trey stopped in front of Patricia. He took her hand and gave a squeeze. "Adam's a very detailed-minded person. He might know something useful to your investigation. I'll have lunch with him as soon as possible and see what he's willing to share."

Progress, of sorts. "Do you know Maywood's father?"

"No, but during school Maywood spoke about him often, and never kindly."

What a shame to grow up that way. "How about Maywood's wife, Abigail?"

"Nope."

She winked at Trey. "I guess we live a sheltered life."

"From what I've heard about Maywood's life, we wouldn't want to have anything to do with that family."

"In what way?"

"Debauchery. Adultery. Excessive booze. Drugs."

"Really? I didn't see any debauchery at his garden party."

Patricia shrugged. "Just Savannah social icons, classical music and aerialists."

Trey pushed a hand through his thick, chestnut hair. "That's Maywood's public image, which is very important to him. But I'm told he flies in Vegas 'models' for smaller, more intimate parties for those investors who enjoy more skin."

"Have you been?"

Trey stepped closer and pulled Patricia into a hug. "No. I'd never go to something like that."

"Been invited?"

"Yes."

"How do you know about what goes on at these parties?"

"Some men tend to boast about such things."

"Sounds like a situation ripe for blackmail."

Trey nodded. "It wouldn't be the first time."

Patricia shook her head. "I can't believe he's doing this in Savannah and I haven't heard about it."

He again took her hand. "It occurs everywhere, Patsy."

"I don't like the smell of this, Trey." She gazed into his eyes. "How do we get our money out?"

"Tomorrow, I'll tell Maywood to stop reinvesting our proceeds."

"Those proceeds are just numbers on a page."

"There's also the fund's office building and the warehouse where the automobiles are stored. And there are the automobiles themselves."

"If they exist."

"I've seen them."

"All 130 of them?"

"Yeah, probably that many. And I've seen the seven automobiles we're part owners of. Really nice, high-value automobiles. If Maywood is forced to liquidate, there should be a high payback on our investment."

"But why can't we find records of insurance and security for all those automobiles?"

"Didn't Meredith say Jackson Capital's accounts are too complex for her to decipher?"

Patricia rolled her eyes. "Yes. I fear it needs the experience of a forensic accountant. Meredith is as sharp as they come, but she has a full-time job, and uncovering the anomalies are probably like finding a needle in a haystack."

"That's going to take time."

"That's what I'm afraid of." She rubbed her forehead. She had to tell Trey about what Sonny discovered. "Yesterday, I gave Sonny the serial number of one of Maywood's automobiles and asked Sonny to check the ownership. He got back to me this afternoon with the surprising news Maywood didn't own the car. Never did. The car has been with the same owner for the past thirty years."

"Any chance Sonny got it wrong?"

Patricia raised an eyebrow. "Sonny doesn't make mistakes of fact. But just to confirm his finding, I faxed him the serial numbers for the seven automobiles Hannah invested in."

"And?"

"I just sent him the fax this afternoon."

"It sounds like you're on the right track, Patsy. With the methodical way you're picking at Maywood's organization, if there's fraud, you'll find it."

"My instinct tells me something's fishy."

Trey gave her another hug. "Trust your instincts."

CHAPTER 11

Patricia met with Simon, her longtime security consultant and occasional bodyguard, Tuesday morning over coffee at The Foundry and filled him in on what she knew so far.

"My next step is to verify those investment automobiles actually exist. I'll have to pressure Maywood to let me see them before I invest my mother's inheritance."

"You plan to invest?"

"Not at all." She twisted her coffee cup. "But I figure he'll be more agreeable if he senses a big payday."

"Good idea." Simon sat back in his chair and fixed his brown eyes on her. "How can I help?"

"I'll need a wearable tracking device."

He canted his head. "Why?"

"He keeps the warehouse location secret."

"Okay. I still have that string of pearls I used with Hayley last fall. You know, the necklace with built-in tracking."

"Can you bring it by my house later today?"

"Sure." He ran his fingers through his long dark hair. "Anything else?"

Patricia wrapped her hands around her coffee cup, enjoying the warmth. "Once I locate the automobiles, if they even exist, I want to get into the storage facility to count and verify their true identity. I presume there could be some sophisticated security inside and out. So I need two things. First, I need a way to ferret out the warehouse security details before going in, and then I need an entry team to get me inside."

"I have two suggestions." Simon leaned forward. "First, I recommend you use reconnaissance robotics to identify the imbedded security details. And second, I suggest you use Timnit Araya to get in."

Patricia paused. She hadn't expected Simon to hand off an assignment like this. "Why Timnit? We brought her on to help us with transporting abuse victims. This is a criminal investigation."

"She had a reputation in the military as an excellent infiltrator. Plus, she can help you plan the mission. And if the two of you need more personnel, she'll know exactly who to bring in. She's exceptionally well trained. You should use her expertise wherever you can."

"Do you think she'd be willing to do something like this?"

"She'd jump at the chance."

Patricia wondered how he could speak so assuredly. "Should I ask Timnit to get the robotics as well?"

"Yes. If you want the best." Simon glanced at his flat-black watch, then pulled a cell phone from the thigh pocket of his black cargo pants. "Do you want me to call her? She might be able to join us right now."

"Sure."

Fifteen minutes later, Timnit, dressed in a loose black shirt and black skinny jeans, strode confidently into the coffee shop, pushed her aviator sunglasses into her gray-streaked hair, and looked around.

Seated in a dark corner, Simon waved his hand to get her attention.

When Timnit, tall and striking as usual, got to the table, Simon stood and gave her a polite hug, then she shook Patricia's extended hand before sitting.

"Can I get you some java?" Simon asked Timnit.

"Please. Triple shot, flat latte."

He turned to Patricia. "Need a refill?"

She nodded and offered her half-empty mug.

"Black?"

"Yes, please," Patricia said.

Once Simon departed, Timnit said, "So you want to breach a secure warehouse."

"Yes."

"Why?"

"I'm investigating possible criminal activity, and I'm looking for evidence of wrongdoing."

"What kind of evidence?"

Patricia let out a long breath. "I don't rightly know, but I'll know it when I see it."

"What do you have on this warehouse?"

"Zero. In fact, I don't even know if it exists."

Timnit's eyebrows elevated. "What do you want from me?"

"I need to get into the facility."

"The one that doesn't exist?"

Patricia chuckled. "I'm working on that."

"Have you ever broken into a secure location?"

Patricia's mind went to Beau's medical office, but that little excursion last year didn't actually qualify as breaking and entering. "No, I haven't. Can you help me?"

Timnit looked across the length of the room for a moment, then turned back to Patricia with a big smile. "I'd love to."

Simon returned with their drinks, and a sugary concoction for himself.

"What's that?" Timnit asked.

"Mocha frappe."

"And a million calories." She gave him a grin.

He tapped his abs through his skin-tight, black T-shirt. "I think of it as an energy drink."

"Like you need more energy." Timnit blew on the top of her latte and took a drink.

"Do you two have the warehouse infiltration worked out?" Simon asked.

Patricia put down her coffee mug. "We're just starting."

For the next hour, the three of them enthusiastically debated alternatives and finally settle on how they would penetrate the warehouse. First, of course, Patricia had to get inside and place a reconnaissance robot. With a plan in place, they split up and Patricia went home.

An hour later, the back door chimed. Patricia went to the door. Simon stood outside. She opened the door.

"What are those bowls on your patio?"

"Food for some outdoor cats."

He nodded, then stepped in.

She closed and locked the door.

He gestured toward the deadbolt. "How are those locks working for you?"

"A bit of a bother having to set the deadbolt each time, but I do feel much more secure."

He handed her a shopping bag.

She looked inside to see the pearl necklace and a palm-sized robot. Patricia held up the jet-black miniature robot. "How's this going to map the warehouse?"

"It'll be the eyes and ears of a much larger robot we'll

position on the roof. The big robot will control junior here, sending it all over the warehouse until we know everything about the place."

"It's a warehouse. What if it's dark in there?"

"Hi-res night vision."

"Impressive."

"We own the night," he said, invoking the military term.

M AYWOOD WAS UNAVAILABLE FOR LUNCH, SO P ATRICIA SETTLED for a two o'clock meeting at his office, a restored historic house just off Falcon Square. She had no idea he worked so close to her home, but until Saturday, she didn't even know him.

The door to his office building opened to an elegant lobby of mahogany paneled walls, Persian carpeting and soft, indirect lighting. Jackson Capital had spent a lot of money on the luxurious place.

Just inside the door, Patricia announced herself to a stocky security guard dressed in a black business suit who asked her to be seated while he notified Mr. Jackson she'd arrived.

Patricia took a seat in one of several upholstered chairs arranged in small conversation groups in the lobby. From that vantage point, she catalogued the room item by item just as her father had taught her years ago when they'd played memory games. Innocent days, when life was play and love surrounded her. Strangely enough, she saw no security cameras in the lobby, though she assumed they were there.

Maywood came out of the side hall on the right side of the lobby, hand extended. "So nice to see you again so soon, Patricia."

They shook hands, and Maywood gestured her to the hall

on the other side of the lobby. "Would you like to see our backroom?"

Patricia relished the opportunity to get eyes on the size and scope of his organization. She gave him a polite smile. "Thank you. I would."

They passed through double doors into a space filled with several cubicles made of frosted glass, maroon fabric panels and mahogany trim. Definitely a step above. "This is our accounting department."

"Impressive."

"These people are the best money can buy. We take our fiscal and regulatory responsibilities very seriously."

"What kind of turnover do you have?"

"Great question." Maywood led her back to the hall. "We have very little turnover."

Maywood stopped by an office and knocked on the door-jamb. When the middle-aged lady behind the desk looked up, Maywood walked in with Patricia right behind. "Jane, this is Patricia Falcon. She's considering an investment. Patricia, this is Jane Burns, our customer service manager."

Jane came around the desk and shook hands. "Pleased to make your acquaintance, Mrs. Falcon."

"Jane manages five account managers and their staff. Client satisfaction is paramount to us. And Jane's department delivers on that promise daily."

"How big is your department?" Patricia asked.

"Ten total employees."

That's too many people. There must be something else going on here. "So this is your sales department?"

"And customer service," Jane added.

"That's a lot of people."

Maywood smiled. "We like it that way."

Maywood led the way out of Jane's office and down the hall past what appeared to be executive row, complete with brass nameplates on the doors and private secretaries outside the offices. Patricia memorized the nameplates of each of the six executives, noting that Zeitfeld, Wainright and Stellman weren't among them.

At the end of the hallway, Maywood guided her into his office, a room every bit as magnificent as his home office. "Would you care for something to drink?"

"No, thank you."

He gestured to a leather chair in front of the desk. She sat, then he took the chair next to her.

"Did you receive the prospectus?"

"I did."

"Do you have any questions?"

When she paused, he tensed.

"I'll be buying a share of a pool of seven automobiles?"

"Yes."

"Do you currently own the automobiles?"

"Six of them. The seventh is in negotiation. We'll soon have it."

"I'd like to see them."

He straightened. "That's not how we operate."

"Could a million-dollar investment change your mind?"

He smiled. "It might, if you don't mind dust on the automobiles. Did you bring your checkbook?"

"An electronic transfer would be much safer."

He nodded. "You've done this before."

"Occasionally. For the right investment. So, am I going to see those automobiles?"

He looked at his Rolex. "It would take about an hour to get there. Two or three hours for a round trip. Do you have that kind of time this afternoon?"

"Of course."

"Good. I'll make the arrangements." He went to his desk, placed a phone call and asked to have the van brought around. Soon after Maywood's call, his cell beeped. He looked at the screen. "Ride's here."

He led her to the front and out to the curb, where a black van idled. A bulky driver held the door open for them.

As soon as Patricia was settled in the chauffeured van, she noticed the side windows were blacked out and the rear window sunscreen was elevated.

Maywood settled in beside her and buckled up. "I'll need you to turn off your phone. Security, you know."

Patricia did as he asked, then returned her phone to her purse. "So, where did you go to school?" she asked as the van pulled into traffic.

"Country Day and Northwood Institute. You?"

"Virginia Tech."

A smile filled his weathered face. "So, you're not from around here."

She nodded. "My family were colonial merchants. They settled in Virginia during the early eighteenth century. Are you Savannah born?"

"Yes. Like the Falcon family, the Jackson family helped settle Savannah. But we don't have a city square named after us."

"Maybe someday."

He chuckled.

The van accelerated as though entering an expressway. She tried looking out the windshield but a dark privacy screen blocked her view. She needed to stay aware of clues as to where they were going in case the pearls stopped working.

Maywood's cell beeped. He consulted the screen, then returned the phone to his pocket. "Trey recently told us to no longer reinvest the proceeds of his investment. Do you have any idea why?"

Rats. She should have coordinated better with Trey. Patricia shook her head. "Not at all."

"Well, I'm glad you're considering an investment with us," he said.

"It does sound interesting."

There was no longer the stop and go of city traffic, just straight and smooth uninterrupted travel. Such a direct route probably meant there was no attempt being made to evade a following car, like Simon's. And besides, the pearls were transmitting, so Simon could hang well back to avoid detection yet still be close enough to respond if something went wrong. After forty-five minutes, the van left the primary roadway and started making a series of turns.

When the van came to a stop and they got out, Patricia was shocked. They were at a small airfield in front of a huge warehouse. Other than a second, smaller building on the other side of the runway, there were no other structures in sight. In fact, there was nothing in sight but farmland.

Patricia looked around. "Pretty isolated."

"Better for security. If anyone gets within a mile of this place, we know it."

Patricia hid her tension. Was Maywood's security already responding to Simon's presence? Well, there was nothing she could do about it now. And Simon was a big boy. He knew how to handle himself. And if Maywood knew there was a security breach, he sure wasn't showing it.

"That's a huge security perimeter." Patricia looked over the warehouse for cameras and saw none.

"We use passive detection. A civilian equivalent to the best military perimeter systems. The civilian version was developed for border security, and has proven to be surprisingly effective on our border with Mexico."

Maywood punched a code into a keypad and opened a door at the front of the building. Interestingly enough, it was the same code he used for his home office. The interior lights came on as they entered. Motion detection?

"Please pardon our dust. We only bring visitors out once a year."

It was a small, bleak, utilitarian office. Steel furnishings from the nineties. Linoleum flooring. No computers in sight. No security cameras. Just those motion detectors, and who knew what else.

They passed though the office and into the warehouse. No motion-detection lighting there. The chilled air smelled of oil and polish.

Maywood removed a schematic map from his coat pocket, went to an electrical panel and, after consulting the schematic, flipped some of the switches, flooding a small section of the warehouse with lights.

"Those are your automobiles," Maywood said as he ushered her past row after row of cars to the illuminated section. "The first six automobiles from the end."

"I thought the contract was for seven autos."

"The seventh is in negotiation."

"Oh. That's right." Patricia stopped at the first. "I see what you mean about dust. What is this?"

"It's a 1953 Ferrari 250 Europa."

"Why is there an extension cord?" She gestured toward a cord running from the engine compartment to an in-floor receptacle.

"All the automobiles are on battery tenders that keep the batteries fresh."

She walked to the door. "Can I get in?"

"Of course." He opened the door for her.

She put her oversized purse on the concrete floor so the drone could get out while she distracted Maywood. Then she settled into the Ferrari. Leather seats. Pure luxury.

She looked up at Maywood. "What's the value on this one?"

He consulted his schematic. "A bit over three million."

She grasped the steering wheel. "Wow. So this is a multi-million-dollar ride."

"Yes indeed."

"Does the engine work?"

He smiled. "Everything works."

She smoothed her palm over the dash. "It's in such good shape."

He nodded. "All original parts."

"They don't wear out?"

"It's a low mileage, collector's car. Hardly broken in."

She got out and picked up her purse. The robot was gone. She gestured to the next car. "What's this one?"

"A 1964 Shelby 289 Lindauer Cobra."

She walked over to the car. "Another million-dollar ride?"

"Yes."

"What's the most expensive car you have?"

He looked into space for a while. "It's probably the 1956 Aston Martin DBR1."

"Where do you get these automobiles?"

He brought his eyes back to her. "Auction."

"You go to auctions?" Patricia trailed her fingers over the door of the Shelby.

"Mostly I bid remotely."

"Sight unseen?"

His brow furrowed. "Not at all. I'm very thorough. I have experts who inspect and authenticate the automobiles before I bid."

"Did you ever overpay?"

He bit his lip. "I've made some mistakes. Mostly in the early years. Not so much now." He cleared his throat. "So what do you say, Patricia? Do you want to see the other four? They're right here."

"Sure."

Maywood explained each remaining car to her, and in no time they were on their way back to Savannah.

"Do you own the entire airport?"

"Yes. And most of the farmland around it."

"What's in the other building?"

"A cargo plane we use to fly the automobiles in and out. And a shop where we do preventive maintenance on the collection." Maywood turned his body more toward her. "I have to tell you, I'm very impressed with your thoroughness."

"Thank you. It's a lot of money. I like to see what I'm buying."

"Do you need any more information before you make your decision?"

"No. Thank you. You've been very forthcoming."

"I have another investor interested in those six automobiles. When that inventory is again fully invested in, I won't be able to accept any more investments until I purchase more automobiles. Which could be a while because we feel the market is generally overpriced. So, if you want to get in, you should make your decision soon."

"How soon?"

"Right now." He laughed. "Seriously. The fractional share is available now. The other investor could make his decision tomorrow or the next day. If you're seriously considering this investment, I wouldn't hesitate."

"I understand. Send me a contract."

"What amount?"

Patricia rubbed her forehead. "Half a million."

"Why not a million? I'll tell you, you'll not find another investment with our performance history."

"It's so much."

"It's just money."

"I'm tempted."

"You can't get a higher return anywhere else."

"Okay. Do this. Send me two contracts. One for half a million and one for a million."

"I'll have them delivered to your home tomorrow."

Patricia got home at four-thirty and noticed the cats sleeping beneath the patio bushes. Shortly after that, Simon called to tell her he got a location fix on the warehouse and Timnit was going to get the robots working after dark. Patricia mentioned the one-mile perimeter.

"Yeah, I heard."

"Heard?"

"There's a mike in those pearls."

She took off the pearls and put them on her desk. Then she called PetSmart and ordered a bag of cat food.

Trey arrived home at six and they went out for dinner at 17Hundred90.

"I saw Maywood's automobiles this afternoon."

Trey swallowed his sip of wine in a gulp. His eyes widened. "How … how'd you pull that off?"

"I intimated I might be willing to invest as much as a million," Patricia said with a proud smirk tugging at her lips.

Trey nodded. "And he took the bait?"

"Yes, indeed. Although he got the message you were halting reinvestment while I was with him. That was awkward, but he seemed to buy that you and I operated separately."

She filled Trey in on the robots and Timnit's mission that night. "We should have an excellent idea of what we're up against in the next twenty-four hours."

"Be careful, honey."

"Absolutely. And Simon's with me every step of the way." Patricia poked at her salad. "Oh. And I'll be joining a Bible study with Abigail Jackson tomorrow."

"What are they studying?"

"Hebrews."

"Have you done your homework?" he asked with a smile.

"I'll do it in the morning." Patricia took a bite of salad, chewed it slowly, and swallowed. "Maywood has his own airfield and a cargo plane out there. He sells less than twenty automobiles a year, but he maintains an airfield and a cargo plane to transport them. Does that make any sense to you?"

"Not at all."

"I wonder what else he's hauling in that plane."

CHAPTER 12

As soon as Patricia turned on the kitchen lights the following morning, the cats came to the back door and peered inside.

Patricia bent to scoop dry cat food into a bowl. When she opened the door, the cats scooted off to a safe distance. Under their gaze, Patricia squatted and placed the food bowl in the middle of the patio. "Good morning my sweet wild ones," she said softly.

The cats stayed their distance until she returned to the kitchen and closed the door. Then they pounced on the food.

After the heartbreaking death of her family's house cat decades ago, Patricia vowed not to have another pet, but these two feral cats had wormed their way into her daily routine and heart. And the cats helped keep her world in balance.

Timnit called Patricia shortly after eight. "The robotics worked perfectly at Maywood's warehouse. His building security is decidedly old-school." Timnit chuckled. "Actually, it's prehistoric. There'll be no problem getting us in there undetected."

"Maywood said his perimeter security is state of the art."

"Not really," Timnit said. "Are you available tonight?"

"Yes."

"I'll stop by at eleven. We'll go over the infiltration plan and modify it as necessary. Wear black and boots. I'll supply all the equipment you need."

"How do we get through Maywood's outer perimeter?"

"Stealth jamming."

"What's that?"

"A wearable device that makes his system think we're just small animals foraging."

"Impressive."

"One of the many things I used to stay alive back in the day."

For the next hour, Patricia reviewed the Bible study syllabus Abigail had sent and read the relevant passages for the meeting, noting how the writer of Hebrews provided the Judaic Christians with reasons to keep Christ primary in their lives. Abigail's study guide indicated the question for the day: 'What is primary in your life?'

Spouse? Parents? Children? Career? Health? Love? Patricia gave the discussion question a lot of thought.

Just as Patricia was walking out the door for Bible study, Sonny called. "Do you have time to talk?"

"I'm on my way out, but I can carve out a few minutes. What's up?"

"I found online matches on five of the seven serial numbers you gave me. Maywood only owned one of the five, and he sold it a couple of years after he bought it."

"No ties between Jackson Capital and the present owners of those automobiles?"

"None that I can find."

Patricia's stomach dropped. *So we all invested in phantom automobiles.* "What about the other two serial numbers?"

"They might be total fabrications, or a clerical error in transcription at Maywood's end. I've run out of places to check."

"Thanks, Sonny. How are you coming on Maywood's cash flow?"

"Both Maywood and Jackson Capital show up in the *Paradise Papers* leaked list of offshore investment accounts, but not in the *Panama Papers*. Together, both Maywood and Jackson Capital own or control at least a dozen off-shore holding companies, with a combined net worth in excess of one billion." Sonny cleared his throat. "Domestically, he has several major overseas investors who just keep sending him huge amounts of capital. I'm talking millions." Sonny paused. "And Maywood is taking way more than one percent off the top of his domestic companies. Much of his skim goes to those holding companies of his. Plus, he's made some humongous personal purchases in the past three years. Lots of antique art. Museum-quality stuff."

"What about rare automobiles?" Patricia asked, her hope for a positive outcome for this case slipping rapidly away. "Is he buying *any* rare automobiles?"

"If he is, they're not showing up in the accounts I'm looking at. Though he's a regular buyer of antique car parts."

"That's probably to maintain his fleet. He's got a maintenance shop at the warehouse."

"If that's the case, he's doing a *lot* of maintenance."

"But no automobiles? Are you absolutely sure?"

"Not that I can find."

"Rats. This is—"

"Shocking. Patricia, I have clients who have money with him. I have—"

"Wait, Sonny. I know. But we have to be careful or people could lose everything. I need to get to the bottom of what is really going on here first. Can you hold on to the information for now?"

"How long?"

Patricia racked her brain. Maybe tonight after they scoped out Maywood's place, they'd have more answers. But there was no guarantee. "Can you give me at least three days?"

Sonny drew a breath. "Fine. Let me know what else I can do."

"Thank you, Sonny. I appreciate it." Patricia ended the call as she pulled up outside the Jackson home. She took a few moments to breathe deeply and affix a mild expression on her face, then she climbed out of her Escalade.

Besides Patricia and Abigail, there were three other women at the Bible study. Their discussion was lively and enlightening, and the two-hour class passed quickly. As Patricia was preparing to leave, Abigail invited her to stay for a few minutes.

Once the other three women had gone, Abigail guided Patricia into a decidedly feminine room done in pale blue with yellow accents. "What did you think of our study group?"

"Your friends are delightful, well-informed and very articulate."

"They're quite outspoken. I hope they didn't offend you."

Patricia shook her head. "Not at all."

"Will you be coming back?"

"Most definitely. Thank you for inviting me."

Abigail settled back in her chair and looked up at the vaulted ceiling. "I wish Maywood was a nice person. If he put faith first in his life, maybe it would help him be a better husband."

Patricia rubbed the back of her neck. She wasn't sure she wanted to get into Abigail's marital problems. It felt deceptive that she was investigating him and becoming friends with her. But she was trapped. "For some people, it takes longer to be sure about the importance of their faith."

"He's forty years old, and he behaves like he's single and in college. It's like I don't exist."

Patricia winced, imagining how awful if would be if Trey acted that way. "Have you talked to him about how you feel?"

"Every time I mention it, he flies off the handle and tells me if I don't like it, I can leave. Leave? He knows I can't leave. I don't have the money to do that. So I'm stuck in this sham of a marriage with a philandering husband who indulges his every whim."

Shocked at Abigail's openness, Patricia looked away for a moment, then returned her gaze to Abigail. "Have y'all considered marriage counseling?"

"He says he doesn't need counseling. I don't know what to do." Abigail covered her mouth. "I'm sorry, Patricia. I shouldn't have unloaded this on you."

Patricia reached out and squeezed Abigail's hand. "It's okay, Abigail."

"I appreciate that. It helps to be able to talk."

"I have a friend who has worked professionally with women in tough situations. Would you like to meet her? She's very easy to talk to, and totally discrete."

Abigail canted her head. "Is she a counselor?"

"Yes. She has a doctorate, a state license and tons of experience. What do you say?"

Abigail gave a faint smile. "I suppose it wouldn't hurt."

Grateful for the positive turn the conversation had taken, Patricia leaned back. "Are you available later this afternoon?"

"Yes."

"I'll ask my friend to give you a call. Her name is Summer."

Abigail pressed her hand to her heart. "That's very nice of you, Patricia."

WHEN PATRICIA GOT HOME, SHE SAW THE JACKSON CAPITAL contract paperwork had been delivered. Maywood even included his bank routing number. Patricia faxed the seven vehicle serial numbers listed in the contracts and the bank routing number to Sonny and asked him to get back to her with research results before ten p.m.

Patricia spent an hour logging the previous day's info into her case file and building relationship maps for both Maywood and Jackson Capital.

Meredith came over at two, and Patricia filled her in on the latest from Sonny and Timnit. "In short, it appears Maywood is selling investments in automobiles he doesn't own."

"Are you sure?"

"Sonny is pretty positive."

"Oh dear, Patricia." Meredith looked pale, and Patricia knew she must be thinking of her clients at the bank with exposure. "Combined with the stuff I just researched, this is way worse than I thought."

"Yeah, I think it might be," Patricia choked out.

Meredith shook her head. "If he doesn't own the automobiles he's offering to investors, then what are those vehicles he shows off in his warehouse?"

"I intend to find out tonight. What you discovered?"

Meredith touched her fingertips together, forming a steeple. "I checked the Georgia registration for Jackson Capital LLC," Meredith said. "It turns out Preston Somerset is listed as the organizer."

"Preston Somerset? I don't think Trey likes him very much. Some sort of a long-running family feud."

"Preston does have a spotty reputation," Meredith said. "Anyway, I also checked the Georgia Securities Division filings, and Jackson Capital isn't listed. There are legal ways for them to operate without registration, but with 350 million of assets, I don't see how they can do it."

"But if it's a scam," Patricia said, "not registering keeps the regulators out of Maywood's hair."

"Until someone like Hannah complains to them."

Patricia let out a long breath. "That's all we need after everything we found out. You don't think she's already contacted them."

Meredith shrugged. "Hard to say."

"This could get messy."

"I'll say."

"Talk about messy." Patricia sat forward. "Maywood's marriage appears to be on the rocks," she confided. "I'm planning to introduce Summer to Abigail to see if Summer can be any help."

"That's nice of you," Meredith said. "With all the progress you're making, are you ready to take this case to the authorities?"

"They'll want hard evidence of illegality, and I'm still building the factual record of that."

Patricia's phone chimed a text from Trey.

TF: Can you talk?

PF: I'm with Meredith. Can it wait?

TF: Possible that Judy Simpson has been sighted in Savannah.

Patricia gasped and the phone almost slipped from her hand. Her mother's killer. Almost *her* killer. She glanced at Meredith. Meredith's almost killer.

"What is it, Patricia?" Meredith asked, her face full of concern.

Patricia turned her phone to face Meredith and watched as Meredith read the text from Trey.

Meredith laid a hand on her chest. "Oh my God."

The phone rang. *Trey.*

"Patricia, are you okay?"

"Yes. Sorry. That was a shock."

"I know. I'm sorry. Beau's home security cameras picked up an image that could have been Judy scouting the exterior of his house late last night."

"When will it be a positive ID?"

"To be safe, we're treating it as conclusive."

"Can I put you on speaker?"

Trey replied in the affirmative and Patricia placed the phone between her and Meredith.

"Sorry for the shocking news, Meredith," Trey's voice emanated.

"It's fine," Meredith responded. "What should we do?"

"Keep your gun handy and be vigilant. And, Patsy, Simon is on his way over. He's not to leave your side until we find Judy."

CHAPTER 13

After Meredith left the Falcon home, Patricia double-locked the doors and checked all the windows. Then she spent some time further researching the automobiles Maywood was offering her.

Maywood had shown her the automobiles when they visited his warehouse, but she hadn't authenticated their identity. Now, with Sonny's revelations about the automobiles Hannah thought she had invested in, Patricia wanted to make sure each car in Maywood's warehouse was indeed the exact car being offered in the contract he'd provided to her. While Sonny looked up all the serial numbers given to her in the paperwork, Patricia wanted to verify each vehicle's identification plate in person to make sure they were the actual automobiles.

Timnit would get her into the warehouse again. Once in, all Patricia had to do was pop the hood and verify the identification plate. Two problems though. How to release the hood on those particular automobiles, and where exactly was the identification plate on each? Fortunately, Google's image library was a big help, including full-sized images of three of the actual ID plates. Patricia made copies of the hood release photos and the ID plate location photos.

The Google image library led Patricia to an online encyclopedia of rare automobiles hosted by Coachbuild, and to the online registries for each make of car. There she found photos and detailed histories for each of the automobiles Maywood was offering her. And in no case was Maywood or Jackson Capital listed as the owner. Not now. Not ever. Excitement rose that she was onto something substantial. Mixed emotions dueled because she and Trey could lose a lot of money if the investment was a fraud. Sorrow was also present because there were a lot of other innocent investors involved.

Assuming the registries were accurate, she finally had proof of fraud. The chassis and engine numbers she found in the registries matched those listed in the contract Maywood had sent over. And according to the registries, Maywood didn't own *any* of the automobiles. So, what exactly were the automobiles he was showing in his warehouse? Since every car had unique engine and chassis numbers, all that remained was to check the ID numbers of the automobiles he'd shown her in the warehouse. After tonight, if the serial numbers didn't match the prospectus, she'd have factual evidence once and for all that Maywood Jackson was a liar.

During a leisurely dinner at home with Trey, Patricia briefed him on the day's findings. "Given what Sonny and Meredith have found, my conclusion is it's highly probable Maywood is selling shares in automobiles he doesn't own."

Trey shook his head. "I've seen the automobiles we own. Several times."

"And I've seen the automobiles he says he's offering me."

"How reliable are those online registries?" Trey asked.

Patricia shrugged. "I can't imagine they'd be of much use to anyone if they weren't reliable."

"Maybe he has the automobiles on consignment from the registered owners."

"Or they might be replicas," Patricia said. "But there's no use speculating. Let's table this until after Timnit and I check the warehouse automobiles."

"I wish you didn't have to do that."

"Simon's coming with us."

"Okay, but let's not wait too long. If this is a scam, we have to take care of it fast."

"We?"

"The Cotton Coalition."

Patricia nodded her understanding at Trey's mention of the secret crime-fighting group he and several of his prominent friends were members of. Of course, they'd need to know. "Why not the Securities Division?" she asked.

"If they get involved, every investor is going to take a bath. A big one. That could have a crippling effect on Savannah. It's better for the Coalition to handle it privately."

"Are you planning to bail out the investors?"

He winced. "We might."

"So Hannah and the rest of us could get our money out?"

"Some."

"Where will that money come from?"

"Maywood's overseas assets, and perhaps, a contribution from the Coalition."

"Okay. On a related subject, did you get a chance to speak with Judge Wainright?"

"I did. It's just as you suspected. Jackson Capital has him on retainer, but he plays no role in the day-to-day operations. He's window dressing. His primary job is to show up at their social events."

"Anything more on Judy?"

"I spoke with Father John earlier today. The Vatican is sending his daughter, Connie, to Savannah to track down Judy. He said the Pope is adamant about bringing Judy to justice for killing your mother. Connie should arrive early tomorrow morning. Also, Chief Patrick has assigned a detective to her case full time and has patrols keeping an eye on her Savannah haunts. So far, the only sighting of her has been at Beau's."

Patricia eyed her purse sitting within arm's reach on the end table. "She made a lot of mistakes the last time around."

Trey nodded. "Amateur mistakes. In fact, getting caught on Beau's security cameras was a typical amateur mistake."

Patricia tapped her fingers on the armrest. "Do you suppose there's any chance she wanted to be seen?"

"I don't see how alerting us to her presence helps her."

"Bear with me, Trey. We know she's unbalanced. Maybe she's taunting us. Maybe she's trying to show us how skilled she is in evading us."

"Well, it's been done before. I suppose this could be part of some sick plan of hers."

"To what end?" Patricia asked.

Trey shook his head. "I don't rightly know."

Timnit and Simon arrived just before eleven that evening.

Timnit, her gray-streaked hair braided and pulled into a tight bun, spread a large hand-drawn map of the private airport on the kitchen table. The outbuildings and perimeter security system were clearly indicated, along with a designated intrusion point.

"We'll drive to this location." Timnit pointed to an X on the only entrance road to the property. "Simon will stay with our vehicle and keep an eye out for unexpected visitors. We'll go cross-country through the forest and penetrate the secure perimeter here." Timnit moved her finger to a spot designated with a Y. "Then we'll proceed to the warehouse. We'll have thick forest cover until we reach the warehouse parking lot. We'll avoid the front office and enter the warehouse at this back door. That entry point is closer to the vehicles you want to investigate, and there doesn't appear to be a motion detector system inside at that point of entry."

Timnit rolled out a large schematic of the warehouse and pointed to a spot marked A. "This is the door we'll enter. According to the robot you deployed, these are the automobiles you're interested in. We'll start with the car farthest from the door, moving back toward the exit with the completion of each inspection. How much time will you need with the automobiles?"

Patricia put the photos of the vehicle interiors on the table. She had circled what she understood to be the hood release of each car. "You release the hood. I'll pull it up and photograph the vehicle identification plate. A couple of minutes per car. Fifteen or twenty minutes total."

Timnit picked up a photo and studied it. "This is perfect. Where did you find photos like this?"

"Online."

"Clever." Timnit put the photo down. "Okay. You need twenty minutes. Let's schedule thirty minutes to allow for contingencies."

Patricia stared at Timnit. "What could go wrong?"

"Something always goes wrong." Timnit gestured, palms up. "Someone shows up. We can't get a hood open. Your camera battery dies."

"Yeah," Simon said. "Always plan for the unexpected."

"Do you think someone could walk in on us?"

"I've only had surveillance on the target for twenty-four hours," Timnit said. "We don't know their routine. That's one of the reasons we're going in at night. Less chance of someone coming by. And if someone does appear, we'll know about it because of the drone."

"Who's running the drone?"

"Simon."

Patricia nodded. "Okay. Thirty minutes."

"We'll exit the same way we came in." Timnit turned to Simon. "You have anything to add?"

"No. I think you have it well-covered."

Timnit held out a gallon-sized plastic bag. "We'll leave our phones here. They're too easy to track and there's no telling who's interested in our activities."

Patricia and Simon deposited their phones with Timnit's.

Timnit folded the map and schematic. "An hour to get to the property, fifteen minutes of cross-country to the warehouse, half an hour inside, fifteen minutes back to the truck, and an hour drive back to town. Three hours total. Let's go."

On the way out, Trey gave Patricia a kiss on the forehead. "Be safe."

Timnit shoved the maps into a carry case and led them outside to a black Ford F-150 Raptor parked in front of Patricia's house.

"Nice ride," Patricia said.

"Thanks," Timnit said as she slid into the driver's seat. Simon took a back seat, leaving the front passenger seat for Patricia. Timnit fired up the Raptor. Forty minutes later, the navigation system advised them to turn off the Interstate at Exit 127. Within five minutes, they were on the dirt road heading toward the airport. At fifty minutes into the mission, Timnit backed the Raptor well off the road.

Next to the truck, Timnit helped Patricia into tactical gear, including the stealth jamming equipment, communications gear, a camera and night vision goggles.

"No moon tonight," Timnit said as she slipped on her equipment.

Simon deployed the drone, then showed Patricia the monitor screen. "Those three green dots are us."

"Comm check," Timnit said.

"Alpha here," Patricia said, using the tactical name she'd picked.

"Bullet here," Simon said.

"Kat here," Timnit said. "Switch on jamming."

Patricia depressed the switch. "Jamming on."

"Switch to night vision," Timnit said.

Patricia pulled down her goggles and the surrounding forest came to life. Every tree. The bushes. Timnit. Simon. "Night vision on."

"Let's roll," Timnit said as she took off into the forest with Patricia behind.

Fifteen minutes later, they were at the back entrance to the warehouse. Timnit tapped in the security code and pulled the gray steel door open.

Patricia stepped inside and hesitated in the chilled air as if waiting for the lights to come on.

Timnit recovered the mapping drone Patricia had left in the warehouse, then walked past Patricia and made her way to the 1953 Ferrari 250 Europa. After briefly consulting Patricia's photo, Timnit got in the car to release the hood.

"Wait," Patricia said. "The hood is partially open. Probably to allow the battery tender wires to be attached." Patricia looked at the automobiles around her. "All the hoods are partially open."

"That will speed things up," Timnit said as she exited the car.

Patricia raised the hood fully, then fished out her tactical flashlight and looked for the ID plate, spotting it immediately. Engine 0307/EU. Chassis 0307/EU. She checked the list she carried. A shiver went through her. The same ID as listed in the contract. The same ID as on a car in the registry. A car not owned by Maywood. Yet here it was in Maywood's warehouse. She photographed the ID plate.

Then she moved a few steps to the 1964 Shelby 289 Lindauer Cobra and lifted the hood. She quickly found the vehicle identification plate and gasped when she read CSX2344. Another match to the contract and to the car's registry. A registry that didn't include Maywood as an owner. Maybe Trey was right that these automobiles were in the warehouse on consignment. She took a photo of the ID plate and moved on, ultimately ending up at the last car.

"Done?" Timnit asked, consulting her watch.

"Yes."

Timnit headed for the back door. Patricia followed.

Timnit stopped and turned to Patricia. "The hoods."

"Oh no." The hoods were still up.

They rushed back to the automobiles, nested the hoods back into partially open position, and returned to the exit.

"Are we forgetting anything else?" Patricia asked.

Timnit opened the exit. "Don't think so."

They stepped out and the door swung closed. Just as it settled into position, the comm line came to life. "Bullet to Kat. Aircraft approaching from the south."

Patricia glanced up to see a huge propeller-driven plane low on the horizon, coming in with landing lights on. Her heart thudded.

Suddenly, the runway lights snapped on.

"Move. Now," Timnit said as she sprinted for the tree line.

Once in the forest, Patricia glanced up again to see the plane skimming the treetops coming right at her, lights blazing. She ducked as the deafening, thunderous roar of four aircraft engines went over her.

Timnit grabbed Patricia's tactical vest and yanked her up,

then ran deeper into the forest with Patricia following, gasping for breath and struggling to keep up. They made it to the Raptor in ten minutes.

Patricia pushed her night-vision goggles up and, gasping for air, sat on the ground next to the truck, utterly fatigued from the sprint.

Simon handed her an iced bottle of water. "You okay?"

"Out of breath." She took a long swallow of water. "Give me a minute or two."

"Sure." Simon went to Timnit and handed her a water bottle.

Timnit pressed the chilled bottle to her cheek. "We need to get the drone over the runway and hanger. Got to see what's going on with the plane."

"Already in position." Simon showed the monitor to Timnit.

Patricia stood on wobbly legs and went over to look at the display as well. The aircraft was already pulled up to the hanger and a forklift was going out to the plane. Patricia looked at Timnit. "Any idea what's going on?"

"Propeller-driven plane making a middle of the night landing on a remote, seldom-used airfield on a night with no moon suggests smuggling," Timnit said as she zoomed the drone in on the 'N' number on the side of the aircraft. "When we get back, I'll Google this registration number to find the owner of the plane."

They watched as the cargo bay of the transport dropped open and the forklift went in, only to reappear with a large crate. "And from the looks of the crate they're unloading, there's likely to be a lot of contraband being taken off that transport."

"This is Maywood's airport, and the cargo is going into his hanger." Patricia took another drink of water. "Clearly, whatever is going on out there has something to do with him. Could we get a look inside that crate after the transport leaves?"

"Who says it's going to leave tonight?" Timnit asked.

Patricia tapped the screen over one of the wings. "They didn't shut down the engines."

Timnit turned to Simon. "What do you think?"

"There were no signs of activity at the hanger before the plane landed. If there are no signs of activity after the plane departs, I say we check out the crate while we know where it is. I'm aware it's risky since we don't know what kind of security they have at the hanger, but there's no telling where that crate will be tomorrow."

"We'll have to wait until whoever is driving that forklift leaves. Check out the parking lot over there and see if there's a car."

"It's a jeep."

"Okay. When the jeep leaves, we go."

"That's quite a hike to the other side of the property and back," Timnit said.

Patricia stared at Timnit. "I can do it."

"Did you not notice what a little ten-minute sprint did to you?"

"But—"

"I think Timnit's right," Simon said. "You'd slow the operation down. We need someone to watch the entry road for us. Your eyes are as good as mine."

Patricia pointed to the drone monitor. "I don't know how to run the drone."

"We'll take the drone controller with us," Simon said. "Are you okay with this?"

Patricia shrugged. "I suppose so."

A half hour later, the plane took off and the jeep left. Timnit and Simon headed back into the forest.

Patricia climbed into the Raptor's passenger seat, noting

the dome light didn't come on, and trained her eyes on the black void where the road should be. She consulted her watch, but couldn't read the time because of the utter darkness enveloping her. She fished out her flashlight and checked the time. Two-fifteen. She stuffed the light back into her vest and leaned back.

Timnit said it would take them at least thirty minutes to get to the hanger. Give them fifteen minutes inside the hanger and a half hour to return. They should be back by three-thirty. Patricia's eyelids drooped. It was going to be a long wait, and to protect their flank, she had to stay awake and totally aware.

"Kat to Alpha. How are you doing?"

Patricia snapped her eyes open. "Bored. Tired."

"There are caffeine tablets in the center console." Timnit's breathing was heavy. "Take one with a half bottle of water. No more than one tablet."

"Thanks. What's with the heavy breathing?"

"Bullet likes to jog. Cuts transit time in half. The sooner we wrap this up, the sooner we—"

"Cut the chatter," Simon said.

"Roger that, Bullet."

The comm line went silent.

Patricia dug out the box of foil-wrapped caffeine tablets, removed one, popped it into her mouth and took a long drink of water.

Twenty minutes after leaving the Raptor, the comm line came to life. "At target. No threats. No significant security. Going in."

"Over here, Kat. Looks like a dozen or so crates. Chinese markings."

"Alpha to Bullet. Get photos."

"You have the only camera."

Patricia shook her head as frustration mounted. Then she

remembered the drone. "Does the drone have recording capability?"

"Yes. Good idea. We'll bring the drone down to record the markings. Kat has a crate open. It looks like auto parts. Frames. Side panels. Another crate has an eight-cylinder engine."

Sonny had said Maywood was spending a lot of money on auto parts. But why deliver them in the middle of the night? "Open another one and try to get photos."

"This crate has axels, bumpers and wheels," Kat said. Patricia heard the screech of nails being pulled from wood. "There's a hood and two doors in this one. There's enough parts to build—" Timnit gasped. "Oh my. They're assembling automobiles here. From the looks of it, old automobiles."

Patricia let out a long breath. "Oh my word. This confirms my worst fears. Replicas."

"Yep. I think they're making replicas with parts from China," Simon concurred.

"China has always had a wealthy, powerful elite," Patricia said. "I suppose they've always imported luxury automobiles."

"This crate has Cuban markings," Timnit said. More nail screeching sounded on the comm line. "There's a fully assembled engine in here."

"Cuba is notorious for preserving old automobiles," Simon said.

"So maybe Maywood is mining these old communist countries for rare automobiles," Timnit said.

"Appears so," Simon said. "I think we can assume what's in the remaining crates. We should put the lids on and head back."

Patricia pulled out her flashlight looked at her watch. Forty-five minutes so far.

"Kat to Alpha."

"Go ahead," Patricia replied.

"How are you holding up?"

"Fully caffeinated."

It was just past four when Patricia crawled into bed.

Trey rolled over. "How'd it go?"

"More questions than answers," Patricia said, wide awake and regretting taking the caffeine. "Maywood has car parts at his warehouse."

Trey yawned. "Maintenance of his fleet."

"Too many parts for that."

"Any idea what he's doing with the parts?"

"I think he's building automobiles, Trey. Fake automobiles. I'm afraid our investment is in jeopardy."

CHAPTER 14

The warble of Patricia's cell phone awoke her from a deep sleep.

"Sorry if I woke you," Timnit said, "but I thought you'd like to know that six people drove up in late model automobiles at Maywood's parts hanger first thing this morning."

Patricia looked at her phone display. She blinked to sharpen her vision. Ten. She'd slept until ten. Oh well. It had been a very late night.

"Are you there, Patricia?"

"Yes, I'm here. I'm just trying to focus. You said there were automobiles at the hanger?"

"Yes. They arrived just before eight."

"It's ten. Why did you wait to call?"

"I wanted to give you some extra time to rest."

"How about you?"

"Didn't go to sleep yet."

Patricia stifled a yawn. "Did you track down their license numbers?"

"I don't have access to the National Motor Vehicle Title Information System."

"Okay. Get those license numbers to Simon and ask him to contact me when he has results."

"Will do. And, Patricia, I had the crate markings translated. The Chinese exporter of those car parts is Chao Ping Auto, a distributor of custom-built automobiles, and the shipping points are several rural cities in Western China. Not places you'd normally expect to find vintage luxury car owners, but possibly automotive assembly plants."

Patricia's fatigued mind was having trouble digesting everything. "Okay. Anything else?"

"No. That's it."

"Thank you for calling."

Patricia returned her phone to the nightstand and sat on the edge of the bed for a moment to get her bearings. Then she slipped out of bed on sore legs, obviously unaccustomed to the sprinting through the forest she'd done when the aircraft flew over, and shuffled into the bathroom.

After showering, she dressed in leggings and a loose-fitting shirt, then went downstairs and fed the cats. She passed on making coffee, pouring orange juice instead.

She spent the rest of the morning contacting the owners of the registry automobiles Maywood wanted her to invest in and had shown her in his warehouse. None had heard of Maywood or Jackson Capital. One of the owners, Nikki Sheldon, lived on Hilton Head Island. Patricia arranged to visit Nikki later in the day to see her Ferrari 250 Europa.

That afternoon, the Escalade's GPS led Patricia and Simon to a narrow road on Hilton Head Island. She turned into the driveway and drove to the front of Nikki Sheldon's home, a modern ocean-front ranch set well back from the dunes. She left Simon in the car and headed for the door.

As soon as Patricia reached for the doorbell, one of the

beveled glass doors swung open to reveal an athletic, silver-haired woman in a navy T-shirt, beige knee-length shorts and worn boat shoes.

"You must be Patricia Falcon," the woman said, extending her hand. "I'm Nikki Sheldon."

They shook, then Nikki led Patricia into the house.

The walls facing the ocean were all glass, making the room bright. Thought the room was huge, the furnishings were sparse and utilitarian. The west side of the room contained a full-sized kitchen. A mammoth breakfast island separated the great room from the kitchen.

Nikki went to a wet bar. "Care for a drink?"

"Water if you don't mind."

"Bottled or tap."

"Tap."

"Ice?"

"No, thank you."

Nikki handed her a glass of water, then filled a glass with water for herself. "So, you're interested in rare automobiles."

"Writing an article on them for *Southern Living*."

"What do you know so far?"

"Very little."

Nikki gave a smile. "You're a newbie."

"I am."

"Every auto connoisseur was once a newbie. You said you wanted to see my Ferrari."

Patricia nodded as her mouth went dry in anticipation.

Nikki walked through the kitchen, opened a door and moved aside. Wired to the max, Patricia stepped through the doorway. Motion sensors triggered the overhead lights, illuminating four antique automobiles in an oversized garage.

Patricia sucked in a breath. There were two old automobiles she couldn't identify, and two identical Ferrari 250s. "You have two 1953 Ferraris?"

"One's a replica," Nikki said. "I occasionally use it for local errands. It's a fun ride."

"And impressive."

"That's a double-edged sword." She grimaced. "To keep it ding-free I need to park it well away from other automobiles. Not always possible. So I only take it out during slow times on the island."

"Which one is the real Ferrari?"

"This one." Nikki gestured to the one closest to the kitchen door.

"How do you tell them apart?"

"The reproduction is so good, I can't. They're absolutely identical, right down to the data plate. I just know where the authentic car is parked."

"How do you register automobiles with identical serial numbers?"

"The replica data plates are purely cosmetic."

Patricia laughed. Why in the world have two? Where was the sense in that, if the only way Nikki could tell the difference was where it was parked? Someone could switch the automobiles' parking places and Nikki wouldn't know the difference.

"Why have two?"

"The real car is an excellent investment. The replica is a great ride. By driving the replica, I let people know I drive a Ferrari without putting miles on the real car."

"Are you sure the investment vehicle is real?"

"Ferrari authenticated it for me."

Patricia pulled out a notebook and a pen as she walked around the real car. "It's beautiful. How long have you owned it?" She jotted down Nikki's answer, then asked several other questions, which Nikki answered without hesitation. "Could I see the engine?"

"Of course." Nikki reached inside and popped the hood.

As the hood rose, Patricia's heart sped at the thought of seeing the telltale vehicle ID plate. "Do you mind if I take some photos?"

"Not at all."

She started with a full body shot, then just the engine and finally zoomed into the ID plate that displayed the identical numbers as the car at Maywood's warehouse.

"How perfect is the reproduction?" Patricia asked.

"Meticulous."

"Really?" Patricia asked, trying to keep a professional tone to her voice. "Would someone be able to sell the reproduction as genuine?"

"Only to a naïve investor," Nikki said. "Smart investors know the pedigree of the car they're buying. I'm the registered owner. You want to buy this car, you have to buy it from me."

"But a naïve investor could be fooled."

She nodded. "It happens. Unfortunately."

"Is your car on the market?"

"Not at all."

So, there it was. Maywood didn't have this car on consignment. He was probably passing off reproductions as investment-grade vehicles. No wonder he couldn't liquidate them. But he had sold some. At least he claimed he had.

"How much does a quality reproduction cost?"

"Depends on the vehicle, but since they're handmade from scratch they're quite expensive. Well north of a hundred thousand. Would you like to take the reproduction out for a spin?"

"I'd like too, but I'd be too nervous."

"I'll drive," Nikki said as the garage door behind the replica opened.

Patricia settled into the passenger seat and Nikki backed the Ferrari out to the drive, then sped off. Patricia didn't know what she'd expected, but the acceleration took her breath away. She forced a nervous grin. "That's some engine."

"These automobiles were made for racing. Ferrari sold a few street versions to help pay for their racing program. In the case of the Ferrari 250 Europa, only twenty-one or twenty-two were produced. Lucky for me, a few survived." Nikki raced the engine.

Patricia felt anxious at the speed, but Nikki quickly slowed for a corner and the rest of the short ride was uneventful. Back at the front of the house, Patricia thanked Nikki for her time and left.

On the way back to Savannah, Patricia thought through how to conclusively prove the automobiles in Maywood's inventory were reproductions. She supposed there were telltale differences an expert would look for, but she wasn't an expert.

Patricia called Nikki who promptly provided the name of a Savannah restorer who routinely worked on rare automobiles. Patricia made an appointment to visit Mr. Knox first thing the following morning.

Later that afternoon, Patricia poured coffee and sat at the kitchen table with her laptop.

She opened her case file and brought up the car photos from Maywood's warehouse and from Nikki's garage.

Three identical automobiles, right down to the ID plates. Same body and engine numbers on each car and, surprisingly, the same scratches on all three identification plates. Whoever had made the reproduction automobiles had gone to great lengths to duplicate absolutely everything about the original. But nothing was perfect. There had to be differences, some oversight that would distinguish the reproductions from the original.

She pulled up the 0307EU photos from the registry and compared them to the three more current ones she'd taken. Side view, interior, engine and front view. All photos were identical. Her eyes sharpened on the screen, then her three sets of photos. "Gotcha!" The back views showed three different license plate numbers. Nikki's real Ferrari and the registry plates matched. The two replicas had different plates.

"So," she said to herself, pleased with her discovery, "there could be vehicle registration and title information on file for each."

After she sent the license numbers to Simon for a trace, she looked out the kitchen window at the two cats sleeping in the bushes. She wondered how Maywood could sleep; taking all those innocent peoples' money.

If no one spooked him before she had completed her mission, Maywood would soon be sleeping behind bars.

CHAPTER 15

Just before eight the following morning, Patricia and Simon pulled her Escalade into the parking lot for the Vintage Auto Shop. The gray storefront had four bays, their doors closed, and what appeared to be an office on the right end of the garage.

Nothing about the place gave any clue that million-dollar automobiles were worked on there. Not that the shop was rundown. It was merely ordinary.

Simon remained in the car while Patricia stepped out into the warm, humid air and went to the office door. Pausing at the entrance, she had a strong feeling she was close to something important for her investigation.

When she walked into the cool air of the office, a gray-haired, wiry man in shop overalls looked up from a cluttered desk. "Can I help you?"

She quickly scanned the office, noting an easel in a corner with a detailed schematic of an automobile, a bookcase with auto manuals, and a Krispy Kreme Doughnut box on the credenza behind him. "I'm here to see Atticus Knox."

The man brushed a gray curl from his forehead, stood,

and came around the desk, hand extended. "You must be Patricia Falcon."

Patricia took his calloused hand, noticing the Masonic tattoo on his forearm. "Thank you for seeing me."

A smile lit his face. "My pleasure. Would you care for some coffee? I import the beans from Sumatra."

"No, thanks."

He gestured to a worn leather chair in front of the desk, then returned to the other side.

"I understand you're interested in vintage Ferraris," he said in a mellow draw as he sat. "You buying or selling?"

"Neither, Mr. Knox." Patricia took out her notebook and pen. "I'm writing an article for *Southern Living* about collectors in the Savannah area."

He nodded. "I know them all."

"Nikki Sheldon?"

"Know her and her automobiles well."

"Maywood Jackson?"

"Yeah, I know he's a collector but oddly I've never done any business with him. He has my card. I send him one every year in my Christmas cards, as I do with all the owners of antique automobiles in the area. I really don't know Maywood, but his daddy, Andrew Jackson, is a right upright man."

"Is Andrew a collector?"

"Not that I know of."

"Would you mind telling me a little bit about vintage restoration. I'm just learning."

"There's much more to restoring automobiles than is apparent to novices," Atticus said. "Each individual item of the restoration can be a puzzle in itself, as each piece to be replaced must match the original equipment as to year and place manufactured. Finding such pieces and proving their provenance is often more elusive than finding the original car. Over time, those of us who do a lot of restorations learn who the reliable parts suppliers are and who are charlatans."

"Quite an adventure," Patricia said.

His brows knitted. "An often frustrating experience. Many required parts ceased to exist long ago and are considered extinct."

"In that case, what do you do?"

"Keep looking. Keep hoping a car with the extinct part is found. It's a long shot, but it's the only honest shot we have."

"So the goal is to find long-forgotten automobiles."

He nodded. "Easier said than done."

"How about China?"

His eyes widened. "A treasure trove lately, but replete with fraud."

"How do you tell a replica Ferrari 250 from an authentic one?"

"Fakery used to be a real problem," Atticus said. "Nowadays, it's all but impossible. Today, any investment-grade vehicle will have a traceable provenance. In fact, Ferrari offers an authentication service. It's the gold standard for classic Ferraris. If a car doesn't have a well-documented history, that's your first tip-off it may be fake. However, occasionally, some authentic automobiles have poor documentation. For example, the Chinese automobiles. With prices in the millions, if there are any questions about a car, a knowledgeable investor would hire a professional to verify the car's authenticity."

"Let's start with paperwork," Patricia said. "What would you look for?"

"First off, if available, I'd want to see a manufacturer's statement of origin. This would show a serial number that should match the number mounted on the frame. Depending on the vehicle, the ID numbers will also appear elsewhere. I'd check each location against the statement of origin. Then I'd want to see a list of all sales of the car and, if possible, copies of each bill of sale and registration, along with a history of all parts replacement and their authentication."

"These are readily available?"

"No. It's relatively rare to have everything. But anyone who understands the value of the car knows to document everything they can. Since these are race automobiles, the provenance will often include race participation data."

"Anything else?"

"I'd want a list of major repairs and who performed them. And, of course, I'd want to see the certificate of authenticity from *Ferrari Classiche,* if one exists. *Classiche* is the division of Ferrari that deals specifically with restoration and certi-fication."

"What do you do if very little paperwork exists on a car?"

Atticus gave a knowing smile. "I'd contact Cathy Roush and Marcel Massini and have them generate reports on the car from their databases. Cathy has the world's largest collection of Ferrari classified ads, and Marcel is the world's top expert on the automobiles. If data exists, they'd know about it."

ON THE WAY HOME FROM THE BODY SHOP, CONNIE CALLED and they made arrangements to meet for lunch later that morning.

Timnit called too. "Two women in black suits visited me right after I called you this morning, produced FBI IDs and wanted to know why I was at Maywood's airport."

Patricia straightened. "What is their interest in Maywood? Why would they be watching his place? And how'd they know it was you who was there?"

"I assume they had someone or something there photographing everything that moved. They got a picture of me and probably you along with Simon. Then they ran their pictures against a computerized facial recognition program," Timnit said. "I'm sure my photo and biometrics are in all the military databases."

"What did you tell them?"

"The truth. It's a felony to lie to them. And they obviously had proof I was there. So I told them I was considering an investment in Jackson Capital's program and wanted to look at the merchandise. They also asked who I was with."

Patricia's throat tightened. "You told them?"

"Of course. So expect a visit from the FBI."

"Strange they haven't called," Patricia said, rubbing her chin.

"They won't talk to you until they know more about you than your own mother," Timnit said. "That's why you have to answer their questions truthfully."

"I understand." Though she had nothing to hide, she couldn't stop her stomach from churning.

"I sure hope so. You don't want to pick a fight with the feds. I wouldn't want to see you sent to prison for lack of candor."

After hanging up, Patricia couldn't get her mind off the FBI interest in Maywood. Did they know he was committing fraud? Maybe she should call them. If they were investigating him, she could tell them what she knew, and then stop her investigation.

WHILE SIMON WAITED OUTSIDE, PATRICIA MET CONNIE, THE investigator the Vatican had sent, at B&D Burgers for lunch. Connie had suggested the shop, observing it was nearly impossible to get a good cheeseburger in Rome.

"It's so good to have you back in town, Connie," Patricia said as they sat at a booth toward the back.

"Your mother was very special to the pope, and he's committed to putting her murderer back in jail."

"Thank you," Patricia said. "My mother loved the pope as well."

Connie nodded.

"How's your father doing back in Vatican City?" Patricia asked after the silver-haired waiter brought water and took their beverage orders.

"He's slowing down," Connie said with a crack in her normally even-tempered voice.

Patricia gave Connie a quizzical look. "Is he okay?"

"Just getting old." Connie, her voice more modulated, put her napkin on her lap. "The mad abuse he's subjected his body to with his investigations on behalf of the Vatican is finally catching up with him."

Patricia nodded while the waiter deposited their iced tea. "It's a tough life."

"I'll say." Connie looked off into space. "Doing the Vatican's clandestine work is definitely a young person's business."

Patricia nodded. Slim, athletic Connie certainly fit the bill.

The waiter took their food order and left.

"Are you enjoying working for the SIV?" Patricia asked in a hushed voice, pretty sure Connie didn't want her affiliation with the Vatican Secret Service broadcasted.

"It's my vocation."

"But are you happy doing this work, *Double O* Connie?"

"Very much so." Connie grinned and removed a notebook and pen from her purse. "Speaking of which, what can you tell me about Judy?" Getting detailed information on Judy was the reason Connie had given when setting up their meeting.

"On the surface, Judy's a charming lady," Patricia said.

"I'm sure Beau, her former husband, would tell you the same thing."

"He did when I met with him this morning."

"Oh. I'm glad you've already spoken to Beau. He probably knows her the best." Patricia let out a long breath. "As much as anyone can know a person like her. I thought we were friends. Good friends. I trusted her. It still haunts me that I never saw that side of her."

"She's certainly a sociopath."

"We all fell for her deceptions."

"You, and as it turns out, many others," Connie said. Their cheeseburgers arrived. Connie sliced hers in half and took a bite. "Delicious."

Patricia, wondering for the millionth time how they had so missed Judy's criminality, nibbled on a crisp fry.

"Like all of us, Judy's a creature of habit," Connie said. "The better I can learn how she operates, the better I can anticipate her next move."

"Do you think she's here to extract revenge for me shooting her hand?"

Connie's alabaster face hardened as her eyes leveled on Patricia. "I don't think she'd come out of hiding for any other reason."

Patricia set down the burger she'd half-heartedly attempted to eat.

"She's a wanted felon," Connie continued. "She's in every database. A simple traffic stop could result in her arrest and permanent imprisonment, if not execution."

The truth of Connie's statement hung heavy over their table. "Do you think she's here just for me?" Patricia managed.

Connie paused for a bit too long. "Maybe Beau as well," she finally offered. "But certainly you."

Taking a sip of water to keep down the meager amount of

food she'd managed to eat, Patricia steeled her nerves. "Then I guess we better find her before she strikes."

"Do you know anything about her habits? For example, does she read?"

"She's a voracious reader."

"How voracious?" Connie took a drink of iced tea.

"She claimed she read upward of twenty books a month."

"Any particular genre?"

"Erotica."

"That's a good lead." Connie jotted a note. "It should be easy enough to identify high-volume erotica readers currently in Savannah. Particularly anyone who recently started buying or downloading a large number of erotic books here."

"Amazon?"

Connie nodded.

"Clever."

Connie smiled. "Any medical issues?"

"Not that I know of." Patricia paused. "Come to think about it, she complained of tennis elbow. Pain killers and shots weren't working. She was thinking about surgery."

"Doctors?"

"Don't know. But since Beau's a doctor, she probably discussed the surgery with him."

Connie made another note. "Any plastic surgery while she was here?"

Patricia nodded.

"What surgeon?"

"Don't know, but again, Beau might."

"Where'd she bank?"

"I thought she banked where we all put our money. At Meredith's bank. But after she deposited money in that Hilton Head Island bank, I can't be certain."

Connie extended her hands in an open gesture. "She's got to have money to live."

Patricia shrugged. "Or a sugar daddy."

"Beau said she had an affair with Preston Somerset. The Cotton Coalition just put round-the-clock surveillance on Somerset in case Judy contacts him."

Patricia was beginning to feel very good about Connie's investigative skills. "That's good."

"Do you know of any other affairs she might have had?"

Patricia took a bite of her cheeseburger while she thought that question through. "I don't rightly know. But she told me often enough how disappointed she was with Beau's sexuality. I wouldn't be surprised if she was seeing others."

They continued to talk and eat without any further hot leads. As they parted, Connie said, "Be careful, Patricia. She's a seasoned killer, and chances are she's after you."

Patricia had just shoved a pan of double fudge dark chocolate brownies into the oven when a call from Summer came in.

"I met with Abigail," Summer said.

"How'd it go?"

"She opened up. Big time. And, get this, she gave me permission to discuss her case with you."

Goosebumps formed on Patricia's forearms. "Great."

"I'll say. Turns out Maywood is abusing Abigail."

"Oh no. How? Physically?" Patricia hadn't noticed any bruises, but serial abusers and their victims were often good at hiding them.

"He hasn't laid a hand on her. He's harassing her electronically. He's turned her life into a nightmare. If anyone is candidate for admission to the shelter, it's Abigail."

"What's Maywood doing to her?"

"Well, apart from some pretty awful-sounding emotional manipulations and a persistent breaking down of her confidence, he's tracking her every move via cell phone, and has cancelled her credit cards to try to control her."

"Yikes. So he definitely knows we've met with her. Thank goodness we have the Bible study cover. Anything else?"

"The Jacksons' home has one of those electronic security systems that can be controlled by a smartphone app. Maywood uses the system to spy on her. Abigail doesn't have access to the security system app, so she's at Maywood's mercy. And he uses the devices to intimidate her."

"How?"

"After he leaves for the office, he'll turn off the air conditioning if he's unhappy with her. Or if she tries to take a nap, he'll start blasting music through the remote-controlled speakers. She feels like she has no control at all over her own home. We've got to get her out of there."

Patricia's pulse surged. "I agree. Is she ready to leave?"

"She's not there yet, but she's close. I hope you don't mind, but I told her we'd be glad to assist when she's ready."

"No. I don't mind at all. What's keeping her from leaving?"

"She says she wants to take Maywood down as a last act of defiance before going into hiding."

Patricia's heart sped. "Did she say how?"

"No. I'm not entirely sure she knows what she should do just yet." Summer sounded exasperated. A first in Patricia's experience with Summer. "I have the feeling she's considering options."

"What kind of options?"

"Nothing specific at this point."

"As she zeros in, do you think she'll discuss the options with you?"

"Absolutely."

"Maywood is the managing partner of Jackson Capital. If there is anything shady going on there and Abigail can get solid evidence of criminal activity, that would certainly qualify as a way to bring Maywood down."

"Good thinking. If Abigail brings up the subject again, I'll let you know."

"And regardless, let Abigail know we'll extract her the moment she wants out. Day or night."

"Thanks, Patricia."

"Anything else?"

"I qualified on pistol."

"That's marvelous, Summer. We'll schedule you into the shoot house as soon as time comes available."

Following the call, Patricia, still troubled by the FBI investigation, checked flight maps, GPS and recent topographic maps of the Statesboro area. Staring at the reflection in her laptop monitor, Patricia watched her face momentarily grimace, then still. Her stomach twisted. Maywood's airfield wasn't shown on any of the recent maps. And the Google Earth image of the property was just an indistinct blur. A hurricane of emotion hit her. Timnit's hand-drawn mission map clearly showed the airfield, but public maps didn't. Someone had gone to great extremes to assure the airfield was off the public grid. Someone with pull. Lots of pull.

Her throat tightened. She could get herself killed by whoever hid the airfield. And if not killed, she'd possibly be arrested for trespassing. The threat of those potential consequences wouldn't stop her, it just made her extra cautious. She needed answers, so with the help of Timnit and Simon she'd be careful to stay well below the airport security and the FBI radars.

After removing the brownies from the oven, Patricia

called Simon. "Maywood's private airport isn't on maps. That's quite a feat for an auto dealer."

"I wouldn't be surprised if Maywood has friends in high places," Simon said.

"Some friends. I'd sure like to know who authorized masking the airfield."

"I'll check right now and call you back."

An hour later, Simon texted.

SX: Authority for erasing Maywood's airfield came from the Deputy Director of the FBI.

PF: Any reason given?

SX: National security.

CHAPTER 16

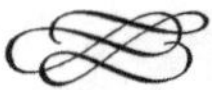

When Patricia entered the kitchen the following morning, both cats were staring in the lower panes of the door like they were canvassing the place.

Patricia squatted at the cat food bin she now kept next to the door, removed the top and scooped a bowl of dry pellets. Before standing, she glanced over at the cats, who were still riveted in place, pink tongues extended a bit from their mouths and their eyes cataloguing her every movement.

As soon as Patricia opened the back door, the cats scampered away to the safety of the edge of the patio and stayed there until Patricia returned to the kitchen and shut the door. Definitely not socialized, but very aware of where their next meal came from and, as befitted cats, eminently curious.

After eating, the cats retreated to the shade of the heather bushes edging the patio, where they preened, then rested.

Simon and Timnit arrived at nine with their laptops and venti lattes all around.

"Thank you," Patricia said to Simon, taking the offered cup. "That was very thoughtful."

"Timnit's idea." Simon sat and opened his laptop.

"Thank you, Timnit." Patricia settled onto her ladder-back chair. "I have to say I prefer getting my caffeine this way rather than those stomach-busting caffeine pills of yours."

Timnit looked up from her laptop and smiled. "Me too."

"So what do you have, Simon?" Patricia asked.

"I've tracked those license numbers you provided. Let's take them in order. The automobiles that showed up at the hanger the morning after our intrusion are all titled to Chao Ping Auto, with a business address in Statesboro."

"That's the same name as on the crates off-loaded from the cargo plane," Patricia noted.

"Yes. But it gets better. The registration paperwork on two of the three Ferrari 250s you photographed also shows Chao Ping Auto as the manufacturer. The manufacturing location is listed as Statesboro. To be more specific, Maywood's airport address."

"Which two were manufactured by Chao Ping Auto?"

"Maywood's and one of Nikki's."

Patricia sat straighter. "And the point of origin for the third Ferrari?"

"Maranello, Italy."

Patricia gazed into space with unseeing eyes, her thoughts racing like Grand Prix race automobiles. "Since Maywood told me that vehicle was one of the automobiles in the contract, that's evidence he's offering a reproduction as an authentic classic car."

"It would appear so," Simon said.

"I've done some checking on Chao Ping Auto," Timnit said. "The US company is wholly owned by a Chinese parent company and they're registered with the Georgia Department of State. They have a sizable showroom in Statesboro, which I've visited. Their display automobiles are clearly identified as reproductions. Despite a night landing at a private airport, on the surface they seem legit."

"We need to establish a paper trail between Chao Ping and Jackson Capital," Patricia said. "Can we determine who bought that reproduction Ferrari from Chao Ping and when?"

"The *when* is easy," Simon said, keying his laptop. "Six months ago. It's on the title. And the who is Preston Somerset, who is listed as the transfer agent for Jackson Capital."

"Print that out for our investigation file." Patricia rolled her stick pen in her fingers and looked into space. "So, Preston is Jackson Capital's point man for Chao Ping transactions. He's got to know what's going on. I mean, why else would Jackson Capital be buying reproduction automobiles?"

"I agree," Simon said.

"I'd like to know a lot more about Jackson Capital's relationship with Chao Ping Auto. How many automobiles has Chao Ping sold to Jackson Capital? How long have they been doing business together?"

"We could ask Summer to approach Chao Ping as a potential customer for a replica car and ask for references," Simon said. "If they offer Jackson Capital as a reference, she could ask how many automobiles they sold to them."

"She doesn't seem like someone who likes rare automobiles," Timnit said. "We need someone more convincing."

"Summer is perfect for this job," Patricia said, drawing out her words. "I've seen her in action. Often. She's a talented and experienced professional. She easily reads people, and is highly skilled at establishing rapport with a wide variety of personality types."

Timnit settled back in her chair. "Impressive."

"Trust me. You don't know half of what she can do."

"She's so quiet. So laid back."

"And so much more," Patricia added. "But your point about being a typical customer is well taken. I wonder what

Chao Ping is going to find when they do a credit check on Summer."

"Let's see." Simon tapped his keyboard. "Damn. An 840 credit score and a high seven figure net worth."

"That should pass muster." Timnit picked up her phone. "Do you want me to contact Summer?"

Patricia nodded. "Now, about this FBI business." Patricia settled eyes on Timnit, who had looked up at the mention of the FBI. "They still haven't contacted me."

"I had a visit from them," Simon said. "Right after you alerted me, Timnit."

"What did they ask you?"

"They wanted to know why I was in the hanger."

"And you said?"

Simon smiled. "Checking out the merchandise."

Timnit nodded. "Did they accept your explanation?"

"Definitely."

"Anything else?"

Simon shook his head. "No. They just made it clear that I shouldn't return to the hanger." Simon paused. "Come to think about it, they also told me not to buy any of Chao Ping's automobiles. I thought that was strange, but I didn't say anything."

"Umm." Timnit looked up, then back at Simon. "Are you sure they never mentioned Maywood's warehouse?"

"Not once. And they never mentioned our drone or our SUV on the entry road to Maywood's airport. It was all about the hanger."

"I'm thinking they must be looking into Chao Ping Auto, not Jackson Capital," Timnit said. "Otherwise they would have asked about the warehouse."

"That makes sense to me." Simon glanced at Patricia. "How about you?"

"Yeah," Patricia said. "I'll go along with that until we know better."

"Now that we have the goods on Maywood, what next?" Timnit asked.

"A lot of my interaction with Maywood has been verbal." Patricia's chest tightened. "That's not going to stand up very well if challenged."

"What about the contract and prospectus?"

"They don't actually say the automobiles are authentic." Patricia pressed her lips together.

"Certainly the valuations Jackson Capital has placed on them implies they're authentic," Timnit said.

Patricia gave a curt nod. "But, there's also a footnote that says the valuations are not to be relied on."

Timnit exhaled sharply. "Legal mumbo jumbo."

"I'd like to see if Maywood will provide authentication for the automobiles he's offering me," Patricia said. "If he does, then we have written proof of misrepresentation. Also, a Ponzi scheme of this magnitude doesn't just happen. It takes a sophisticated organization to implement it. We need to determine what Maywood's key people know. Did you get any information on those names I gave you, Simon?"

Simon again keyed his laptop. "Real people. According to Meredith, their bank records show they each receive a handsome salary from Jackson Capital. Most of them have worked for Jackson Capital from the beginning. Excellent credit reports. No criminal records."

"You think they know Jackson Capital is engaged in fraud?" Timnit asked.

Simon shook his head. "I have no idea, other than the one who told Sonny not to invest with Jackson Capital."

"Cotton McNaly," Patricia said.

"Yeah. That tip says Cotton is plugged in. And, of course, Preston Somerset, who is buying the reproductions."

"Good job, everyone." Patricia shut her laptop and stood. "I'll ask Maywood for authentication papers right away."

After Timnit and Simon left, Patricia straightened the kitchen. The sleeping cats stirred and looked up from beneath the shrubs when Patricia went out to retrieve the food bowl. Fixing her eyes on the gray cat, Patricia cooed.

The cat winked in response. Then, eyes on Patricia, ran his pink tongue over his upper lip.

After she washed the food bowl, Patricia called Maywood and set up a time to see him later that morning. Then she called Simon and asked him if he'd go with her because of the Judy threat.

STANDING IN THE SHADE OF THE JACKSONS' MAMMOTH wraparound porch, Patricia rang the doorbell, then catalogued her surroundings that she hadn't had a chance to when she and Trey had arrived here for the investor shindig. Spotless glass double doors. Polished brass lockset. No trace of tarnish. She looked up, not surprised to see a robin's egg blue ceiling, a color traditionally selected in Savannah to keep bad spirits at bay. To one side, a porch swing was hung from the ceiling. To the other side, white wicker chairs with pale-blue cushions and a bentwood rocker, also painted white. The very picture of Southern hospitality. Yet not a hint of surveillance cameras. Maywood had to have a security system in place. She looked around again. Nothing apparent.

She turned, glanced at the curb where Simon sat in the idling Escalade and shrugged. Then she rang the bell again, wondering if she'd misunderstood what time Maywood had said he'd see her. Just as Patricia turned to leave, one of the doors clicked open.

"How nice to see you." Maywood gave a tip of his head and gestured toward inside. "Won't you come in?"

Patricia responded politely, but her internal reaction to the sight of Maywood after everything she now knew, took her by surprise. Disgust and disappointment in his inhumanity filled her. If Abigail was to be believed, and she had no reason to doubt it, he was an abuser as well as a fraud. It was possible Abigail would require rescuing from him. And if he used deadly force to keep them from picking up Abigail, Patricia wondered if she'd be able to shoot him to protect Abigail. Not a fatal shot, of course. And she decided right then that, yes, yes she could.

Maywood lead her to an ornate sitting room decorated in yellows and indicated an upholstered chair with a lovely garden print reminiscent of the French impressionists.

Wondering where Abigail was, Patricia sat and folded her hands in her lap.

"Would you care for something to drink?" he asked, towering over her. A kindness delivered from an intimidating position. Conversation devoid of corresponding emotion. A psychopathic trait.

"No, thank you."

With apparent nonchalance, he eased into the chair next to her, leaned back and settled his eyes on her. A pair of reading glasses poked out of his shirt pocket. "How have you been?"

"Busy, as usual." She noticed he wasn't wearing the wedding ring he'd worn at the garden party. "I'm still working out some final kinks in the burn center."

As if sensing her examination, he folded his hands. "And Trey?"

"Never a dull moment for him." Patricia leaned forward. "I've looked over your prospectus and the investment contract."

Even though he was still smiling, he seemed to stiffen ever so slightly. Eagerness to do a deal? Or concern he might lose one? "Any questions?"

"As a matter of fact, I do have a few."

He nodded. Gave a smile. "Sure. How can I help?"

"Do you have paperwork authenticating these automobiles?"

He hesitated for a moment. Then his eyes locked on Patricia's as if looking inside her head, and the smile eased from his face. "Of course," he said in a brittle voice. "But why would you question their authenticity?"

"I'm not questioning anything. I'm just engaging in due diligence."

A small vein below Maywood's jaw pulsed ever so slightly. "The prospectus and audited financial statements I provided you aren't enough?"

It was Patricia's turn to pause.

Maywood's jaw pulsing persisted.

Finally, Patricia said, "When can I get the authentication paperwork?"

"Give me a couple of days." Maywood consulted his watch, a different timepiece than the one he'd sported at the garden party, and stood. "You'll have to excuse me. I have a client coming over shortly."

"Why not give me the copies right now?"

"My attorney has the originals locked up."

Patricia stood. "Of course."

At the door, Maywood stepped close to her, blocking her exit. Too close. "Patricia," he said in a soft voice, "if you have any additional concerns about this investment please don't hesitate to discuss them with me."

Patricia nodded, eased past him and left.

No, she'd have no problem shooting him to protect Abigail.

CHAPTER 17

*I*t was morning feeding time for the feral cats. Patricia hadn't figured out which was the dominant partner of the pair who'd taken up residence on the back patio, but the one with the black markings had begun to show less fear of her.

Over the past few days, Patricia had spoken to the cats each morning and evening without any evidence they acknowledged the conversation. She hadn't minded. They were well-behaved, and she enjoyed having them around. Still, Patricia couldn't ignore the recent heightened boldness of the black cat, and decided to slowly extend a hand after putting the food bowl down.

Much to Patricia's surprise, the black cat stepped closer to her and briefly rubbed his cheek against her hand before slinking back to the edge of the patio. Patricia's heart sped. She knew the odds of domesticating a feral cat were against her, but this small welcoming gesture by the black cat was a huge first step. Patricia returned to the kitchen elated.

As soon as she closed the door, both cats went to the bowl, circling it while brushing their cheeks against each other. Then they crouched and fed, with Patricia watching through the door and beaming with delight.

Patricia sipped coffee as she gathered her thoughts, then called Maywood.

"Hello, Patricia," he said warily. "What can I do for you?"

"The authentication papers. You said two days. It's the morning of the third." She eyed the cats feeding on the patio.

"There's been a small problem." His voiced sounded rehearsed.

"Are you still planning to give me a copy of the papers?"

"Of course." His words were clipped.

"When?"

"Later today. Tomorrow morning at the latest."

"I'm glad to hear that."

"I'm a man of my word," he said coldly.

PATRICIA MET CONNIE AT THE GREEN TRUCK PUB FOR LUNCH and an update. "Any more sightings of Judy?" Patricia asked.

"Not a one." Connie raised her eyebrows as she glanced at Simon sitting by the door.

"No attempts on her ex-husband's life?"

"Nope. We haven't confirmed it yet, but she may have left on a flight to New York yesterday. I'm beginning to think Judy may no longer be in Savannah."

Disbelief surged. "Why was she at Beau's in the first place?"

"To wrap up some loose business or to distract us?" Connie ventured. "Maybe to make us concentrate our resources here before she disappeared again. Maybe to give her a measure of who was on her case and how we were deploying our resources. Who knows?"

"What's next?"

"If something positive doesn't pop up in the next day or

two, the Vatican wants me back in Rome. But wherever Judy is, she's a loaded gun with a hair trigger. I wouldn't let my guard down if I were you, just in case she hasn't left, or if she has but comes back."

"We're taking precautions. We've increased security at our home. Simon has become my shadow. I'm carrying. The Cotton Coalition has had their resources looking for Judy and hasn't seen any evidence she's still around. Whether she's here or not, I need to go about my investigation."

"Good, but err on the safe side."

Maywood called later that afternoon. "I have your papers. Do you want me to mail them?"

"Could you drop them off?"

"I'm in the middle of something right now."

"Could I pick them up?" Patricia asked, miffed at Maywood's lack of urgency.

"If you wish."

She shivered, not from what he'd said, but from the icy, ominous way he'd spoken. "I'll be right over."

Fifteen minutes, later Patricia and Simon pulled to the curb at Maywood's house. Once she turned the Escalade off, Simon buttoned a microphone under her collar. She left Simon in the car and went to the house. Much to her surprise, Maywood answered the door on the first ring. Patricia gave a smile.

"Won't you come in?" He led her to his office. When he offered coffee, she politely declined then sat across the desk from him.

Maywood pushed a thick manila envelope toward her. "The information you requested."

Patricia removed the papers and paged through them to those documenting the Ferrari 250 Europa. Her breath caught. "The last transaction for the Ferrari indicates Nikki Shelton is the owner."

"Yes. I have her car on consignment."

Patricia clenched her jaw and locked eyes with Maywood. "How can a car be two places at the same time?"

Maywood's eyes widened. "What … what do you mean?"

"Two weeks ago, you showed me this very car in your warehouse. This week, I visited Nikki Shelton and saw the same car in her garage."

He looked away, shaking his head. "Miss Shelton owns a reproduction as well as the original. She bought the original as an investment. She drives the reproduction. She's made quite a bit of money on her investment vehicle and asked me to sell it for her. Which is what I'm doing."

Patricia gave what she hoped would come across as a look of utter disgust. "You're selling shares in a car you don't own?"

"Once enough people subscribe to this set of automobiles, my company will buy all seven of them."

Well, it did make sense to get a firm commitment from the investors before buying the automobiles. Patricia nodded her understanding.

"Do you have any other questions?" he asked.

"No."

"I'm looking forward to your investment."

"I'm not going to invest," Patricia said, determined to panic Maywood and see who he contacted after she left. "There are just too many questions."

"I assure you—"

Patricia huffed. "I'm perfectly capable of drawing my own conclusions, thank you very much."

"What exactly are those conclusions, Mrs. Falcon?" he

asked in a reedy voice.

"Bad investment." She swallowed hard. "Possible fraud."

His cheek reddened. "That's absurd."

As soon as Patricia left Maywood's home, she called Nikki Sheldon. "Are you selling your Ferrari?"

"Heavens no," Nikki said. "I love that car."

"Have you consigned the original to anyone?"

"You've got to be kidding. Why would I do that?"

There it was. Maywood didn't have Nikki's car on consignment. He was selling shares in a reproduction car and representing the car as genuine. He was a slick talker and a complete fraud. "Is there a price that would cause you to change your mind?"

There was a pause, then Nikki said, "I have a personal attachment to my car. There's no price that would cause me to part with it."

After talking with Nikki, Patricia called Timnit. "Do you have the Slingshot call logging device in place at the Jacksons'?"

"Yes indeed."

"What were Maywood's calls in the last ten minutes?"

"He just made a call to Preston Somerset and mentioned your name. Apparently, Maywood knows you're investigating him."

"That's not surprising. I just told Maywood I'm not buying his scheme. Any other calls?"

"No. Just Preston. Maywood's phone has been silent since that call."

That evening, Patricia and Trey had dinner at Huey's, then moved to Rocks on the Roof to watch the sunset.

They were led through the rooftop lounge toward a patio table. As alert as a sentry dog, Patricia catalogued the patrons, then, seeing no threats, she relaxed and admired the aged wood, the rustic hues and the stunning oyster shell chandeliers. She guessed Simon might be close by, but she couldn't see him.

Trey ordered a bottle of chardonnay. Patricia settled back, marveling at how the setting sun had colored the clouds above the Talmadge Bridge with reds and pinks and oranges. "We certainly have a blessed life, Trey."

Seated next to her on the sofa, Trey settled his arm on her shoulders. Goosebumps prickled her skin. She closed her eyes, enjoying the deep, abiding sense of security filling her, as it always did when she was in his arms.

"With no new leads on Judy, Connie's heading back to Rome in a couple of days," Patricia said.

He gave her upper arm a gentle caress. "I understand. She has other work. The Cotton Coalition has had extensive resources looking for Judy, and we're cutting back on them as well."

Patricia rested her head on Trey's arm and looked up at the pink-hued sky. "I feel so bad for the Jackson Capital investors. I'm sure more than a few put way too much of their money into that scheme. Have we recovered our money?"

"No. I'm afraid that's impossible until the assets are sold." He shook his head. "Unfortunately, we're like all the rest of the people Maywood has deceived for so long."

Their wine arrived. Patricia took a sip. "I suppose those reproduction automobiles have some cash value."

"Unless they're heavily mortgaged."

Indignation rose. "This is going to be a financial disaster for Savannah. Thank goodness Meredith is having some success locating Maywood's overseas accounts."

CHAPTER 18

Willie, the dogged investigative reporter for the *Savannah Post*, called Patricia first thing the following morning. "I hear you're investigating Jackson Capital."

Patricia had a good idea what admitting to that could lead to. "Oh?"

"Come on, Patricia. You've always been open with me."

"I'm not investigating Jackson Capital."

"According to my source, you've been asking a lot of questions about the company."

She knew better than to ask him to name his source. "Not anymore."

"What happened?"

"I closed my investigation."

She heard Willie let out a long breath. "Why did you open an investigation of Jackson Capital in the first place?"

"Curiosity. Trey's an investor."

"Why did you close your investigation?"

"No longer curious."

"Should I look into Jackson Capital?"

She knew he'd probably take a 'no' as an indication she was hiding something, and thus, an invitation to investigate. "Feel free to do whatever you want, Willie."

He chuckled. "I intend to."

As soon as Willie was off the phone, Patricia called Trey and brought him up to date.

"I'll take care of Willie," Trey said.

"Another involuntary vacation?"

"We have other, less dramatic ways to close his investigation down."

Summer called midmorning. "Abigail needs us right now," Summer said in an uncharacteristic tight voice.

"I'm on it." Patricia grabbed her purse and headed for the garage. "Where is she?"

"At home."

Patricia's thoughts scattered. Had something she'd done or said incited Maywood to abuse his wife? Too many unknowns. She needed to focus. "Is she okay?"

"So far."

"How much time do we have?"

"As much as we need."

"I'll pick you up in five minutes and you can fill me in. Call Meredith and Timnit and let them know we need them."

"Will do."

Patricia went into the dining room, Simon's control center. "The girls and I are doing a pickup."

He pushed back from his computer and stood. "I have orders from Trey not to leave your side."

"We've got it, Simon." She patted her purse.

"Orders are orders."

"It never hurts to have more power. Thanks."

They went to the garage, got into the Escalade and backed down the driveway. Patricia was cautious not to let her surging emotions cloud her driving.

Summer, wearing her vest and utility belt, was at curbside when Patricia pulled up. She climbed in the passenger side. "Meredith and Timnit are available. They're both at Meredith's. Mornin', shadow," she added looking over her shoulder at Simon.

"Mornin', Doc."

Patricia wheeled the SUV into traffic. "What happened to Abigail?"

"Maywood beat her."

Patricia clenched her hands on the wheel, mindful to keep her focus on her driving. "What a damn monster. Is Maywood still there?"

"He's an insecure coward. Abigail said he stormed out. Never came back."

It took mere minutes to get to Meredith's. She and Timnit both smiled on seeing Simon. Then they shuffled into the back and suited up while Summer briefed them.

Rage mounted as Patricia heard for the second time that Maywood had beaten Abigail. Then Patricia's mother's words came. "Focus on rescuing the victim. Show compassion and support. Let the authorities deal with the abuser." Rage gave way to an iron-willed determination to get Abigail to a safe space at all costs.

Patricia pulled up in front of Abigail's house. "Simon, please stay by the car. Summer, you take the door. Timnit and I will cover your flanks. Meredith, take the wheel."

Hand on her holstered weapon, Patricia moved toward

the right side of the wraparound porch as Summer approached the front door.

Abigail, her lower lip swollen, emerged with a wheeled suitcase.

Summer embraced Abigail wordlessly, then lead her to the SUV with Timnit and Patricia following. At the SUV, Patricia gave Abigail a hug, then put her suitcase in the back and motioned with a wink for Simon to join it.

Timnit got in the passenger side. Patricia and Summer sat in the back, with Abigail in the middle. Patricia patted Abigail's hand.

As the SUV pulled from the curb, Abigail reached into her purse, pulled out a ledger book, and handed it to Patricia.

"What's this?" Patricia asked.

"Revenge."

"Revenge?"

"Maywood's overseas accounts ledger. Account locations and numbers. Passwords. Transactions. Mostly deposits. And a list of his biggest investors."

Patricia's heart sped.

CHAPTER 19

$\mathscr{P}$atricia, still wearing her assault gear, and Meredith arrived at Sonny Carothers' accounting firm to review Maywood's ledger. Simon waited outside in the Escalade.

As they entered the conference room with his receptionist, Sarah, Sonny stood. He wore khakis and a pale-blue, button-down shirt. His sleeves were rolled to just below his elbows. His black hair, which he normally wore long, was trimmed more closely, and he sported a fair amount of facial stubble.

His mouth tipped into a slight smile. "If you don't mind, I'll have Sarah make working copies of the ledger."

Patricia handed the young woman the book.

"Three copies as soon as possible," Sonny said, then gestured for Meredith and Patricia to sit. "Have you had a chance to review the ledger?"

"Not yet." Patricia rolled her chair closer to the table. "We just received it and came right over."

Sonny sat. "I hope the ledger clarifies what I've already learned. As I mentioned earlier, Maywood and Jackson

Capital own or control offshore holding companies with a combined net worth in excess of one billion dollars. I have no idea how he managed to put together that empire."

"That's a lot more than can be accounted for selling shares in rare automobiles," Meredith said. Meredith wore a black shirt over black jeans, her standard outfit for picking up victims. Her long, dark hair was loose, covering her scar. "Were you able to locate any other significant income sources for Maywood?"

"He has several overseas entities that keep sending him huge sums of money, but they don't appear to be affiliated with his holding companies." Sonny shrugged. "I can't figure out what those entities are getting in return. It could be entirely legal. He could be selling those reproduction automobiles overseas. Or it could be money laundering or drugs. I just don't know."

Meredith sat back. "You mentioned he's buying museum-quality art. Is there any evidence he's resold some of those pieces?"

Sonny shook his head. "Not that I can tell. But these large entities have to be getting something from Maywood. He's not a bank."

Meredith bolted forward. "Maybe he is. Maybe he loaned money or assets and is getting paid back at exorbitant interest rates. Maybe the deposits are loan repayments. Or maybe he's holding money for them."

He paused, then nodded. "I suppose anything is possible."

They sat in silence for a moment.

Patricia turned to Sonny. "Let's talk about the connection between Chao Ping Auto and Maywood. Why would Chao Ping build automobiles in the United States?"

"Car parts have a lower value and a lower customs duty than fully assembled automobiles," Sonny said.

Sarah came in, deposited a tray with cups and a coffee

carafe on the table, distributed the copies, returned the ledger to Patricia and left.

Sonny asked, "Coffee anyone?"

It had been a long morning. Patricia didn't know about Meredith, but she could use some coffee. She and Meredith pushed cups toward Sonny.

Sonny poured theirs, then filled a cup for himself.

Coffee cup in hand, Patricia watched Sonny quickly page through his copy of Maywood's ledger.

"There's nothing in here about his holding companies," he said. "Just offshore bank accounts and a list of clients of some sort. I can't believe the size of these deposits." When Sonny reached the end of the pages, he looked up with a smile. "Big picture is that in addition to his overseas holding companies, he also has several hundred million on deposit overseas."

The corner of Sonny's mouth twitched. "But more importantly, this ledger fills in some of the missing pieces in his overall financial picture. I had most of Maywood's domestic finances figured out, including domestic monies transferred overseas, but this ledger reveals more of the international part."

"More?" Patricia put her cup on the table.

Sonny gave her a long look. "He has much more in these offshore accounts than I can attribute to Jackson Capital transfers or to the clients listed here." Sonny's brown eyes narrowed as he examined the first page. "So, this list of depositors is incomplete."

"Maybe there's another ledger," Meredith said as she slowly flipped one page after another.

"Maywood obviously has other sources of income," Sonny continued. "Jackson Capital only accounts for a small percentage of what he's placed overseas."

Meredith scowled. "We don't know if any of that additional money is tainted, but his rare car scheme certainly qualifies as fraud."

Patricia's gaze lingered on an entry on the page she'd just turned to. She sighed to herself. It wasn't the massive cash balances Maywood had amassed. Nor was it the extensive list of clients who had invested money with him. Rather, it was the huge investment Preston Somerset had made a decade ago when Jackson Capital was first formed.

"What do you suggest we do next?" Meredith asked.

"I'll put all this data together into a financial report," Sonny said. "Give me a couple of days to do that. Then I think it's time y'all give what you have to the authorities."

Patricia turned in her chair and stared at Sonny. "Do you think we have enough for them to put Maywood away?"

"He's misrepresented reproduction automobiles as originals using counterfeit authentication papers and solicited investors based on those representations. That's fraud," he said.

She turned to Meredith.

Meredith nodded. "I agree."

"Can the authorities seize that overseas money?" Patricia asked.

Meredith nodded again. "Yes. Eventually."

"Would seized assets mean investors will get at least their initial investment back?"

Meredith frowned. "They may, but it depends on where all this money came from and how much of it is owed to the US government."

Patricia picked up her mug again, inhaled the bold aroma and took a sip. Maywood was a fat trout on a solid hook. Now, as long as they could ensure he was quickly fished out of the water, she might be able to give Hannah some good news, and the burn center might get a lovely donation.

However, the problem with catching a fat trout was how slippery they could be.

It was midafternoon, and Patricia was at home putting ledger details into her case file when her phone rang.

"I'm across the street from Chao Ping Auto's showroom in Statesboro," Summer said with excitement in her voice.

"Great," Patricia said. "Have you got the information on Chao Ping's customers that we want?" Patricia knew they'd have to cross-reference everything to make a watertight case to turn over to the authorities.

"No. Statesboro police have blocked access to Chao Ping's parking lot. FBI personnel are carrying boxes out of the office building. Looks like it might be a raid of some sort."

Patricia began pacing. "The FBI?"

"Yes. FBI are coming and going from the office. Statesboro police are guarding the perimeter."

A herd of questions trampled Patricia's concentration. She stared into space trying to clear her mind and center it on the situation. "What do you see besides FBI carrying out boxes?"

"Television crews and unmarked SUVs inside the perimeter. Lots of spectators outside."

Patricia let out a long breath. "Ask the local police blocking the entrance what's going on."

"I did," Summer said. "They told me 'no comment.'"

"Try talking with the spectators. See if they saw more than you. Then check out Chao Ping's hanger at Maywood's airport. It's not on GPS maps. I'll send you directions. I'm guessing the FBI will be there as well."

"Didn't the FBI tell Timnit and Simon to stay away from that hanger?" Summer asked.

"They never banned *you*. If you get stopped, just say you're lost, turn around and come back to Savannah."

As soon as Patricia hung up, she called Willie. "Do you know anything about an FBI raid in Statesboro?"

"Sure do. I'm here."

Anticipation of finally getting answers rose. "That was fast."

"The FBI gave the media a heads-up a couple of hours ago."

"What's going on?"

"You're lucky I'm more forthcoming with you than you are with me. It's trademark infringement involving unauthorized reproductions of high-end classic automobiles. Apparently, they've arrested several people here and are seizing records and property."

Patricia's stomach churned. An FBI raid of Chao Ping would certainly spook Maywood. What a screw up. "Who's the lead there?"

"An FBI Financial Crimes Unit."

Who else were they coming after today? Jackson Capital? "Any other locations involved?"

"All I've heard about is here and an assembly plant in a hanger outside of town. I've got to go, Patricia. It's about time for a scheduled press conference. Turn on your TV. I'm sure Savannah stations will carry the press conference live."

"Okay, Willie." She knew the ledger had Maywood's account numbers and passwords. If he didn't have a duplicate, he couldn't get the money, but he could still flee. If he did, she hoped he wouldn't destroy evidence before he left.

. . .

SHE CALLED HER CLOSE FRIEND, STATION CHIEF ALGENON Melfive, at the FBI. The call rolled into voicemail, so she left a message.

We haven't talked for a while. A friend asked me to look into Jackson Capital. In light of the raid on Chao Ping Auto, who supplies cars to Jackson Capital, I'm concerned Maywood Jackson might try to flee the country. Please give me a call.

She disconnected the call and turned on the kitchen TV. Sure enough, the first station she tried was covering the FBI raid. They ran raw footage of men and women being escorted out of the office building and placed in unmarked black SUVs. There was footage of quite a few boxes being removed from the building as well and a reporter voiceover that a press briefing was upcoming.

Patricia watched the short press briefing where Savannah FBI special agent in charge Algenon thanked his partner organizations for their support on the lengthy investigation that culminated in arrests and the closure of Chao Ping Auto. When asked if there would be additional arrests, Algenon replied that there could be depending on what they found in the evidence they had just seized.

If Maywood Jackson was watching this, she needed to be watching him.

TIMNIT CALLED. "THE PHONE INTERCEPTOR AT THE JACKSONS is going crazy."

"I can imagine," Patricia said. "I bet he's anticipating an imminent FBI action against his company." She filled Timnit in on the news of the FBI raid on Chao Ping.

"What do you want me to do?" Timnit asked.

"Stay tuned in. I need to know Maywood's plans while I figure out how to make sure the information we have on Maywood gets to the FBI soon enough that we are not obstructing, but not before we've done all we can to assure the investors will be protected." Patricia was going to have to ask Trey, with all his legal expertise, to figure out a way through this minefield.

"I'll keep you posted," Timnit said.

WHEN PATRICIA WENT TO THE PATIO TO RETRIEVE THE FOOD and water bowls that evening, there was a gold chain with an emerald pendant on the mat at the doorstep. Recognizing it immediately, her heart sped. It was the high school graduation gift she'd received from her parents. Something she'd worn often after arriving in Savannah, but had lost shortly after marrying Trey twenty years ago. The thin chain was broken an inch from the clasp.

Had one of the cats discovered it and brought it to her as a gift?

After washing the bowls and the treasured jewelry, she settled down in the family room with Trey.

"Remember when I lost my graduation necklace at that party here shortly after we were married?" Patricia asked. "It showed up."

"Just showed up?"

"I think one of the cats found it and brought it to our back door." She held the chain up.

He took it. "It's broken."

"Just the chain."

"Do you mind if I get this fixed for you?"

She gave him a heartfelt smile. "Not at all."

"I'll take it to Levy's tomorrow."

Patricia filled Trey in on Maywood's ledger and the raid on Chao Ping. "So, should we tell the FBI right now we have the ledger, or wait?"

"I'll call my contact first and get confirmation that everything is playing out like we think. Then we can make a better determination. I'll also fill the Cotton Coalition directors in."

Trey immediately contacted his friend at the Savannah FBI office and got confirmation of what Patricia had told him. Nothing more. Patricia's cell vibrated. She checked the screen. A text from Summer.

SK: Abigail just checked herself out of the shelter.

PF: Where's she going?

SK: Don't know. She gave up her cell at the shelter. I called her home phone. Maywood answered. Abigail isn't there. I'm going to check her Bible study friends.

PF: Let me know when you locate her.

SK: Will do.

Patricia called Simon. "Can you do a quick relationship map and profile on Abigail Jackson? I'll text you some names."

"Of course," he said. "What's going on?"

Patricia filled Simon in.

"Give me a couple of hours," Simon said.

Leaving Abigail's safety in Summer's capable hands, Patricia attempted to return to putting the last of the ledger details into the case file.

A HALF HOUR LATER, TREY'S PHONE CHIMED.

"It's Isabel," Trey told Patricia, putting the phone to his ear.

The head of the Cotton Coalition would only call Trey at night if it was urgent.

The call was short, and Trey said nothing. When the call was over, he turned to Patricia, his face grim. "The Coalition has had round the clock surveillance on Preston Somerset since Judy showed up. He went to the Jacksons house midafternoon. He visits there often, but never for long. As far as we can tell, he hasn't left. We're going to give him until midnight, then we're calling the police."

"We just discovered Preston made a huge investment in Jackson Capital a decade ago, when it was first formed."

A text chime from Trey's side of the bed woke Patricia. She rolled toward Trey in the dim light as he sat up on the edge of the bed to look at his phone.

"What is it?" she asked his back. She could tell his muscles were bunched tight. Tense.

"Emergency meeting of the Cotton Coalition directors."

Patricia shivered. "Did something happen to Preston?"

"No. Not Preston. Maywood Jackson. He's dead."

CHAPTER 20

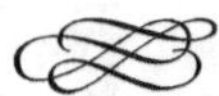

Patricia came downstairs the following morning dressed in black yoga pants and a black tee-shirt. Trey was seated at the kitchen table, nursing a coffee.

"Did you get any sleep last night?" Patricia asked, enjoying the cool terrazzo tile on her bare feet.

He looked up. His unshaven jaw bristled with whiskers. "Last night's Coalition meeting on Maywood's death ran long. Chief Patrick gave us a detailed briefing. I only got a couple of hours or so. I slept on the sofa so I wouldn't wake you when I came home."

"I wish you'd come upstairs. I had a fitful sleep with you gone." She went to him and gave him a good morning kiss. "Going to work today?"

He nodded.

"Would you like some biscuits and gravy?"

A smile filled his face. "That would be perfect, Patsy."

Patricia set the oven to 425 degrees. "So, how'd Maywood die?"

"Murdered. Single shot. Perfect placement."

A hit. She shuddered.

"From the look of things, Chief Patrick thinks it was a professional hit." Trey confirmed her fears.

Patricia scooped kibble into the food bowl, put the bowl outside, petted the head of the gray cat, then returned to the kitchen. "I didn't know Preston had that kind of gun training," Patricia remarked as she washed her hands, then assembled the ingredients for the biscuits.

Preston had always seemed genteel, if a bit slimy. She didn't like him much, but that didn't make him a murderer.

"In truth," Trey said, "other than a lipstick-smudged champagne coupe that may have DNA, Chief Patrick doesn't presently have anyone in particular in his sights other than Preston." He shook his head.

She knew Trey wasn't easily disturbed, but he was clearly shaken this morning. "Should I give Chief Patrick my case file?"

"I think that would be wise."

Patricia cut butter into the dry ingredients. "I figured as much. My case file is up-to-date. The only physical evidence I have is Maywood's ledger and the fake authentication papers on the automobiles he wanted me to invest in. Sonny is doing a report on Maywood's financial situation, but with the sudden appearance of Maywood's ledger, he needs a couple more days to wrap up his report. And Simon is doing a relationship map on Abigail, who's missing."

"Turning your case file over to Chief Patrick means you're done on this case."

Patricia made a well in the flour mixture, added milk, a raw egg, and a shot of vodka to assure the biscuits were moist. Then she kneaded the dough. "Well, Sonny said there is probably another ledger that carries on from the first. I'd like to look into that loose end."

"Only if you don't interfere with the murder investigation."

"Of course." Bits and pieces of her investigation whirled like a hurricane. But one piece stood out. "Abigail told Summer her home has cameras and microphones all over. She couldn't go anywhere inside without Maywood knowing exactly what she was doing. Maywood's murder has to have been recorded on that system."

"Chief Patrick's crime scene investigators looked at the Jacksons' security system right away. It was shut off when they found it, and the memory was wiped clean. They've sent the hard drive to the Georgia Bureau of Investigation for a forensic analysis."

"Why would someone thorough enough to wipe a security system leave a telltale glass?"

"Maybe they were interrupted." Trey stared into space. "Or maybe Maywood previously wiped the system in preparation for getting out of town."

Patricia rolled out the dough and cut it with her grandmother's biscuit cutter. As soon as she put the biscuits in the oven and set the timer, she began to crumble sausage into a hot skillet. "Who found the body?"

"Savannah Police." There was a pause. "Mmm. That sausage sure smells good."

She looked over her shoulder and gave him a smile. He stood, walked over to her, wrapped his arms around her and squeezed.

She let go of the pan handle and wrapped an arm around herself, holding him to her. For a moment, they both stood still. She leaned her head back into him, then turned to face him.

"You sure know how to pamper me, Patsy." He gave her a long, slow kiss.

"I think we both need comfort food this morning," she said softly.

As he released her, she gathered her senses and returned

her attention to the skillet, adding a little flour to the crumbled, cooking sausage. "Did the CSIs get into Maywood's computer?"

"It was wiped clean like his security system and his cell phone. Patrick sent both devices to GBI for forensic analysis."

Patricia added milk and flour, and stirred the gravy. "Did your man ever reconnect with Preston?"

"Preston was at his home this morning. He left for his law office at the same time he always does. Since Preston was the last person seen at Maywood's yesterday, Chief Patrick plans to question him later today."

Patricia rubbed her lower lip. "I wonder how he got out of Maywood's house without your man knowing."

"He could have gone out the back," Trey said. "We only had one person on surveillance, and he was covering the front."

"Any chance the Jackson home is connected to the tunnel system?"

"I hadn't considered that." Trey put a message into his cell. "We'll have to look into it."

Patricia adjusted the stovetop to keep the gravy warm, then checked the timer on the biscuits. Ten minutes to go. She grabbed the coffee pot and refilled both their cups, then plopped in a chair across from Trey. "I hope Summer found out more about where Abigail went after she left the women's shelter yesterday. I need to check in with Summer and find out if she has any leads."

Trey shook his head. "Abigail is still MIA as far as I know. And definitely also a person of interest." Trey picked up his cup and took a drink. "Abigail, Preston, … and whoever's DNA is on that champagne glass."

"So y'all believe Maywood was drinking champagne with

a woman sometime yesterday, and either she may have seen something, or she's the killer?"

Trey swirled the coffee in his cup. "It appears so."

"Hopefully her DNA will be in the national database."

AFTER TREY LEFT FOR WORK, PATRICIA CLEANED UP THE kitchen, then went upstairs to get ready for the day. An hour later, dressed in a blue Lilly Pulitzer shift, she was back downstairs. She poured coffee and sat.

The kitchen had a nostalgic feel to it. How many hours in the past two weeks had she sat at that table reviewing case files and sorting out theories and leads? She'd felt so alive investigating, but with the exception of the second ledger, the case was now out of her hands. She wasn't going to be able to help Hannah after all.

Patricia stared into her steaming cup and let out a long sigh. She supposed she'd have more time now for the burn unit. And maybe help Summer become a marksman.

Her phone chimed a text.

TF: I'm on the way home with Chief Patrick. Should be there in 5 or 10.

TF: They found what could be the murder weapon.

TF: It's your gun, Patsy.

CHAPTER 21

In utter disbelief that she might have misplaced her gun, Patricia dashed across the kitchen to the countertop by the back door and pulled her Kimber 45 from the concealed compartment of her purse. With a quick glance at the distinctive initials Trey had put on the grip, she confirmed it was her gun. Relief swept through her. Whatever weapon the cops had found, it wasn't hers. She returned the Kimber to the hidden compartment.

So what gun had Chief Patrick's guys found, and why did they believe it was hers?

She paced to the other side of the kitchen and turned just as Trey, dressed in a dark suit, came in through the back door, followed by Chief Patrick.

Patrick, a big man and good friend, wore a dark-blue suit, a light-blue tie, and a crisp white shirt. His expression was somber.

Patricia glanced at Trey, trying to get a read on his state of mind. He appeared completely at ease. Good. Patricia took further strength from that and extended her hand to Patrick.

The chief took it and gave a gentle shake. "Sorry for the intrusion, Patricia."

"It's not my gun, Patrick."

He nodded his acknowledgement. "Okay. Can we just sit and talk for a while?"

Trey led them into the family room, where they sat in upholstered chairs around the glass-topped coffee table.

Patricia took another quick look at Trey. He had repeatedly warned her on being careful in conversations with authorities. Be truthful. Always. But be brief. And always have a lawyer present. But Patrick was a good friend.

"Patsy," Trey said, "the chief is going to ask you some questions. If I feel any question is inappropriate, I'll let you know. As long as Chief Patrick is here, I'll be functioning as your attorney."

Patricia's eyes darted from one to the other. "I understand."

The chief removed a notebook and a stick pen. "This is purely voluntary."

"Go ahead," Patricia said.

"Where were you last night between six and midnight?"

"Here. With Trey." She gestured to her husband.

Patrick's gaze shifted to Trey.

Trey nodded.

Patrick returned his focus to Patricia. "Did you leave at any time between six and midnight?"

"What's this got to do with the gun you found?"

"We'll get there. Now tell me, Patricia, did you leave between six and midnight?"

"No."

"Did Trey?"

"No."

"What time did you go to bed?"

"Nine."

The chief turned to Trey. "What time did you go to bed?"

"The same time as Patricia."

Patrick brought his attention back to her. "Do you own a handgun?"

Finally. "Yes."

"How many do you own?"

"Only one."

The chief frowned. "You've never owned another gun?"

"Correct."

"Describe your weapon."

"A Kimber 45."

"When did you purchase your handgun?"

Patricia assumed Patrick already knew everything but was just covering the bases and getting an interview pattern established. "Trey purchased it shortly after we were married."

"That would be twenty years ago?" Patrick asked.

"Yes."

"Is your Kimber registered?"

"Yes. Twenty years ago."

"Where is this weapon?"

Patricia gestured to her purse, sitting on the kitchen counter by the back door.

"May I see it?"

She stood, retrieved her purse and offered the gun to Chief Patrick.

He examined it. "Why are you so sure *this* is your gun?"

She showed him the initials *VJ* engraved on the grip. "I can't imagine these initials being on any weapon but mine."

"Whose initials are those?" Patrick asked.

"It's an inside joke," Trey said.

"That's not convincing, Trey. What's the story on those initials?"

"Vigilantes for Justice."

Patrick's brow furrowed. "Why?"

"Patricia and her friends rescue abused women," Trey said. "They coined the term Vigilantes for Justice to describe themselves."

"Okay. I'll accept that." Patrick turned to Patricia. "How many handguns did you say you own?"

"I already told you. One. Just one." She held her Kimber up. "This one."

"Yet we found a handgun registered to you twenty years ago less than a block from Maywood's home. A gun that's the same caliber as the bullet that killed Mr. Jackson."

"That's impossible. I have my gun right here."

"Let me see your gun again." Patrick made note of the serial number and returned the weapon to her. Then he removed his phone and punched out a text. "The handgun you're holding has a serial number that's not the serial number of the gun registered to you twenty years ago."

"What?" Trey asked.

A lump formed in Patricia's throat. "How can that be?"

"I don't know, Patricia. We'll do a quick trace on the serial number for this gun," he said as he slid the phone back in his jacket pocket. "Maybe that will give us a better idea of what's going on here."

She let out a long breath. "Maybe there was some sort of clerical mistake in the registration or your lookup."

"My goodness," Trey said. "Is there a chance someone may have stolen the original gun and replaced it with the gun in your purse? And when? I only had it engraved about a year ago."

"Who would have had access, or motive?" the chief asked.

Her mind whirled through her recent cases, but they were all neat and tidy. Only Judy, the woman who murdered her mother, was still at large.

"Since I carry my weapon in my purse, anyone with ready

access to my purse could be the thief. Any number of people fit the bill, but my guess is that it's Judy Simpson."

The chief jotted a note. "Why do you suspect Mrs. Simpson?"

"Trey had *VJ* engraved on the gun in my purse shortly after Judy was arrested. So, the theft of my original Kimber had to have occurred before that. At the time, I was investigating the murder of my mother, unaware that my former good friend, Judy, was responsible." Patricia paused for a moment. "I know this might sound out there, but now that I'm thinking about it, it makes perfect sense. I have a strong suspicion Judy stole my gun and replaced it with an identical weapon, hoping to use the original to frame me for something that would distract me from my investigation."

The chief frowned, but somehow refrained from the skeptical look Patricia was expecting. "Why would she or an accomplice use the weapon now?"

Patricia shook her head. "Perhaps lack of opportunity until last night."

The chief looked at Trey. "Do you have any other explanation for how Patricia's Kimber became a suspected murder weapon?"

Trey shook his head.

Chief Patrick rubbed his chin, staring into space. "I suppose we can go with your theft theory for the time being." He put his notebook and pen back in his coat pocket. "About the gun in your purse, since it may be evidence in this investigation and is not your, I'd like you to turn it over to me. And I'd like you to come down to headquarters sometime today to give us a current set of your fingerprints."

Yet again, she glanced at Trey.

He twisted his lips, then nodded.

"Of course," she offered.

"And you have a detailed case file on your investigation of Jackson Capital. Correct?"

"Yes."

"Trey says it has information that could implicate Mr. Somerset in financial fraud."

"Yes."

"Bring your case file with you when you come to the station. I'd like to make a copy of it."

"It's missing a couple of important last-minute reports."

"That's okay," Patrick said. "You can add those reports when you receive them. We want to review what you currently have right away."

Patricia nodded.

The chief removed his cell and read a message. "The gun in your purse was purchased fifteen months ago by Herman Stockford. Does that name ring a bell with either of you?"

Patricia's mind raced until it settled on who Herman was. "That's Judy Simpson's brother."

"Well that certainly helps with the theft theory. Did Mr. Stockford have access to your purse?"

"Not that I know of. I've never met him."

The chief reached for his pen. "I don't suppose Judy ever shared an address or phone number for him?"

"No. And remember, he died a year ago from the same poison Judy used to kill my mother."

"Oh, that's right. What a shame. I would have liked to have spoken with him." Patrick stood. "Well, that does it for me. Thank you for your cooperation, Patricia."

"I'll just walk Patrick to his car," Trey said.

She handed the gun to the chief and followed the two men to the back door.

Trey gave her a smile. "You did good." Then he left with the chief.

. . .

"Doesn't Patrick already have my fingerprints from my concealed carry application?" Patricia asked as soon as Trey returned.

"He does, but they take prints electronically nowadays and the digital images they obtain are much sharper than ink prints. He's completely within his rights to request a new set of prints."

"Then we need to give him my fingerprints promptly."

He nodded. "Yes, indeed. And I wouldn't be surprised if he asks for your DNA while we're there."

"Let me make a copy of my case file, then let's get down to headquarters right away."

Sonny called on their way to police headquarters. "I have to delay wrapping up the final report on Jackson's financial profile," he said. "I hope it won't inconvenience you."

Patricia put her cell on speaker so Trey, who was driving the Bentley, could hear. "What's up?"

"Cotton McNaly, Jackson Capital's treasurer and Maywood's CPA, may have been skimming profits from Jackson Capital. I've asked Meredith to locate as many of his bank records as possible. She says she needs a couple of days."

"Good work, Sonny. Take as much time as you need to do a thorough job."

"Only the best for you, Patricia."

Patricia disconnected the call and turned to Trey. "Doesn't that just beat all?"

"I'll say. As thorough as Maywood was with his financials, I'm surprised he didn't figure out he was being swindled."

"Maybe Maywood did eventually figure it out. Maybe he confronted Cotton and threatened to turn him over to the authorities. Maybe, in panic, Cotton murdered Maywood to avoid being turned in."

Trey stopped for a family in the crosswalk. "Lots of

maybes there. Plus, if Maywood was committing fraud, I'm not sure he'd want to get the authorities involved in his business dealings."

"I wish we knew who, besides Preston, was in Maywood's house in those final hours," Patricia said. "And what they did."

"Preston should be able to shed some light on that. And if he doesn't, the Cotton Coalition recently put a geo-fence on Maywood's home. In a couple of days, we should have a list of cell phone numbers pinged there and what times the phones were at Maywood's house."

"Why were you monitoring Maywood's house?" Patricia asked.

"Once you documented fraud, the Coalition decided to support your investigation."

"When are you going to be briefed on Preston's interview with the police?" Patricia asked.

"Chief Patrick said I could speak directly with the lead detective anytime I wished."

"Since I'm a suspect, isn't that unusual?" Patricia asked.

"You have a strong alibi. Patrick's on our side and appreciates any help we can give him on promptly solving this murder."

"Do you think the lead detective will be there when we get to headquarters?" Patricia picked up her cell as Trey pulled to a stop at a red light.

"Let me make the call." Trey hit the Bluetooth display, speed-dialed Patrick and made an appointment to speak to the detective.

On arriving at police headquarters, Patricia and Trey met with Detective Rodriguez. He wore jeans and a white golf shirt.

"Hello, Mrs. And Mr. Falcon." Rodriquez gave a broad smile as he shook her hand, then Trey's. He gestured to chairs around the conference room table and they all sat.

Rodriguez removed a notebook and placed it on the table. "The chief asked me to get the Maywood Jackson case file from you, Mrs. Falcon."

Patricia handed him the thumb drive.

He cocked his head to one side. "And the physical evidence?"

"I'm sorry. I forgot. We left in a hurry. I'll bring it over later today."

"No problem. So, I understand y'all are interested in my interview of Mr. Somerset."

Patricia and Trey nodded.

Rodriguez consulted his notebook. "I spoke with Mr. Somerset this morning at eight. Unfortunately, there's not much to share. Mr. Somerset lawyered up as soon as I started questioning him."

"Was he charged?" Trey asked.

"No. We didn't have sufficient probable cause." Rodriguez fixed his gaze on Patricia. "The chief said you may have some information that might implicate Mr. Somerset in financial fraud."

"Are you familiar with Jackson Capital?" she asked.

"I'm coming up to speed on that."

"Preston Somerset handled Jackson Capital's corporate filing with the Georgia Department of State. He's also listed as the transfer agent for their principle asset, a fleet of counterfeit rare automobiles that Jackson Capital has repeatedly represented and valued as authentic."

"Do you have proof?"

"As I said, he's the registered agent on the corporate papers on file with the Secretary of State and the transfer agent on the vehicle registrations." Patricia decided not to mention that Preston had also received a sizable monthly check from Jackson Capital since its founding, as that information came from Meredith who probably broke some laws obtaining it.

The detective jotted some notes. "How did Jackson Capital misrepresent the automobiles?"

"In a prospectus and in counterfeit authentication documents. Plus, Maywood Jackson hosted investor tours and parties where the automobiles are stored and represented them as authentic."

"Are those documents on the thumb drive you just gave me?"

"Yes."

"I'd like physical copies as well," Rodriquez said.

"Those documents are at home. I'll bring them to your office with the rest of the physical evidence."

"How did you come by the authentication documents?"

"I was considering making an investment. Mr. Jackson provided them to me as an inducement to invest."

He raised his eyebrows. "I was told you were investigating Jackson Capital."

"That too." She felt her cheeks flush.

The detective made a note on the notepad. "So, your assumption is that Mr. Somerset, as a corporate insider, is fully aware of the misrepresentations regarding the counterfeit automobiles?"

"Yes."

He studied Patricia for a moment. "Do you have any proof that Preston Somerset *personally* represented the automobiles as authentic?"

"No."

"Well, your information might be sufficient probable cause to obtain search warrants for evidence of his insider status. Is there anything I can do for you?"

"Have you located Abigail yet?"

He shook his head. "Not a clue. Anything else?"

"No. That does it for me."

He nodded. "Then let's get those fingerprints and DNA taken care of, and y'all can be on your way."

ON THE WAY HOME FROM THE POLICE STATION, SIMON TEXTED Patricia.

SX: Judy Simpson shows up on Abigail's relationship map. Call me for details.

CHAPTER 22

*P*atricia put her phone on speaker so Trey, who was driving, could hear, then she speed-dialed Simon. "What's the scoop on Judy and Abigail?" she asked.

"I just learned that shortly after the first time Judy came to Savannah, she joined Abigail's Bible study group," Simon said. "She attended weekly discussions and, according to one of the members, became quite close to Abigail."

Patricia cringed. *There could only be one reason for Judy doing that.* "Don't tell me they played tennis."

"As a matter of fact, they did. Weekly. At Abigail's club."

Patricia's chest tightened at the implications. "How long did this go on?"

"Several months. Then Judy dropped out of the Bible study group."

"No more contact with Abigail after that?"

"No evidence of further contact."

"Anything else, Simon?" Patricia asked, relieved.

"No. That does it. I'll send you the completed relationship map for Abigail in an hour or so."

Patricia disconnected and, her mind whirling, settled

back in the passenger seat. "Abigail is lucky she didn't have any money to invest with Judy," Patricia said. "Otherwise, she would probably be among the dead at this point."

"Very lucky."

"You know," Patricia said, "whoever killed Maywood with that single shot was either well-trained or very lucky. And, according to the chief, they seem to have covered their tracks pretty well, including planting evidence meant to misdirect. I can't believe Judy is a trained assassin. There's no evidence for that. I've seen her on the firing range. She's not that good of a shot. And after I put the 45 slug through her right hand, I'd bet she's shooting left-handed. A single, perfectly placed kill-shot seems like too much for Judy. Sure, she's a killer, but in the past she used poison."

"But your gun is most likely the murder weapon," Trey said as he pulled the Bentley to a stop at a light. "It's pretty clear to me that Judy stole your Kimber. If Judy isn't the murderer, it's likely the killer is someone she knows or hired."

"Judy's got to be fully aware she would be arrested as soon as she showed her face," Patricia said. "Yet, rather than hiding from the authorities, she's messing with us. She knows very well how capable we are, yet she's still coming after us. It doesn't make sense she'd risk prison again. She's used surrogates before. Why not now?"

"Who?"

"Abigail? Preston? A paid killer? Who knows."

Trey slowed to make a right turn. "Where would Judy get the money to hire an assassin?"

Patricia swiped a hand down her face. "Do you suppose she has a horde of cash somewhere? She did live a lavish lifestyle."

Trey shook his head. "I think Beau was bankrolling that."

"You said he was broke."

"After being married to Judy, he was," Trey said. "So how would Judy have the means to hire a killer? Maybe she got the money from a lover. Remember, Beau claimed she was sleeping around."

"I do remember." Patricia closed her eyes and rubbed her temple. "What if … what if Judy's involvement with Abigail was just a pretense to get to Maywood. After all, he was the person with money. Plenty of it, if we can believe his journal."

"Maywood as Judy's target and lover. Hmm. Unfortunately, Maywood isn't around to shed more light on that theory."

"Nor is Judy," Patricia said. "But for some reason, Abigail suspected Maywood was unfaithful. Do you suppose she actually found hard evidence about Judy and Maywood, then flipped out and killed Maywood?"

"Hard to tell, Patsy. But where would Abigail get your gun?"

"Which brings us back to a paid killer."

Trey paused to let a group of SCAD students cross the street. "Look at how your gun was thrown in a public trash can a block away. That's not something a professional hit man would do, unless told to do so. This was well planned to point the blame at you."

"I agree."

Trey pulled into the garage. "With Judy still on the loose, I'm not sure it's wise to have Hayley come home after she finishes her summer forensic internship."

"We keep talking about this, Trey, but we don't make any decisions." Patricia looked out the window at their dust-covered bicycles stowed on the side of the garage. "We're her parents. We have to protect her. What bothers me is that because of our work there will *always* be life-threatening dangers for every member of our family. You taught me not to run from that danger. And, sooner or later, we'll have to teach Hayley how to live with the dangers as well. But now?" She shook her head. "No. Not now."

Then she thought of Hayley having a life of always looking over her shoulder, like she herself did, and slammed her fist on the dash pad. "Why not now? Let her come home. Pair her with Simon or Timnit. Teach her real-time situational awareness and close-combat skills. We *have* to do this, Trey," Patricia said resolutely. "I don't want her going back to college in September without those skills. Not as long as Judy and who knows who else is out there looking to kill us."

"We should have fully trained her long ago." Trey leaned back and exhaled. "As soon as she gets home, we'll start."

"I wish we could locate Judy and put her away first."

"It's not like a lot of us haven't been trying, Patricia."

"Well, this Judy/Abigail link is new information."

"True. We should let Connie know before she heads back to the Vatican."

"How about having her over for dinner tonight?" Patricia asked. "I could make shrimp and grits."

Trey turned off the car and opened his door. "You want me to call her?"

"No. I'll do it," Patricia said as she stepped out of the car.

Once inside the house, Patricia called Meredith. "Would you check Maywood's bank accounts and see if he transferred any money to Judy Simpson? Start with that shadow account she and her brother used to bilk my mother." Abject sadness invaded at the mention of her mother.

"Will do, Patricia. Anything else?"

"No. That will do for now. Thank you."

Patricia assembled the physical evidence on Maywood's investment scheme and slipped the items into a large manila envelope.

"I'll drop those off for Detective Rodriguez on my way to work," Trey offered.

She gave him a warm hug, then handed him the package. "You sure it won't be a problem?"

"No problem." Trey grabbed his leather satchel.

Patricia stepped to Trey and adjusted his open collar tucked under his navy blazer. "Would you like some red velvet cake tonight?"

He gave her a broad smile that pleased her no end. "For sure."

She kissed him and enjoyed the little shiver the touch of his lips gave her. Somehow, after all these years, kissing Trey was still a treat. She wished he could stay, but knew he couldn't.

As the back door clicked behind Trey, Patricia took her phone from her purse, called Connie and invited her to dinner.

Patricia made herself a tomato sandwich and had just taken a bite when a thought hit her. The shelter took Abigail's phone when she checked in. Did Abigail take it back when she checked out? If she wanted to get off the grid, she had probably left it there because her phone would be easy to track.

Patricia called the shelter. "Did Abigail Jackson leave with her phone?"

"No. We offered it to her, but she said she didn't need it."

"Hang on to the phone," Patricia said. "I want to look it over. By the way, how did Abigail leave the shelter?"

"By Uber."

"Booked from her phone?"

"Yes. It was the last thing she did before returning the phone to us."

"Any idea where she was headed?"

"None at all, but it's probably in her phone app."

Patricia finished her sandwich, then drove with Simon to Ambos Seafood to get fresh shrimp for dinner. On the way home, she stopped at the shelter and picked up Abigail's phone. As luck would have it, the phone wasn't locked.

Shortly after she returned home, Simon provided Patricia with the completed relationship map on Abigail. She printed out a copy and went through it relationship by relationship. On the surface, nothing seemed extraordinary, other than Abigail's relationship with Judy.

Patricia matched the names from the relationship map to names in Abigail's phone contact file, recording cell phone numbers and street addresses for each name. Then she reviewed Abigail's call history, making note of those numbers Abigail called the most. The last call Abigail made was to Uber. Patricia brought up Abigail's Uber app and checked the ride history, discovering that after leaving the shelter, Abigail went to a local drug store, then to an address in Richmond Hill. Where Abigail went after Richmond Hill was an open question. Patricia checked the Richmond Hill address against Abigail's contacts and came up empty-handed.

So, what did Abigail do at the drug store? Patricia called Timnit and asked her to visit the store and see if there was any way to get a look at the relevant security video. She then called Summer.

"I know it's short notice, but do you have a couple of hours available this afternoon?"

"Sure do," Summer said. "Another pickup?"

"Not today. I found a lead on where Abigail went after she left the shelter. I'd like you to visit her destination and see what the people there know about Abigail's whereabouts."

"Sounds interesting."

Patricia gave Summer the Richmond Hill address. "Call me once you're done."

"Will do."

As soon as Summer was off the line, Patricia called Trey, filled him in on the latest info, and asked him if he had someone who could keep an eye on the house in Richmond Hill and if he could put a geo-fence on the home.

"I can get surveillance in place within the hour," he said. "Getting the geo-fence set up may take longer, but it should be complete sometime this evening."

"I'll take what I can get," she said.

Patricia spent the rest of the afternoon making the red velvet cake. Baking allowed her mind to focus and distracted her from worry. Still, as she stirred red food coloring into the cocoa powder, she couldn't help thinking she was missing something about her gun. She could either worry herself into high anxiety or relax her mind and hope the missing puzzle piece revealed itself.

Around three, Timnit called. "We struck gold at the drug store."

"Really?"

"An ex-military is the assistant manager," Timnit said. "She gave me full access to the security video. Even allowed me to make a copy of the pertinent sections. We have Abigail coming into the store, buying a Boost prepaid phone and a carton of cigarettes, and leaving."

"I didn't know Abigail smoked," Patricia said.

"I contacted a friend at Boost. He's checking local phone activations in our timeframe."

"Good call. When do we get the activation information?"

"Anytime."

"Abigail went to Richmond Hill after the drug store," Patricia said. "Have your friend at Boost check where those newly activated numbers are pinged and isolate those pinged in Richmond Hill. That should narrow the list considerably."

"Sounds like a plan," Timnit said.

Shortly after four, Summer called. "I just left the address in Richmond Hill. The owner says she doesn't know Abigail and that Abigail never came to her house. In my professional opinion, the woman is telling the truth."

Disappointment surged, then a string a questions. "We need to find out where Abigail got out of that Uber."

"They're not going to give us that information."

"I know. I'm hoping she activated her prepaid phone and we can trace her that way."

By the time Trey arrived home shortly after five, Patricia was already working on the shrimp and grits. He came into the kitchen and gave her a hug and little kiss. She so enjoyed having him home.

"I could use a drink," Trey said. "How about you?"

"Sure."

He pulled a bottle of chardonnay from the fridge, poured two glasses and handed one to her. "That andouille sausage smells great."

Patricia looked at the skillet. "Lots of special flavors in there. How did your afternoon go?"

"I talked to the chief when I dropped off your evidence. He told me the ballistic tests on your Kimber show a match to the slug recovered from the crime scene. And your thumbprint is on each of the bullets in the magazine."

Her stomach clenched. "I can't say I'm surprised. I loaded the gun with those cartridges. I suppose the gun hasn't been used for anything until now." Patricia set the fried sausage aside, turned up the heat and dropped several strips of bacon into the hot pan. "I always store my gun with the magazine separate from it. Since the recovered gun included my magazine, that means the gun was stolen when I was carrying. I have to tell you, Trey, this evidence against me has me worried."

"Don't worry. The chief also told me again he's still open to our alibi despite the hard evidence."

"That's a relief. How about the DNA on the glass?"

Trey forked a piece of fried andouille, blew on it and took a bite. Once his mouth cleared, he said, "He's expediting the DNA testing."

She turned the bacon. "How soon for results?"

"Next week, earliest," Trey said.

"When are you getting the geo-fence data on Maywood's house?"

"Tomorrow." Trey took a sip of wine. "That data is key. It'll show what phones were in Maywood's house at the time of the shooting. However, a phone being there doesn't prove the registered owner is present as well. We're going to need more than those phone numbers." Trey grabbed some plates and silverware. He took the place settings to the dining room and returned.

Patricia's hand shook as she set the crisp bacon aside and put green, yellow and red peppers into the hot skillet. Then she added a diced onion. "What about video from neighbors? Traffic cams? Commercial firms?"

"I suspect the chief is already canvasing everyone close to the crime scene for video. I'll check with him. He said he'd share info with the Cotton Coalition, and I don't mind sharing that with you."

"Speaking of which, I picked up Abigail's phone from the shelter. It wasn't locked. I got contact information off it and her call history showed she took an Uber to Richmond Hill the night of the murder. Interestingly, when Summer spoke to the homeowner, she said she didn't know Abigail."

"We need to find out where she got out of the Uber."

"Abigail bought a prepaid phone on the way," Patricia said. "Timnit is trying to get the phone number and location."

"I can get Simon to help." Trey took a drink of wine.

"Let's see what Timnit comes up with before you involve Simon."

"We'll need to give that phone to the chief."

"Yeah," Patricia said. "I was surprised he hadn't come across it. By the way, have they brought Preston back in on the fraud charges?"

"The chief said a prosecutor is going to the grand jury for an indictment tomorrow."

Patricia added shrimp and sausage to the cooked vegetables. "A lot going on tomorrow."

Trey nodded. "I'll say. When is dinner?"

"Connie should be here anytime."

Trey held their chairs as Connie and Patricia settled themselves at the dining room table.

Patricia passed the bowl of grits to Connie. "How is your investigation going?"

Connie scooped grits onto her plate. "Slow. Just wrapping up loose ends."

"Whatever came of finding people in Savannah who read a lot of erotic e-books?"

"We couldn't get the information from Amazon."

"Sorry that didn't work out for you," Patricia said. "Simon was doing a relationship map on Abigail and Judy popped up." Patricia handed Connie the shrimp and vegetables. "Were you aware Judy knew Abigail?"

Connie shook her head. "That's new information for me. What was the nature of the relationship?"

"Shortly after Judy first arrived in Savannah, she joined Abigail's Bible study group and played weekly tennis with he for several months."

"I didn't realize Judy was religious."

"Probably just a ploy to get close to Abigail," Trey said.

"Or to Maywood," Patricia added. "He was the one who controlled their money."

Connie handed the serving dish to Trey. "Speaking of Maywood, I heard Patricia's Kimber may be the weapon that killed him."

"Ballistics just came in," Patricia said. "My Kimber is definitely the murder weapon. The working theory is that Judy stole it more than a year ago. However, we don't have a clue on who actually pulled the trigger."

"Or why," Trey said. "But we initiated a geo-fence on Maywood's house the day before he was killed. I'm supposed to get information tomorrow on what phones werepinged at his house."

"That should be helpful." Connie took a bite of sliced red pepper. "Ohh. This sauce is so good." Connie swallowed. "You said Simon was working on a relationship map on Abigail. Considering the relationship between Abigail and Judy, would you mind giving me a copy of the map when you get it?" Connie forked a shrimp.

"Just got it this afternoon," Patricia said. "Remind me before you leave."

Connie took a bite of the sautéed shrimp. "This is delicious. How's Hayley doing with all this Judy business?"

"Thank you. Hayley's been in Nashville since the end of May on a five-week internship at the University of Tennessee Forensic Anthropology Center."

"Is she thinking about going into crime scene investigation?"

"As far as I know, she's still pre-law," Trey said.

"It's good she's not involved in this Judy chaos," Connie said.

"Unfortunately, she comes home Monday," Patricia said.

"Poor child," Connie said.

"We're planning to pair her with Simon or Timnit for the

rest of summer," Patricia said. "With Judy on the loose, we want to get her trained in countermeasures fast."

"I'd be glad to help," Connie said. "On-the-job training. I learned so much shadowing my father. In fact, I wouldn't mind a roommate for a month or two."

"Sounds good to me. What do you think, Trey?" Patricia asked.

"You sure it wouldn't slow you down?" Trey asked.

"Not at all."

"Let's put it up to Hayley when she gets home."

CHAPTER 23

Worry over the potential personal consequences of the police investigation gnawed at Patricia all night. Deep concern about what additional mischief Judy might be whipping up piled on top of her worry.

Trey had already left for work by the time Patricia, still exhausted, climbed out of bed and padded in a stupor downstairs to feed the cats.

True to form, the cats were sitting at the back door, looking inside at the empty kitchen. They stirred on seeing her and, as they did every morning, began brushing their cheeks on the base of the door. Both fled to the edge of the patio when Patricia opened the door. As soon as the bowl of kibble settled on the concrete, they inched closer.

Still squatting, Patricia extended her hand as they approached. Each cat sniffed her outstretched fingers, but today neither allowed her to pet their head.

As petting was an on and off thing with them, Patricia thought nothing of their hesitancy and returned to the kitchen. The black cat pounced on the food, but the gray cat held back which was so unusual it alarmed Patricia. Neither cat had ever refused food.

She poured coffee and watched the cats for a few minutes, during which the gray cat simply sat on the edge of the patio.

Was someone else feeding them? Had it caught a snake, frog or another small varmint? Was it sick? Not knowing troubled Patricia, but there was nothing she could do about it, so she went back upstairs to prepare for the day.

She had just finished blow-drying her hair when Meredith called and suggested coffee at Goose Feathers. An hour later, with Simon in tow, Patricia strolled into the restaurant and crossed to the back table Meredith occupied.

After greeting her good friend, Patricia stepped to the counter and returned to the table with a steaming cup of much needed coffee.

"That was an excellent tip on Maywood possibly funneling money to Judy," Meredith said as Patricia sat. "Turns out he was making modest monthly transfers to Herman's account on Hilton Head Island beginning well before Henrietta was murdered."

The mention of her mother's murder turned Patricia's stomach.

"Deposits stopped shortly after Judy was arrested."

Finally a break on Judy. "And Judy had access to her brother's account?"

"Yes. She made periodic withdrawals from it during that time." Meredith took a sip of coffee. "Once Henrietta transferred money to the account, Judy's withdrawal amounts went up, but they were never substantial. Of course, all activity on the account stopped when the authorities seized the assets."

"Well, that certainly establishes some sort of relationship between Judy and Maywood."

Meredith adjusted the neck of her black shirt. "On a hunch, I checked Beaufort County real estate transactions and found that Maywood bought a condo on Hilton Head Island about the time Judy escaped. Actually, shortly before. I haven't had time to talk with neighbors or view security video, but it's possible Judy may have spent time there since escaping. In fact, she may still be using the place. Here's what's interesting about that condo deal; Maywood bought the condo *before* Judy escaped, suggesting prior knowledge of the escape. Too many coincidences here."

Patricia reached for her phone. "We need to talk with her neighbors and get surveillance on the condo right away."

"I've already asked Timnit," Meredith said.

Patricia put her phone back on the table. "This is great news. Will you also let Connie know?"

"Sure will, but I wanted to tell you first." Meredith smiled. "It gets better, Patricia. Not long after Judy escaped custody, a new account was opened at the Hilton Head Island bank in the name of Melody Henning, a fictitious name, with a substantial initial deposit, and Maywood began depositing monthly amounts again."

"Has Judy been withdrawing money from that account?"

"Someone has." Meredith took a sip of coffee. "It's either Judy or a new mistress."

"Great work, Meredith. Thank you. I'm sure the bank has cameras, I just don't know how to access them. Maybe Connie or Trey would know."

"I could help with that," Meredith said.

"Thank you."

Patricia briefed Meredith on Abigail's trip from the shelter.

"Where's Abigail getting money from?" Meredith asked.

"No idea."

Meredith took a pad from her purse and made a note. "I'll do some looking."

Once Patricia returned home, she put the new information in her case file, then lay down for a much needed nap. Sleep came immediately.

Patricia's chiming phone awoke her.

TF: You available for lunch?

PF: Sure. What's up?

TF: Geo-fence data just came in.

Patricia's pulse surged.

TF: How about Flying Monk at two?

PF: Perfect.

Patricia was already seated in the back of the restaurant when Trey, dressed in a summer-weight, light-blue business suit, came through the front door and nodded at Simon sitting by the entrance.

Patricia brushed a strand of blonde hair from her face and stood. They hugged. Trey gave her a polite little kiss and bright smile, then held the chair for her to sit.

"Thank you," she said.

Trey removed two reports from his satchel and handed one to her. Butterflies filled her stomach in anticipation as he settled into the chair beside her.

A waiter arrived, and they ordered Singapore Noodles to share and Thai tea.

Once the waiter left, Patricia motioned toward the geo-fence report in front of her. "Have you been through it?"

Trey nodded.

"Why don't you give me an overview before we dig in?"

He leaned forward. "The basic problem is that two of the logged phone numbers are prepaid phones." Trey ran fingers through the side of his salt and pepper hair. "And the other three numbers are owned by Jackson Capital."

"I assume the phone numbers are in the report?"

"Yes."

The Thai tea arrived. Patricia took a satisfying sip. "We know Preston and Maywood were in the Jackson house that day, so chances are good two of the Jackson Capital numbers belong to them."

"They do."

"For starters, I can check the other three numbers against the contact file in Abigail's phone." Patricia pulled out her laptop. "Show me the numbers."

He opened the report and directed her attention to the list as her laptop booted up. "You copied Abigail's contact list?"

"I copied Abigail's entire phone."

He gave her a smile.

As soon as her laptop was up, she went to Abigail's contact data, checked the remaining Jackson Capital number against the list and got a match. "It's Cotton McNaly. He works for the CPA firm that handles Jackson Capital's accounting."

"Why he would have a Jackson Capital phone?" Trey asked.

"Hmm. Let me check something." Patricia consulted her case file. "Yeah. Here it is. McNaly is Jackson Capital's treasurer."

"But assuming the CPA firm provides him a phone, why would he have one from Jackson Capital as well?"

"To keep his business interests entirely separate," Patricia suggested.

Trey nodded.

"So, three key officers of Jackson Capital were in the house," Patricia said as she checked the two other prepaid numbers and came up empty-handed. "Do you know what prepaid company the other two phones are registered to?"

Trey thumbed through the report, paused midway, and read. "Boost."

"Timnit says she has a contact at Boost," Patricia said. "Maybe she can get us a ping report on the two numbers and find out where the phones spend the night."

"Sounds like a plan." Trey smiled. "And if Boost doesn't cooperate, Simon just got Timnit Signit-7 clearance so she can access their files using counterintelligence protocols."

Patricia raised her eyebrows. "Wow. Is that because of her military background?"

"More to make her more helpful to you, though her stint at Cyber Command made the approval process a breeze."

"Does your report have 'time of day' ping data?"

"Yes." Trey paged through the sheets, then stopped. "Here it is. Page eighteen."

Patricia turned to the page. "Which is Preston's number?"

Trey gave her the corresponding names for each of the Jackson Capital numbers.

"So, Preston arrived at least an hour before Cotton and was alone in the house with Maywood during that time. Then Cotton arrived and all three were together for two hours. Didn't you say Maywood's security system, computer and phone were reset to factory settings?"

"Yes. Completely erased," Trey said. "But the chief sent the devices to the Georgia Bureau of Investigation to see if any data can be recovered."

"I bet Preston's and Cotton's phones were also reset."

"Don't know."

"So, Preston and Cotton left the geo-fence around six p.m. Of course, Maywood remained. Then around eight both Boost phones were pinged several times inside the house, and the pings on those phones stopped at eight thirty-five. Do you have a time of death for Maywood?"

"No. The chief is expecting autopsy results tomorrow."

"Okay. So once the Boost phone pings stopped, only Maywood's phone was pinged inside the geo-fence for the rest of the night."

"Correct."

"We have to track those Boost phones," Patricia said. "I'll call Timnit as soon as we're done. Oh, by the way, we got a possible lead on Judy's whereabouts," Patricia said.

Trey's eyes widened.

"Apparently Maywood had a financial relationship with Judy that terminated on her arrest. Then shortly before her escape, Maywood bought a condo and opened a new bank account in a fictitious woman's name. We're thinking the condo and new bank account could have been for Judy."

"Hypothetical, but certainly an intriguing theory."

Patricia took a long drink of tea. "We asked Timnit to interview neighbors at the condo complex and review security videos there."

"We have to give all this to Detective Rodriguez."

Patricia nodded. "Yes. If it pans out."

"Sounds like you've covered all your bases." Trey forked some Singapore Noodles. "If you locate Judy, I'm sure the chief will be happy to pick her up immediately."

"That would be a relief."

As soon as Patricia got home from lunch, she called Timnit, who was on her way to Hilton Head Island, and gave her the two Boost phone numbers from Trey's ping report.

"Both of these Boost phone numbers were pinged inside Maywood's home on the evening he was murdered. It would be incredibly helpful if your friend at Boost could give us everything he has on those numbers, including ping location data, particularly at night."

"He's been cooperative so far," Timnit said. "With any luck, these are subscriber phones and he'll be able to give me names as well as ping data."

"Thank you. And good luck at the Hilton Head condo."

Patricia spent the next hour adding the new information to her case file and straightening up the kitchen.

AROUND FOUR-THIRTY, TIMNIT CALLED PATRICIA. "I GOT strong positive identification of Judy from two of her condo neighbors. However, there have been no sightings of Judy in the last week. But the neighbors say that's not unusual."

Success was so sweet. "We'll take what we can get. How about the condo complex security video?"

"Got quite a bit of Judy parking a black Lincoln Navigator and going into the condo over the past two weeks," Timnit said. "Also video of her leaving the condo and getting into the same SUV, as well as the Navigator coming and going from the condo complex. The vehicle is registered to Melody Henning. South Carolina plates."

"Yes!" Patricia gave a fist pump. "That's the name Maywood used to funnel money to Judy. We're on the right track."

"I'll do some more checking on the name."

"Meredith can give you Melody's banking details."

Excitement mounted in anticipation of finally apprehending Judy. "Is Judy in the condo now?"

"No. Security video indicates she left in the Navigator around seven this morning."

"Let Connie know. I'll pass the information to Detective Rodriquez. And Timnit?"

"Yes?"

"Great work."

As soon as Timnit was off the line, Patricia called Detective Rodriquez and shared the information on Judy.

"Thank you, Mrs. Falcon," Rodriquez said. "We'll take it from here. I'll advise the Beaufort County Sheriff. They'll put a surveillance team on the place and catch her." Patricia heard paper shuffling. "You know, this is a murder investigation, and that makes this dangerous work for you and your friends to be engaged in. As much as I appreciate your considerable help, I think for your own well-being you should devote your talents to something else."

"I appreciate your concern, but we plan to stick with our investigation," Patricia said, irritation stirring. "After all, this is my freedom on the line."

"I don't think that's wise. You've done enough. Far more than enough. In fact, you're dangerously close to interfering with my murder investigation."

"I'm a suspect," Patricia said, fighting to control her rising indignation. "I'm entitled to conduct my own independent investigation. I'm not interfering, I'm protecting my interests."

"Okay. I get it. But I'm going to need real-time updates from you."

"We can do that," Patricia said, her agitation cooling.

"Real time," Rodriquez said. "No more delays. You find out something, anything, I want to know immediately."

"Will do."

CHAPTER 24

Bowl of kibble in hand, Patricia looked down in surprise at the red-tipped cigarette butt at her backdoor. She jerked back, scanned the yard and reached for the gun that wasn't there. "Lord, have mercy."

Judy? She was the only woman Patricia knew who still smoked. Patricia stepped over the cigarette and put the food bowl on the patio. The black cat sidled up to the food and began to eat, but the gray cat just watched from the edge of the patio.

"Are you okay?" she said to the reluctant cat, extending her hand.

The gray cat inched closer and sniffed her fingertips, then went to the door and sniffed the cigarette butt.

"Is that from you?" Patricia asked softly, recalling the missing necklace the cats had deposited.

The cat looked up and meowed.

Patricia looked more closely. The butt appeared fresh. Had someone, perhaps Judy, tossed it aside last night? Sensing the cigarette butt could be important, Patricia went inside, took a paper lunch bag from the pantry and returned to the patio, where, using a clean spoon, she nudged the butt into the bag. When Trey came down, she'd ask him to get the DNA checked.

A few minutes later, Trey came into the kitchen dressed in a tan cotton suit and gave her a kiss on the cheek. She wrapped her hands around his head and kissed him on the lips, lingering a bit longer than necessary.

"What's getting into you today, Patsy?"

"Can't a girl be romantic now and then?"

He pulled her closer. "Of course you can."

Oh, the delight of this man. "Do you want some red velvet cake for breakfast?"

He let out a sigh. "Are you trying to kill me? How can I say no, though? Such sweet death. Yes, Patsy, I would *love* cake for breakfast."

While Patricia sliced the cake, he poured two cups of coffee and sat. She sat as well and they both began on the cake. "Could you get a fast DNA test for me?" she asked between bites.

He put down his fork. "What's the source of the DNA?"

"Cigarette butt."

Trey starred out the window as if in thought, then let out a long breath. "If there's sufficient DNA and it isn't contaminated or degraded, we could get results as fast as nine hours using our new Rapid DNA equipment. Otherwise, two or three days. Why the rush?"

"The same cats that found my missing necklace brought a fresh cigarette butt to our backdoor this morning. I think someone was in our backyard last night."

"Have you checked our security videos?"

"Not yet," Patricia said. "I just finished bagging the evidence."

Trey pulled his laptop from his satchel. "Let's take a look."

Patricia came around to Trey's side of the table and watched as he logged into the video archive file.

"It would take hours to review this in real time, so I'll fast motion it." The timestamps on each of the four back cameras whirled, but nothing but black night appeared. Then, a couple of minutes later, dawn lit the yard scenes and Trey stopped the videos. "Nothing unusual. I'll have Simon take a closer look at these today. Meanwhile, where's the evidence?"

Patricia gave Trey the paper bag. "The cigarette butt had red lipstick."

Trey turned off his laptop. "Are you thinking Judy?"

"Could be. I recall her smoking."

Once Simon came downstairs, Trey shoved the laptop into his satchel, took a last sip of coffee and, with Patricia by his side, went to the front door. "I'll see if we can get Rapid DNA on this."

Timnit called shortly after Trey left. "Not only does the fictional Melody Henning have a well-funded bank account and a brand-new Lincoln Navigator, she has a valid South Carolina Driver's License, a Social Security number, and a couple of high-limit credit cards. Meredith is checking the transactions on those cards. And I just received data from Boost on local phone activations after Abigail's purchase of a burner phone, and ping data on the Boost numbers from Maywood's."

"Have you looked at the Boost data?"

"Not yet. I think the four of us should get together this morning and go over our findings."

"Good idea, but I think we should include Connie. Any ideas on where to meet?"

"We'll be discussing sensitive material," Timnit said. "We need somewhere completely private."

"Since Simon is here, how about my house?"

"Sounds good to me. What time?"

Patricia glanced at the microwave clock. "Let's try for ten. If not that, maybe noon."

"I can do either."

"I'll let you know."

Patricia called the girls, and everyone could make ten. She sent them all a confirming text, then prepared a batch of double dark chocolate brownies before heading upstairs to freshen up.

Just as Patricia took the last heated roller out of her hair, her phone chimed an incoming text.

TF: Check your email for copy of Maywood Jackson autopsy summary.

PF: Will do. Thanks.

TF: Also, geo-fence in place at Richmond Hill and Hilton Head addresses. Physical surveillance of Richmond Hill reports no sighting of Abigail.

PF: Any luck with Chief Patrick on videos from Maywood's neighbors?

TF: Nothing meaningful yet on neighbor videos. Prosecutor obtained warrant from grand jury to bring Preston Somerset in on fraud charges. Preston due to surrender later this morning.

PF: Cigarette butt DNA?

TF: Lab says there is sufficient fresh, uncontaminated DNA for a Rapid DNA test. Hopefully they will find a match on CODIS.

PF: Judy's DNA is on CODIS?

TF: Most certainly.

PF: Thank you.

Patricia checked her email, brought up Maywood's autopsy summary and gasped as she read the cause of death: poisoning. Judy's *modus operandi*. So, someone poisoned Maywood, and then shot him with a gun registered to Patricia to implicate her in the murder. The summary listed the chemical, and though Patricia searched her mind, she couldn't come up with what chemical Judy had used to kill Herman and Henrietta.

She texted Trey.

PF: What chemical was used to kill my mother?

TF: The same one that was used to kill Maywood.

A chill went through Patricia.

TF: Hopefully you're off the hook.

PF: Thank God.

TF: I know.

PF: But Judy's still out there and she's gunning for me.

TF: That's why Simon is with you. Either the sheriff or us will get her, dear.

PF: Thank you.

Patricia set her phone down and let the tension bleed from her shoulders. It didn't relieve the sadness and confusion over becoming one hateful woman's target, but now she could get one hundred percent focused on getting rid of the threat of Judy once and for all.

THE GIRLS HAD JUST SETTLED DOWN AROUND PATRICIA'S kitchen table with coffee and warm brownies when Patricia's phone chimed an incoming text.

TF: Judy's Lincoln Navigator and purse with fake ID were found at the Hilton Head Airport. After the federal marshals found Judy's car, they raided her condo. Completely empty. No personal effects. No trace of Judy. It's as though she knew we were onto her and cleared out.

PF: Last time we pursued her, she fought back.

TF: That didn't turn out well for her.

PF: I hope she learned her lesson.

TF: Me too, but just in case, stay home today.

PF: Will do.

"Well, girls," Patricia said, "thank you for getting together.

I just figured because there are so many moving parts here we should meet, review where we're at and who all is involved in this investigation and who is leading each segment. It's a multiheaded snake we're dealing with—the FBI, US Marshals and sheriffs from two counties."

"So lay it out for us," Summer said. "Who's doing what?"

"The FBI and marshals are focused on apprehending Judy. The Chatham police are focused on Maywood's murder, and I'm still a suspect, but …" Patricia filled them in on Maywood's autopsy results. "The FBI is also looking at Maywood's fraud. It's our job to make sure we share everything with the authorities. We are obligated to share our information in a timely manner."

"So, what are we focused on?" Summer asked.

"Judy is our focus," Patricia replied. "The latest information on Judy is that she has fled the Hilton Head condo and abandoned her brand-new SUV at the Hilton Head Airport."

"That SUV left the condo complex at seven this morning," Timnit said, looking at her laptop screen. "There aren't many flights that time of day out of the Hilton Head Airport."

"I'm not certain she took a flight," Patricia said. "You need photo ID to board. She left her purse and ID in the abandoned SUV."

"I don't know," Meredith said. "According to my data on Molly Henning's credit cards, she bought two airline tickets yesterday."

"Who's Molly Henning?" Summer asked as she scribbled the name on the pad in front of her.

"Fictitious name Judy is using," Meredith answered.

"Well, that underscores why we're here," Patricia said. "We need to get everything we know out on the table, starting with the day Maywood was killed. Let's do this one by one. I'll start."

After summarizing Judy's relationship with Abigail and

passing out relationship maps on Abigail and Judy, Patricia went through Abigail's journey from the abuse shelter into oblivion, the five phone numbers pinged at Maywood's, the planted gun and the suspicious cigarette butt.

Meredith outlined financial transactions linking Judy and Maywood.

Summer detailed her fruitless interview at the Richmond Hill home Abigail had directed the Uber to.

Timnit went through the data on the two Boost phone numbers pinged at Maywood's house. One of the numbers was activated shortly after Abigail bought a Boost phone, the other was registered to Molly Henning.

"I have ongoing ping surveillance on both numbers." Timnit clicked her laptop to a surveillance map.

Patricia leaned over to see two overlapping red dots.

"The two dots are together," Timnit said, "and have been since they joined up at eight."

"Judy and Abigail are together," Patricia said, surprised to have her unconscious fears confirmed. She'd known there was suspicious overlap in all their investigations, but this was an unpleasant development.

"Oh my word," Meredith said.

Timnit zoomed the view in. "They're presently on I-95 just north of Jacksonville."

Connie stood. "I guess Timnit and I need to get down to Jacksonville."

Timnit remained seated. "I can say with certainty the two target phone numbers are headed south on I-95. But I don't know their intended destination, and I don't know how many people, if any, are in that vehicle. Also, based on distance traveled in the last two hours, the vehicle is traveling at the speed limit which makes vehicular pursuit from here problematic."

"Are you saying we should ignore this clue?" Connie asked.

"Not at all," Timnit said. "But I don't need to go with you. You and I can set up communications, and I can keep you appraised of the real-time location of the phones."

"Before you leave, Connie," Patricia said, knowing Connie wanted Judy behind bars as much as Patricia did. "It troubles me that Judy fled the condo before the marshals raided it. It's as though she knew we were onto her. Now, if you assume she believes we're on to her, why would she hang on to her phone? This a clever woman. She booked flights and parked her SUV at the airport, clearly intending to mislead us. Who's to say the southern-bound phones aren't another attempt to mislead?"

"It's the only concrete lead we have," Connie said. "If it doesn't pan out, I'll come back to Savannah and your team will probably have more leads. Right now, someone has to follow-up on this lead."

"Have you been sharing everything on Judy's whereabouts with the FBI, Timnit?" Patricia asked.

"Yes indeed."

"Then I think we can safely assume they or the US Marshals are going to follow up on it," Patricia said.

Connie exhaled. "It's possible their Jacksonville office is already arranging to intercept." Connie pulled out her phone. "I should check before I go flying off." Connie stepped into the study, punching numbers on her phone.

"Must be nice having those kind of contacts," Timnit said.

Connie returned, frowning. "FBI stopped the vehicle. A UPS truck. The phones were in a parcel shipped to a repair company in Jacksonville."

Summer raised her eyebrows. "And we have bang-on instincts. You were right that it could be a decoy, Patricia."

"Let's focus on what happened this morning." Patricia

inclined her head. "Timnit, you said the Navigator left the complex at seven?"

"Yes."

Patricia rolled a stick pen in her fingers. "Were Judy or Abigail in the SUV?"

"I have remote access to the security video," Timnit said. "Let's see." She glanced at her laptop for a moment. "Yes. Judy is driving the SUV."

"Anyone else in the SUV?"

"No."

Patricia tapped the end of the pen on her lower lip. "The two phones joined up at eight?"

"Yes."

"Where?"

"Hilton Head Island. Some industrial park."

"Probably UPS." Patricia glanced off in space for a moment. "What time did the marshals raid the condo?"

Timnit consulted her monitor. "Nine-thirty."

"So the marshals found Judy's SUV sometime before then. Which raises the question of how Judy left the airport parking lot."

"The airport has got to have security video," Timnit said. "You want me to check it out?"

"Can you do it remotely?" Patricia asked, eager to get back on Judy's trail.

"I don't know, but with my Signit-7 clearance it wouldn't hurt to try." Timnit started to key her laptop.

CHAPTER 25

From across the kitchen table, Patricia saw the weight of trying to get back on Judy's trail in Timnit's eyes as she moved her computer search from one secure portal to another. Getting remote access to the airport security video would definitely speed things up.

Suddenly, something clicked in Timnit's face. Her jaw set. "Got it," she said. "A white Cadillac XTS driven by a woman pulls up behind Judy's parked Navigator in the airport parking lot at nine this morning. Judy transfers three suitcases to the Cadillac, then gets into the passenger seat."

"Abigail drives a white Cadillac," Patricia said, adrenaline surging. "Anything else in the video."

"Judy did everything with her left hand. Is she left-handed?"

"No." Patricia shook her head. "She's right-handed, but I shot her in the right hand last year when she was trying to poison me."

Timnit raised her eyebrows over the top of the computer screen.

"True story," Patricia said. "Now, can you see the plates on the car?"

"Georgia plates. I'll run them."

Patricia brought her hand to her throat, fingering her heirloom pendant while she waited for the results of Timnit's search.

"Plates are registered to Jackson Capital," Timnit said.

"Criminy," Summer said. "That was fast."

The corners of Timnit's mouth tipped up.

"Make sure Detective Rodriquez gets that information right away." Patricia looked at her Rolex. "So, about two hours ago Judy and Abigail left the Hilton Head Airport. Any ideas on where they were going? Or why they were together? What's drawing these two together? Maybe they schemed to kill Maywood, but why are they still together?"

"Twice today," Connie said, "Judy planted evidence that she was fleeing the area, so it's entirely possible she's doing the opposite and sticking around. But why would she stay? She knows we're onto her. Maywood's dead. She's not getting any more money from him."

"Money. Hmm." Meredith keyed her laptop, then looked up. "Just as I suspected. Judy drained her Molly Henning account. All one hundred thousand dollars. Transferred it to a numbered account in Belize. So, if money isn't keeping her here, what is?"

"Revenge," Summer said, growing somber. "Patricia is the reason Judy was arrested for murder. Patricia is the reason Judy's on the run. Patricia is the reason Judy can't use her right hand. Judy is a psychopath. Once you cross a psychopath, you're in for a whole lot of hurt. She's not going to leave until she evens the score."

Patricia had figured as much, but hearing it put into words wasn't pleasant. Not helpful at all. On the other hand, it *was* one of Judy against five of them. Way more than five.

The Cotton Coalition. The Catholic Church. The sheriffs. The US Marshals. And the FBI. Patricia took some comfort that she had numbers and talent on her side.

"Let's get back to Abigail's Cadillac. There's only one road off of Hilton Head Island and that road is blanketed with traffic cams, Timnit."

Timnit gave an okay and returned to her keyboard. Moments later she looked up. "At nine-thirty, a traffic camera at the foot of the bridge to the mainland picked up a white Cadillac XTS headed west."

"It doesn't take a half hour to go from the airport to the bridge," Connie said. "I wonder what else they were doing in that half hour."

Timnit shrugged.

"Is it Abigail's car?" Patricia asked.

"Can't read the license plate."

Patricia massaged her forehead. "That was an hour ago. She could be in Savannah by now, or halfway to Charleston."

"As I said before," Summer said, "my bet is Savannah. Judy's not going anywhere until she gets even."

"We need to locate Abigail's car." Patricia looked at Timnit. "Can you get into the Cadillac GPS network?"

"Don't know, but I can sure try."

While Timnit searched for the Cadillac GPS portal, Patricia turned to Summer. "Do you think Judy would be bold enough to come here, to my house? Right now?"

"Like many psychopaths, she's a planner," Summer said. "She's not going to make a move on you without some sort of a plan. So, no. She's not coming here right now. She'll study you. Probably has been studying you, hence the cigarette butt in your backyard, looking for vulnerabilities."

Patricia swallowed. "She certainly does an excellent job of anticipating us."

"We know she's bright," Connie said, "but she doesn't

have telepathic capabilities. We share our information with the authorities. Could she have an accomplice within the Chatham Police who's tipping her off to leave the condo and abandon the Navigator?"

Sweet mother. "Is there no limit to her scheming?" Patricia asked.

"She's a con artist," Summer said. "She conned your mother and you and Maywood. Apparently, she conned Abigail. Who knows who else has fallen under her spell?"

Patricia sucked in a breath on the thought there could be more people out there helping Judy with her sinister plans. And poor Abigail. She'd only just escaped one abusive situation with her husband, only to be in another one. Abigail could end up dead once Judy had finished with her. As disconcerting as it was, Patricia shook it off. "How do we beat Judy?"

"Her singular focus is her vulnerability. She's not going to give up. She'll come at you with everything she has and keep coming at you until she succeeds, or she or someone close to her makes a mistake. And if we catch it, we'll be able to capture her."

Goosebumps rose. "Until then?"

"Until then, we do everything we can to frustrate her plans and to keep her off her game," Summer said in a determined tone. "She'll have plans, but they will be superficial because we'll be constantly forcing her to change them."

If only it were that easy. They'd had a good run so far of interrupting Judy's plans, but she still had an hour head start on them. Patricia looked at Timnit. "Anything yet?"

"Almost there."

Patricia turned to Meredith. "Judy's money that's in Belize, can you freeze it? That would certainly throw Judy off her game."

Meredith nodded. "We have international banking protocols to freeze criminal transfers, but we also have monitoring protocols which could be much more useful in this case. Sooner or later, Judy's going to need money. I suggest we monitor the Belize account, and when Judy brings money back here, we identify the domestic bank and focus surveillance there."

"Got it!" came Simon's voice from the dining room.

The girls, minus Timnit, scurried into the room where Simon had set up shop and clustered behind him.

"What do you have?" Patricia asked.

"The person smoking a cigarette in your backyard last night."

Oh Lordy. Curiosity surged. Patricia focused on the computer screen. "All I see is a black screen."

Simon pointed to the far left of the field of view. "See the small red dot? That's the glowing end of the cigarette. See how it glows more brightly when she's puffing."

"She?"

"Lipstick on the cigarette butt you found. I realize it could be a man in drag, but I'm old school. I'm going with *she*."

Patricia drew closer and focused on the spot. Now she could see the faint glow. "Where's the woman's face?"

"Black mask," Simon said. "And notice how she stays nearly out of our field of view. This gal knows what she's doing."

Definitely sounds like Judy's MO. Patricia watched as the glow went to the study window, then dropped three feet. "What's she doing?"

"Could be squatting to avoid being seen from inside," Simon said. "A good precaution, but totally unnecessary because it's well past midnight and y'all are upstairs sleeping."

The glow then elevated to its former height and went to

her kitchen window. A shudder went through Patricia. How creepy.

"Why is she looking in your windows when everyone is asleep?" Connie asked.

Patricia had been mulling the same thing. Then a hunch hit her. "Maybe she's retrieving something."

Simon stood and headed for the back door with the girls trailing behind him. Once outside, he went to the study window and stooped where the glow had stooped. Directly in front of him was a small black box attached to the corner of the window.

"Is that one of ours?" Connie asked.

"No," Simon said.

"What is it?" Patricia asked.

Simon leaned forward. "It's a digital audio recording device."

"Is it recording us right now?" Summer asked.

"Afraid so," Simon said.

"Hi, Judy," Summer said.

"She can't hear you." Simon pointed to the end of an SD memory card. "Everything is being recorded on this memory card, which I'm guessing Judy picks up each night. I suspect we'll find a similar device on the kitchen window."

"Oh. My. Word," Patricia said. "So that's how she knows our every move. Didn't you sweep the house for listening devices when you arrived?"

"I did. That's the beauty of the devices she used. They don't emit any signals, so my detector doesn't pick them up. Very clever of Judy to employ this kind of listening device."

"Thank goodness we found this," Connie said, "or she would have been privy to all our plans we discussed today."

"Why didn't our motion detector turn the external lights on?" Patricia asked.

Simon looked up at the roof line. "The flood lights have been removed."

"If Judy can get on your property unobserved, why hasn't she tried to shoot you through your window?" Summer asked.

"Judy would know we have bulletproof windows," Patricia said. "We both had them installed around the same time."

"So, what's the plan?" Connie asked.

"We let the US Marshals know," Simon said. "Then wait for Judy to make her pickup tonight and be arrested by them."

"Well done, Simon," Patricia said with a lilt to her voice. A world with Judy behind bars was a better world, particularly Patricia's. And it felt darn good to be ahead of Judy for a change.

When they returned to the kitchen, Timnit looked up, grinning. "I found Abigail's Cadillac."

Patricia loved when a search bore fruit. "Where?"

"I lost the vehicle GPS signal at the Ellis Square underground parking garage, but I located garage security video of Abigail taking her parking ticket and various garage security videos of the car finding a parking space. There's a poorly lit video of Abigail exiting her car, but no indication Judy got out."

"What?" Patricia asked, totally blindsided.

Timnit shrugged. "Apparently, Judy got out of the car somewhere else."

"What does the Cadillac GPS show on other destinations?" Connie asked, sitting at the kitchen table.

"GPS archive is consistent with the Cadillac going directly from Hilton Head Airport to the Ellis Square Garage in Savannah."

"We all saw Judy get in to the Cadillac." Summer sat. "So what happened?"

"There are plenty of stoplights along that route," Patricia said. "A flick of the door handle when the car was paused and Judy's in the wind again."

"That girl is as slippery as an eel," Summer muttered.

"We still have a shot at her tonight," Patricia said. "Let's get back to Abigail. Why Ellis Square?"

"I have security video of Abigail taking the elevator up to Ellis Square," Timnit said. "I also found a video of her leaving the square on Barnard, heading toward Bay Street."

Summer stood. "Let me see the video of her leaving the square."

Timnit opened the file and a full-motion image came up. "Abigail is the woman in white jeans and a pale-blue top." Timnit pointed to the screen. "Right here. You can see she turns left at Barnard and disappears from the field of view heading toward Bay."

"Her gait shows determination." Summer peered at the screen. "Slightly faster than normal and leaning forward a bit. She has a destination in mind and is eager to get there."

"There are plenty of hotels on Bay," Patricia said. "Meredith, would you mind checking Abigail's credit cards to see if she recently reserved a hotel room. In fact, check Molly Henning's cards as well."

"I can tell you right now that Molly's cards weren't used for a hotel room." Meredith's fingers raced over her keyboard. "I went through them with a fine-toothed comb once we learned of them. Of course, I'll take another look in case Judy snuck something in just before she left her purse at the Hilton Head Airport. Abigail is an entirely different story."

"Timnit, there are condos in that area as well," Patricia pointed out. "Check the property records and see if

Maywood or Jackson Capital own any property in that area. But, before you do that, could you bring up the video of Abigail getting her Ellis Square parking ticket?"

"Sure."

Moments later, the video clip started rolling.

"Freeze it as soon as Abigail reaches for the ticket." Patricia stepped behind Timnit to see the laptop screen.

"What are you looking for?" Connie asked.

"I want to see if the passenger side is visible and confirm Judy left the car before Ellis Square."

Timnit froze the footage. "Hard to see the passenger side in such dim lighting, but there's no indication of Judy in this frame."

"But notice Abigail's left wrist." With excitement mounting, Patricia pointed to the screen. "That's a smartwatch. If she has a smartwatch, she has a smartphone on Bluetooth with the watch."

"That fits her recent credit card purchases," Meredith confirmed. "No hotel bookings, but a sizable purchase at Verizon yesterday."

"Can you get into Verizon, Timnit?" Patricia asked.

Timnit rubbed her hands together and then wiggled her fingers. "Don't know why not."

Patricia nodded. "Let's track that phone and the address Abigail gave for billing."

"Do you still want info on condo purchases in the area?" Timnit asked.

"Track Abigail's phone first, then the condo purchases," Patricia said. "Meredith, did you find where Abigail is getting the new credit card and funding from?"

"Yesterday Abigail moved three-hundred-thousand dollars from an offshore account to the Cotton Mercantile Bank on Bay and got a credit card from the bank."

"Don't tell me that money came from Belize," Connie said.

"No. From the Caymans."

"Abigail has an offshore account?" Summer asked.

"It might be one of Maywood's many overseas accounts. One from the missing second journal," Meredith said. "If the second journal is anything like the first, it contains account numbers and corresponding passwords."

"Abigail's own piggybank," Summer said.

"Wherever Abigail's phone is, it's not pinging," Timnit said. "But her billing is going to an address on Barnard Street."

"Find out who owns that property," Patricia said.

Moments later, Timnit said, "Jackson Capital."

"Bingo," Summer said in an excited voice that echoed Patricia's feelings.

CHAPTER 26

"I'll contact Trey to get a geo-fence on the Barnard Street building," Patricia told the ladies seated around the kitchen table. She texted the request to Trey.

"Abigail just made a three-hundred-dollar withdrawal from the Cotton Mercantile Bank on Bay," Meredith said from behind her laptop. "Timnit, can you get the ATM video?"

Timnit nodded. "Right on it."

"We need physical surveillance on the Barnard condo address," Patricia said. "Can you handle that, Connie?"

Connie grabbed a brownie, wrapped it in a paper napkin and tossed it into her crocheted bag. She stood, smiling. "Happy to."

"And keep an eye out for Judy," Patricia added as Connie, sandals clacking on the hardwood floor, scurried to the front door.

"Be safe," Summer called after her.

Patricia's phone chimed an incoming text. She checked her phone. "Trey says he's setting up the geo-fence at the Barnard location for us."

"I really need to learn how to do that," Timnit mused.

Patricia flashed Timnit a smile. "You're doing plenty."

"Thank you," Timnit said. "Okay. I have the ATM video. Abigail is on foot. No one appears to be with her. She leaves the Bay Street ATM in a direction consistent with a return to Barnard."

"Thanks, Timnit." Meredith starred off into space. "Why isn't Abigail's phone pinging?"

"She could have it turned off," Timnit suggested. "It's a standard military tactic for special ops. To avoid detection, we set scheduled times for communications. We turn on our satellite phones, communicate, and then immediately turn them off. If our communication is detected, by the time the enemy responds we're long gone."

"So, at some point her phone will ping."

"Yes," Timnit replied. "And, if she's smart enough to keep it turned off, she'll be smart enough to not turn it on when she's close to her home base."

Patricia shook her head. Not a good situation. "Let's hope she's not that smart."

"Thing is," Summer said, "there are two of them. To beat one, we have to beat both."

Patricia straightened in her chair. "Do you think they're true partners in this, or is Judy using her?"

"I don't think Abigail knows she's being used. She thinks they're partners and will likely do anything for Judy. I can assure you Judy doesn't feel the same way about Abigail. You saw what Judy did to her brother when he was no longer useful to her."

"So, Abigail is in danger." Patricia shook her head, her brows pinched with worry.

"Not as long as she's of value to Judy." Summer looked out the bay window at the yard. "Hmm. It's possible Judy found out about the second journal. That would explain why Judy is chumming up to Abigail."

"But if Abigail is Judy's pawn, why hasn't Abigail given the journal to Judy?" Meredith asked.

Patricia twirled her pen on the table. "Maybe we've underestimated Abigail."

"Girls," Summer said, "I think Patricia's right. I think we've underestimated the supposedly poor widow of Maywood Jackson. We may be dealing with two psychopaths. Two sinister women who have teamed up."

"Teamed up to get Maywood's money," Patricia added.

Summer nodded. "Two dogs. One bone. And if I'm right, and I think I am, by sticking our nose into that dogfight we're going to have to be at the top of our game just to survive. The two are likely to turn on us. And, let me tell you, those two together are significantly more dangerous to us than those two individually."

Patricia's chest tightened. "You said *us*."

"Correct," Summer replied. "Judy's revenge is directed specifically at you. But, to the extent we protect you or block Judy's access to Maywood's money, we all become targets. And Abigail sees us as a threat as well. One of those two, or both, probably poisoned Maywood. They're not going down without a fight. A fight that's likely to become deadly."

Oh Lord. Patricia's hands shook as she reached for her glass of water and scanned the somber faces of her friends. "I'm so very sorry it's come to this. If any of y'all want to drop this case and go into hiding, I certainly understand."

"I'm with you to the end," Meredith said.

"Me too," Timnit echoed. "I've had far worse trying to kick my butt."

"You can count on me," Summer chimed in. "Let's put those two behind bars where they belong."

Patricia's heart pounded with appreciation for their priceless support.

Patricia's phone chimed an incoming text.

C: In place.

PF: Take precautions, Connie. Abigail may be armed and dangerous.

C: Copy that.

Patricia put her phone down. "Lunchtime is coming up. Anyone feel like carryout from Goose Feathers?"

They all gave Patricia their preferences. She notified Simon of their lunch plan, got his order and phoned the order in, requesting home delivery.

"All right," Patricia said. "Since we're not going to walk away from this case, let's get back on the initiative. Any ideas?"

"I think Connie should get into that condo and see if it's currently being lived in and by whom," Meredith said. "From what I know, she certainly has the skills."

"I respectfully disagree," Patricia said. "That space could be equipped with intrusion sensors, cameras or silent alarms that would tipoff Abigail, or possibly Judy, that we've found their new hideout. I suggest we just keep an eye on the place like we're doing. Once we round up Judy and Abigail, we can check the condo out."

"We're making a big assumption the Barnard condo is active," Meredith said.

"Okay," Patricia responded. "How about this? If there is a security system at the condo, there should be some external evidence. Let's have Connie look over the perimeter."

Meredith smiled. "Sounds good."

Patricia punched in Connie's phone number.

"Connie here."

"Would you be willing to covertly check out the condo

perimeter?" Patricia asked. "Specifically, the extent of external security in place."

"Sure. I'll do it right now and call you back."

"Thanks, Connie." Patricia returned her phone to the table. "We need to get back on the phone lead again. Abigail ditched her phone, but she has a new one as far as we know. Timnit, can you get Verizon's records on Abigail's phone? Call history. Contacts. GPS data."

Timnit nodded. "Coming up."

"If Abigail has a new phone and she needs to communicate with Judy, it stands to reason Judy has a new phone too." Patricia turned to Meredith. "What Verizon store did Abigail buy her phone at, Meredith?"

Meredith keyed her computer. "Cellular Sales, Hilton Head Island."

The back of Patricia's neck prickled. So that's what the two were doing in the half hour before leaving the island.

"Meredith, can you check their merchant credit card sales activity and identify transactions they recorded just before and just after Abigail's? It's possible Judy bought a new phone at the same time and place as Abigail."

"Of course." Meredith went to work on the request.

Patricia's phone rang. "It's Connie." Patricia put the call on speaker phone.

"The Barnard building has two external security systems," Connie said. "One is standard. The other is military grade. All the bells and whistles."

Timnit's eyebrows raised. "How did Abigail get military-grade stuff?"

"No idea," Connie said. "Anyway, I didn't go inside for fear of being identified."

"I don't think Abigail or Judy know you," Patricia said.

"I hope not, but I'd rather err on the side of caution. My professional opinion is that whoever goes into that building without prior clearance is going to be identified as a hostile long before they ever get close to Abigail's condo."

Goosebumps prickled on Patricia's arms. "I can't imagine Jackson Capital needing that level of security, Connie. Can you see anything that suggests a need for high security?"

"Ground floor is a Chinese restaurant. The rest of the building looks to be condos. Restaurant is entered through the front. Main entrance for the condos seems to be in the back. Either end of the building has ground-level exits. Probably for fire escape. I'm going to put one of my surveillance nano drones on one of the fourth-floor window ledges and see if I can link to Abigail's Wi-Fi network."

"Okay, Connie," Patricia agreed. "Give us a call if you see Abigail or Judy."

As soon as Patricia ended the call, Timnit spoke up. "Li Construction LLC bought the Barnard Street building five years ago and still owns it. Their LLC registration shows Ken Li as managing member."

Patricia's mouth dropped open. "Small world."

"Isn't that your hairdresser?" Meredith asked.

"Yes," Patricia said. "I know he and his children have other business interests in Savannah, but he has never mentioned a construction business. I always thought his family favored restaurants."

"As Connie said, there is a restaurant there, called The Mandarin Room." Timnit peered at her screen. "According to their website, it's an upscale Asian fusion place. Business license is in the name of Pearl Enterprises LLC. They own four restaurants in Savannah. Managing member is Ken Li."

Patricia nodded. "Ken is quite proud of The Mandarin Room. Apparently, it's well-regarded by visiting Chinese."

Timnit keyed her laptop. "Second floor of the building is home to the Chinese-American Club of Savannah, a non-profit registered to Ken Li."

"That computes," Patricia said. "I've heard Ken is the patriarch of the local Chinese community."

"Condos on third through seventh floors have been sold to some major Savannah corporations," Timnit read off. "The penthouse on the eighth floor is deeded to Li Construction."

"Is that where Ken Li lives?" Summer asked.

Patricia checked her contact file. "Yes."

"Get this," Timnit exclaimed. "According to the architectural plans on file with the city, there's a privately owned subterranean pedestrian passageway from Li's Barnard Street building to the Ellis Square garage."

"Easy come, easy go," Summer said. "And completely beyond Connie's surveillance."

"Where does the passageway terminate in Li's building?" Patricia asked.

"Basement," Timnit replied.

"See if you can get security video from Li's building," Patricia said. "We're looking for Abigail and/or Judy coming and going from the building in the past twenty-four hours."

Patricia's phone rang.

"Hello, Connie. What's up?"

"My nano drone just got zapped," Connie said.

"Not good."

"I'll say. That drone is state of the art. It's supposed to be indifferent to all known countermeasures. Sorry, Patricia. Without the drone, I'm down to my eyes on the place, and because the main condo entrance is on the back of the building, I'm having trouble finding an out-of-sight place to observe from. Whoever put this place together sure knew what they were doing."

"It's worse than that, Connie," Patricia explained. "There's also a subterranean pedestrian passageway to the Ellis Square garage."

"Do you think I should come back?" Connie asked.

"Give us a half hour," Patricia suggested. "Timnit is trying to get security videos."

"Okay."

Patricia thought of calling Ken Li to solicit his assistance, but decided to wait until she had the results of Timnit's search for security videos. Patricia glanced at her wristwatch. "Lunch should be here shortly." She stood and grabbed a pitcher of homemade sweet tea from the fridge.

With the exception of Timnit, the girls cleared their files and laptops from the table.

The Goose Feathers' sandwiches arrived and Simon joined the girls for lunch. Timnit grabbed her sandwich and returned her attention to her search for Li's security videos.

"What are you working on?" Simon asked Timnit.

"Security videos."

"Need any help?"

Timnit shook her head. "Not yet."

Patricia poured iced tea all around, sat and unwrapped her *Barnard Street Club* sandwich, a delicious blend of ham, turkey and swiss cheese on an exquisite baguette.

"Look at that." Summer pointed to the back patio. "You have a pair of cardinals at your water bowl. Did you know they mate for life?"

"I've heard that." Patricia looked out to the patio to see a male cardinal splashing around in the cats' water bowl and a female feeding on the cat kibble. She couldn't see the cats. "Those are the first cardinals I've seen this season."

"It's so kind of you to feed and water them," Summer said.

"Actually, those are the cats' bowls," Patricia corrected.

"You have cats?" Timnit asked between bites. "Outdoor cats."

"They adopted us," Patricia said. "They're at the back door every morning and spend most of their afternoons sleeping on the back doormat. They're cautious around me but allow me to pet their heads."

"Do they have names?" Meredith took a sip of iced tea.

"We haven't got around to that yet," Patricia said.

"I'm in," Timnit shouted. "Oh no." Timnit's fingers pounded on her keyboard. "No. No. Nooo!"

CHAPTER 27

*P*erspiration wet Timnit's brow as she and her security software fought the Barnard Street building's electronic security system. "This one's good," she mumbled as she typed commands at blinding speed. Everyone around Patricia's breakfast table watched in nervous fascination.

"How far?" Simon asked Timnit.

"Just the outer layer," Timnit replied without looking up. "Our software has the virus pretty well isolated but, for some reason, can't seem to kill it. Oops. The virus just mutated."

"Why is Ken Li's system attacking us?" Patricia asked.

"The best defense is a good offense," Timnit answered.

"Why does a sweet, unassuming hairdresser to Savannah's genteel society have an aggressive antihacking system?" Patricia mused. "What's he doing in that building?"

"Is access to your next security layer locked down?" Simon asked.

"Tight as a drum and powered off," Timnit answered.

Simon pointed to a cable connecting two external drives.

"Why's this physical connection still in place?" Simon reached for the cable.

Timnit pushed his hand away. "Leave it connected. It's the honeypot."

"Honeypot?" Summer asked in a soft voice.

"It's a trap for the virus," Simon said. "A huge pool of succulent, but utterly meaningless data designed to attract the virus. Once the virus and its clones move into the data, the electronic door snaps shut behind them and the physical connection is broken, isolating the virus. Well, most of it is isolated, making dealing with the bits and pieces of the remaining intruders an easier task."

"Is it working?" Summer asked.

Simon glanced at Timnit's screen. "Partially. Problem is, not all the virus is going for the phony data. For some reason, the basic virus is mutating outside the trap and just sending mutants into the honeypot. Timnit is trying to isolate the breeder virus, but it's not cooperating."

"Lord have mercy," Patricia said. "Is it going to take your entire system down?"

"So far, it's a standoff," Simon said. "Timnit is throwing everything she has into this battle."

"What happens if she runs out of weapons?" Patricia asked.

Simon interlocked his fingers and flexed them. "Then I get a shot at taming the beast."

Patricia looked into his eyes and saw a quiet confidence she envied. He exuded strength and assurance. He knew what he was doing at each step of the investigation. She was flying on fumes. Maybe someday investigating would be old hat to her as well, but right now she was making it up as she went. Patricia gestured toward Timnit. "How long is this going to take?"

"As long as necessary," Timnit said.

"This virus came from Ken Li's security system?" Patricia asked her.

"It appears so."

"Can he turn it off?"

"He probably has a kill code that's fatal to the virus," Simon said.

"Should I call him?"

Simon paused, apparently mulling the question. Then he took another close look at Timnit's screen and shook his head. "No. Don't call him. Timnit's getting the upper hand. There's no point in tipping off Mr. Li that we were hacking his security system."

"Well, we *are* trying to locate an escaped murderer and her accomplice who might be hiding out in his building." Patricia tilted her head back. "I think he'd help us. He's a good friend."

Simon gave a tight smile. "That's a fact, but it doesn't explain why we didn't ask for his help from the get-go."

"Good point," Patricia acknowledged. "I assume he'll know someone tried to hack his system."

"Most definitely," Simon shot back.

"Well, this is as bad of a twenty-first century social *faux pas* as I've experienced. Will he be able to tell who?"

Simon shook his head. "I don't think so. But there's no guarantee. That virus he's using is extremely advanced. Who knows what other security technology he possesses. The problem I'm having with all this is why does he have this kind of advanced technology in the first place?"

"Me too," Patricia said. "What is Ken Li hiding in there and who is he hiding it from?"

Simon stroked his chin. "I probably should talk to Trey about this because of the advanced nature of the system."

"It wouldn't hurt." Patricia exhaled. "And I will as well tonight."

"Speaking of tonight," Simon said. "Tom Reed of the US Marshals Service wants to come by this afternoon to work out the apprehension of Judy."

"Judy's arrest? I'm cautiously optimistic, but are we ready?" Patricia gestured to the chaos of the files on the table. "I think we should delay."

"That's what I told him." Simon flashed a rare smile. "He said he didn't need much of your time. Just wanted to get a good look at your backyard in the daylight so they could get their logistics set."

Patricia nodded. "In that case, he can come over anytime."

Simon took out his phone. "I'll let him know."

"Got it!" Timnit barked.

Patricia gave a fist pump. "Well done."

"Good work," Simon added as the girls all came over to Timnit to congratulate her.

When everyone had returned to their seats, Timnit lowered the lid to her laptop. "We survived his attack on us. But I can say with certainty we're not hacking into Ken Li's security system today."

"No problem, Timnit." Patricia consulted her notes. "Did you get Abigail's Verizon call history on her new phone?"

Timnit straightened, pulled her laptop to her and flipped the lid back up. "Give me a moment. I've been busy." Timnit typed in some commands. "Yes. Here it is. Just a couple of calls. Two different numbers. Short calls. Less than a minute each. Both in the same timeframe. Then nothing."

"Chances are one of those numbers is for Judy's new phone," Meredith added. "Cellular Sales Hilton Head sold two iPhones this morning. One was Abigail's. I assume the other was Judy's."

"Right on, Meredith," Timnit said. "One of these numbers was activated this morning."

"Did you get a billing address on that number?" Patricia queried.

Timnit swung into action. "The billing address on Judy's phone is the Barnard Street condo."

"Ken Li's building," Simon confirmed.

Patricia stared hard at Simon. "What name is Judy's phone registered under?"

"Abigail's. Same as the first one."

Summer raised her eyebrows. "So, the question is, are they at home or not?" Summer said.

"We're not accessing the security cameras and our drone doesn't work, so how do we get in to find out?" Patricia added.

"If we cover the condo exits thoroughly," Timnit answered, "we don't have to get in. We can just wait for them to come out."

"There are four exits, including the tunnel." Meredith paused as she let that set in. "We could each take an exit and have Timnit stay here on the computer."

"We are dealing with killers," Patricia said.

Meredith patted her purse.

Patricia turned to Simon. "When's the marshal going to be here?"

"He's on the way over."

"Timnit, since you have access to the Ellis Square Garage video system," Patricia said, "can you see if they have a camera covering where the Barnard Street passageway exits into the garage?"

Moments later, Timnit looked up from her computer. "I found a garage camera that includes the door to the passageway. Abigail's Caddy is parked near it. But the orientation of her car is different than earlier. Previously, the car was parked front-first. Now the car is backed in. Someone has driven the car since Abigail first parked it there."

"Run through the archived footage on that camera." Patricia came around to look over Timnit's shoulder. "There. It's Abigail. The time stamp is a half-hour ago. She comes out of the passageway, repositions the car, removes a suitcase from the trunk, then goes back into the passageway. Can you zoom and slow the video to see what passcode she used to open the tunnel door?"

Timnit backed up the video and advanced it slowly.

Patricia made a note of the four-digit passcode.

"Since Abigail took one of Judy's suitcases back to her condo," Summer said, "chances are Judy is there or planning to be there."

"Okay." Patricia returned to her seat. "I'll let Detective Rodriquez know Abigail is at the Barnard Street condo. Timnit, keep an eye on the tunnel door. Meredith and Summer, head over to Barnard and watch each fire exit door. I don't know how long it will take Detective Rodriquez to get a warrant on Abigail, but we want to keep her bottled up until he apprehends her."

THE FRONT DOOR RANG.

Simon went to the front of the house and returned with a somber-faced, middle-aged man with thick, deeply tanned forearms peeking out from his Air Force blue button-down. He had a military buzzcut.

The man took a couple of quick steps toward Patricia and extended his hand. "Tom Reed," he said in a thick swamp drawl. "US Marshals Service. Sorry for the interruption."

She took his hand. "Patricia Falcon."

His shake was firm. His brown eyes firmer.

"Pleased to meet you, Mr. Reed. Would you care for some iced tea?"

"No, thank you."

"How can we help?"

"I just need to look over your backyard. Take some pictures."

She led him to the backdoor and opened it. "Anything in particular you're looking for?"

"No." He stepped outside. When she began to follow him, he held up his hand. "I can take it from here."

She returned to the kitchen table. "That's one serious guy," she said to Timnit.

Timnit nodded. "I'll say."

"I'll be in the dining room," Simon said.

Meredith and Summer put their files and laptops away, said their goodbyes to Timnit and, with Patricia, went to the front door.

"Stay as far away from the Barnard Street building as you can." Patricia released the deadbolt, then opened the door. "We don't want them knowing we have the building under surveillance."

"Understood," Meredith said as she and Summer exited.

Patricia stopped by the dining room, where Simon sat at his security console. Marshal Reed's image filled a couple of monitors. "He's thorough," Simon explained unapologetically.

Patricia watched Reed check corners and nooks behind the bushes. "I sure hope so. What's he doing?"

"Probably looking for the best places to hide when Judy comes into the yard tonight. With the high brick walls surrounding the yard, it's a perfect trap. One way in. One way out. Perfect. She won't stand a chance."

"I can't wait." Patricia rubbed her hands. "You want a refill on that iced tea?"

Simon shook his head. "I'm fine."

Patricia returned to the kitchen.

"All's quiet in the garage," Timnit said.

Patricia sat. "I can't wait until Judy and Abigail are in custody."

"Which one do you think killed Maywood?"

Patricia leaned back in her chair. "It was Judy's poison, so she's at least an accomplice, but either of them could have administered it."

"Speaking of which," Timnit said. "How do you suppose the poison was administered?"

"There were two champagne glasses on the scene." Patricia looked out the window at the treetops against the cloudless blue sky. "Hmm. No one mentioned a champagne bottle on the crime scene. If one wasn't there, the two glasses of champagne might have been filled elsewhere and brought into Maywood's office."

"Which would provide an opportunity for the killer to doctor one of those glasses," Timnit said.

"Precisely."

The back door opened and Marshal Reed, mopping his brow, came in. A blanket of hot, moist air followed him. "I'll take that iced tea now, if it wouldn't trouble you, ma'am."

Patricia poured a glass and handed it to him.

"Thank you kindly." He took a sip, and then another. "Is Simon available?"

Patricia gestured to the hall. "He's in the dining room."

Reed didn't move. "Actually, I'd like to talk with both of you."

"Is it okay if my associate sits in on the conversation?" she asked.

"Certainly." He put his drink on the counter and walked over to Timnit, hand extended. "Marshal Tom Reed."

She scrapped back her chair, stood and took his hand. "Timnit Araya. Pleased to meet you."

"I'll get Simon," Patricia said.

Moments later, she returned with him in tow. While

Simon sat with Timnit and Reed around the table, Patricia refilled glasses, placed the rest of the brownies on the table and sat.

"We plan to apprehend Mrs. Simpson tonight in your backyard," Reed said.

Though Patricia knew that was the plan all along, hearing the words spoken out loud by the marshal gave her much satisfaction. She couldn't wait to have Judy out of her life and to have a modicum of normalcy restored.

"Because Mrs. Simpson is a wanted murderer, we consider her dangerous." Reed scanned his audience, settling his gaze on Patricia. "Therefore, for your safety, we want no one in this house tonight."

Patricia straightened, stifling an objection. She so wanted to witness Judy being taken down, but knew the marshal was right. At the very least, she'd be able to watch a recording on one of Simon's cameras. "What time?"

"As early as possible," Reed said. "But certainly before sunset."

She turned to Simon, who nodded.

Patricia smiled. "We can do that."

Reed stood. "All right then. We'll take it from here."

Patricia, Timnit and Simon stood and Reed shook hands all around.

"I'll show Marshal Reed out," Simon said.

Once Simon and Reed had departed, Patricia turned to Timnit. "Oh my goodness. I forgot to call Detective Rodriquez about Abigail."

Timnit glanced at her monitor. "Her car is still in the garage."

Patricia placed the call. Detective Rodriquez answered on the first ring.

"This is Patricia Falcon. You asked for real-time updates."

"What do you have for me?"

"We're pretty certain we know where Abigail Jackson is," Patricia said with grateful assurance. "Do you have a pen?"

"Go ahead."

She gave him the Barnard Street address and the condo number.

"How do you know she's there?"

"We saw her go into the building less than an hour ago and she hasn't come out," Patricia said.

"Do you have eyes on the building now?"

Patricia looked over at Timnit's monitor. "Yes."

"I'll send someone right over. If she leaves before we get there, let me know."

"Will do," Patricia said. "By the way, there are at least four exits, including a subterranean passageway to the Ellis Square garage."

She heard Rodriquez exhale. "What level in the garage?"

Patricia handed the phone to Timnit, who filled Rodriquez in on the garage details, then returned the phone to Patricia.

"Thank you for the tip, Mrs. Falcon," Rodriquez said.

"You're welcome. By the way, we believe Abigail is with Judy Simpson and is either assisting her or being forced to assist her."

When the call was over, Patricia let out a long breath. "Let's hope that pickup goes smoothly."

Timnit frowned. "You know better than that."

Patricia's mouth went dry. "I sure do."

CHAPTER 28

S eated at the table with her friends, Patricia stared out the kitchen window at the cats sleeping on an afternoon sun-drenched patch of grass just beyond the patio. Not a care in the world.

But Patricia had plenty of cares. For her friends. For herself. Anything could happen during the afternoon at the Barnard Street condo where Abigail and perhaps Judy were hiding. For that matter, anything could happen in her back-yard when the sun went down and Judy came around to retrieve the memory from the listening device. But she and her team had done everything they knew to do to assure their safety. It was now up to the authorities and to fate.

"We have people coming out of the Barnard Street passageway to the garage." Timnit angled her laptop so they could both see. "Civilians. Middle-aged. Well-dressed. Mostly men. Some women. Mainly Asian."

Patricia studied the flow. People were walking normally, saying farewells and moving off-screen as if a business meeting had just broken up. She didn't see Ken Li or anyone she knew among the mix, but the lighting was poor and the milling crowd made it hard to see for sure. Patricia's phone rang. It was Connie. Patricia switched to speakerphone.

"Abigail just left the main exit of Barnard Street with two other women I don't recognize," Connie said. "They got into a late model Volvo. One of the strangers is driving. I'm following as best I can, but they have a good head start on me and traffic is thick."

Patricia's frustration mounted. The idea of losing Abigail in traffic was unacceptable. "Did you get a license number?"

"No," Connie replied. "But I'll try to."

Timnit's fingers tapped at her keyboard. "I just linked to your GPS, Connie. Try to keep up and we'll see where she leads you."

"Great," Connie said. "I'll let you know if anything develops."

"Stay safe," Patricia said before disconnecting the call. She turned to Timnit. "I'll let Detective Rodriquez know." Her call to Rodriquez rolled into voice mail. She called Chief Patrick and explained the situation. He said he'd let Rodriquez know.

Moments later, Rodriquez called. "I understand you have the follow car on GPS?"

"Yes," Patricia replied.

"Can you give me the link?"

Patricia handed the phone to Timnit, who provided Rodriquez the details then returned the phone to Patricia.

"Let your follow car know we'll be tailing the Volvo shortly," Rodriquez said. "And thank you again for your help."

"We make a pretty good team," Patricia said with a lilt.

"It's a real pleasure working with you, Mrs. Falcon."

When the call was over, she turned her attention to Timnit. "Something tells me this is a long way from over."

Timnit smiled. "I was thinking the same thing. What do you want to do about Summer and Meredith?"

"Keep them in place at the Barnard Street building until the police show up."

"Now that Abigail has left, do you think the police will still surveil it?"

Patricia took a moment to consider the alternatives. "Let's keep our people in place. Judy could still be in there."

"Good point. But we have no coverage on the main entrance."

"I'll move Meredith from the side exit to the entrance." Patricia texted Meredith with instructions.

"We've got a lot of balls in the air," Timnit said.

"I'll say. By the way, where's Connie now?"

Timnit studied her screen. "She just made the turn toward Islands Expressway. Heading east."

Patricia dialed Connie. "Do you still have the Volvo in sight?"

"Yes. Barely. Traffic's not cooperating. And the tourists are out in force."

"Detective Rodriquez has your GPS details and is dispatching a car to join the chase." Worry for Connie's safety simmered. "Stay safe."

Connie chuckled. "I kind of enjoy dodging in and out of traffic, but running those red lights is downright sobering. And not exactly helping me keep a low profile."

Patricia's breath caught. "Lord have mercy. You've run red lights today?"

"Just a couple."

Patricia shook her head. No way was catching Abigail worth Connie's life. "I really wish you wouldn't do that, Connie. It's too dangerous. You could kill someone, or yourself."

"I'll be careful, Patricia."

"You do that." Patricia took a deep breath. "And let me

know when Rodriquez's pursuit car shows up." Patricia disconnected the call.

"Trey and I need to go to a hotel for the night," she said to Timnit. "For safety reasons, the marshals don't want anyone here when they apprehend Judy."

"Good luck with that. It's the height of tourist season."

Patricia shrugged. "Doesn't hurt to try."

"And you're overdue for some good luck," Timnit said with a nod.

Luck. Some well-timed luck could really help her investigation, which was mostly built on circumstantial evidence. But, if bad luck occurred, and it certainly did, then why not believe in good luck as well? Patricia picked up her phone and called the general manager of the Hyatt, a close friend they'd used for countless parties over the years. Sure enough, he had a room available, the penthouse, which she quickly snapped up.

Connie called fifteen minutes later. "The Volvo just went into a gated estate on the north end of Tybee Island. Looks like there's some sort of a party or big meeting going on. Lots of security at the gate. I won't be able to crash it."

Losing sight of Abigail was a huge setback. "Any sign of the police?" Patricia asked.

"None what so ever, but they might be using an unmarked car." Connie paused. "I'll stay here in my car on the street until the Volvo comes back out."

"Did you get a license number?"

"Yes." Connie gave Patricia the digits from the license, the color of the Volvo and the street address of the estate, then terminated the call.

Patricia passed the information to Timnit, then dialed Detective Rodriquez. He answered promptly. "Did the car you dispatched get eyes on the Volvo?"

"Yes."

"Then you know the Volvo pulled into a gated estate."

"Yes. We're trying to get a warrant to go in after Mrs. Jackson."

"Do you want me to pull my person off surveillance of the estate?" Patricia asked, pleased that Rodriquez seemed to be on top of things.

"Probably ought to," he said. "She's not going to see anything we don't see."

"Will do," Patricia said. She disconnected the call and sent Connie a text to break off surveillance and head home.

"I've got an ID on the owner of the Volvo," Timnit said. " Hannah Hunter."

Shock sent a chill through Patricia. She had no idea Hannah and Abigail knew each other. Hannah, who had come to Patricia with utter contempt for Maywood Jackson and his corrupt investment scheme, was out partying with Abigail? What was going on? And who was the third woman in the Volvo?

"The party location is owned by Judge Adam Wainright," Timnit added.

The Georgia Supreme Court judge who, along with two others, fronted Jackson Capital? Was this party a wake for Maywood? Patricia was surprised Abigail would have anything to do with any of the operators of Jackson Capital. Unless Abigail was in on Maywood's scheme all along. Patricia stood. "I want to ask Simon something." She went into the dining room.

Simon put down the handgun he was cleaning and looked up.

"Hannah Hunter just chauffeured Abigail to a party at Judge Wainright's estate on Tybee Island. Would you mind digging into their profiles to find out what they might have in common beyond knowing Maywood Jackson?"

Simon tapped his keyboard. "Mrs. Hunter and Judge

Wainright don't show up in my relationship map for Abigail. But Judge Wainright was at Jackson Capital events at the Jackson home and might have had some interaction with Mrs. Jackson during those times."

"How reliable is that mapping software?"

Simon shrugged. "I think it is quite reliable. But I also have plenty of old-school resources to ferret out a relationship, if there is one."

Patricia smiled. There was little that evaded Simon. Sometimes he had to dig deeper and longer, but eventually he'd get the facts.

"When do you want this?" he asked.

"Yesterday."

He chuckled.

Patricia's phone rang as she headed back to the kitchen. It was It was Detective Rodriquez.

"We've run into a problem with the warrant for Mrs. Jackson," he said in a glum voice. "I can't find a judge who'll let us arrest Mrs. Jackson at Judge Wainright's estate. No one will say so, but I think the judges we're talking to are reluctant to disrupt Judge Wainright's party. Talk about an old boy network. No sweat. There's only one exit, so we'll wait out here and pick her up on her way out."

"But you don't have a warrant," Patricia said.

"Trust me. We'll have plenty of probable cause to arrest her and her friends."

"DUI?"

"That if they overconsumed at the party or any number of other offenses. So far we haven't been able to talk to Mrs. Jackson about where she was on the night her husband was poisoned."

"Are you sending officers over to the Barnard Street building to watch the exits for Judy Simpson?"

"They're already in place."

That surprised Patricia. "Even the garage exit?"

"Yes."

"Okay. I'll pull my people off surveillance there. And good luck with Abigail and her companions."

Patricia texted Meredith and Summer that they could stop surveillance and go home. Then she excused Timnit and walked her to the front door. "I'm so impressed with your cyber skills."

"Thank you, Patricia." Timnit flashed a bright smile. "I thought I was done with cyber-sleuthing when I left Cyber Command. To tell you the truth, it's just as much fun operating as a civilian, perhaps more so."

Patricia returned the smile. "You seem to have a passion for it."

"I do." Timnit stepped to Patricia and gave her a warm hug. "Thank you for the opportunity to pursue my passion outside the service."

"It's my pleasure."

Timnit stepped back. "Let me know how tonight goes."

"Will do." Patricia opened the door.

Once Timnit had departed, Patricia went upstairs and packed an overnight bag for her and Trey, then returned to the kitchen and updated her case file.

Around four, Simon came into the kitchen. "Got a minute?"

"Absolutely," she replied.

"Hannah and Abigail have no relationship that I can document other than an abundance of phone calls in the past two weeks, most of which were originated by Abigail. But Abigail seems to have a social relationship with Judge Wainright and his wife. More so with Mrs. Wainright."

CHAPTER 29

*A*round six p.m., Patricia, Trey and Simon left for the Hyatt, where they checked in. To maintain security, they took the hotel freight elevator to the penthouse.

After asking Patricia and Trey to wait in the hall, Simon dropped his bag off at his adjoining room, then escorted them to their suite, where he did a full security sweep before they stepped inside.

Afterward, Simon handed Trey the key card. "Everything's clear," Simon said, then left for his room.

Patricia and Trey deposited their bag in the master bedroom and returned to the living room.

Patricia let out a long breath. By morning, Judy and Abigail would be in jail. For now, it was just her and Trey in a luxurious suite with nothing to do but finally relax and enjoy each other.

"Would you like a drink, Patsy?" Trey asked.

She loved the gentle way he said her name. "Maybe a little champagne."

Trey called room service and arranged to have two splits of champagne and a mini-bottle of single malt scotch delivered to Simon's room, then called Simon to give him a heads-up.

"Why Simon's room?" Patricia asked.

"Security," Trey said. "We'll do the same thing with dinner. If someone means us harm while we're here, they won't have direct access to us when everything goes through Simon."

Trey walked over to her, a mischievous smile on his handsome face. She stepped closer to him, fixed her eyes on his and hugged him to her.

After a minute, she pulled back and looked up at him. "You're the best, Trey," she said softly. "Simply the best."

"You mean the world to me, Patsy."

"Thank you," she murmured.

The entrance bell chimed.

Trey went to the foyer, checked the peephole and opened the door to Simon, who pushed in a cart with the two bottles of champagne in twin chillers, the bottle of scotch, glasses and a crystal bucket of ice.

"Would you care for a drink?" Trey asked him.

"Not while I'm on duty."

"Okay. I'll let you know when we order dinner."

Simon left and Trey wheeled the cart into the living room. He poured a flute of champagne and handed it to Patricia, then he made himself a scotch on the rocks.

They took their drinks out to the terrace overlooking the Savannah River. Sun, low in the western sky, shone on the river, turning it golden. A light breeze took the edge off the lingering late-afternoon heat.

She turned to him, the compassionate man who meant more to her than life itself. The man who fed her soul. "To us," she said, raising her glass.

"To us," he replied.

She took a sip and let the champagne settle on her

tongue, enjoying the effervescence before swallowing. She sighed. Soon this Judy business would be over.

"What do you know about Ken Li?" Patricia asked as she sat on the wicker sofa overlooking the western horizon.

"Nothing, other than he's your hairdresser, and I have him to thank for amplifying your natural beauty." Trey winked.

Patricia smiled at her endearing husband. "Yes. Other than that. Like have you heard about him in the Cotton Coalition context?"

"No. Why?"

"He owns a building on Barnard Street that has highly advanced security."

Trey tapped the side of his crystal. "How advanced?"

"Timnit says his system is the latest military grade. It took down Connie's nano drone, a Black Hawk 8."

Trey's eyes widened. "The eight is supposed to be indestructible."

"That's what Timnit said, but obviously Connie's drone met its match at Li's Barnard Street building." Patricia swirled her champagne. "And when Timnit tried to breach the building's surveillance video system, Li's security software fought back and almost took Timnit's system down."

"That's some serious defense."

"Way too much for a residential building," she said between sips.

"I can look into it," Trey said. "Thanks for the heads-up."

"I don't think I'm going to sleep well tonight."

"It's going to go smoothly, Patsy. The marshals have assigned their best people and have a sound plan for this situation."

"But stuff happens."

"And the marshals plan for contingencies."

"I wish I had your confidence, Trey."

"I asked Chief Patrick to text me as soon as he gets Judy into custody. We can binge watch *Game of Thrones* tonight waiting for the text."

She flashed him a smile. "I'd like that."

Trey finished his scotch and set his glass on the bistro table next to the sofa. "Are you ready for dinner?"

"I am," Patricia said.

Trey went back into the penthouse, returned with the room service menu and handed it to her. They ordered a shrimp and grits each, and a fresh peach cobbler to share. Trey refilled his glass, came to the patio sofa facing the river and sat next to Patricia.

The moment Trey sat, Patricia's cell phone rang. "Detective Rodriquez," Patricia said, her pulse spiking. She set the cell to speakerphone and placed the phone on the table in front of them. "Good evening, Detective," Patricia greeted.

"Evening," came the tinny voice. "We apprehended Mrs. Jackson and her two friends in Mrs. Hunter's car when they left Judge Wainright's party. Unfortunately, one of Mrs. Jackson's companions is a criminal defense attorney, so we didn't get a word out of Mrs. Jackson, and because we didn't have grounds to charge her, we had to release her and her companions."

"What about Judy?" Patricia asked. "Was she with them?"

"No. We don't know where Mrs. Simpson is."

Disappointment soured Patricia. "Where is Abigail now?"

"The three women are in the Volvo, heading back to Savannah."

"You're following them?"

"Yes. We won't harass Mrs. Jackson, but we're keeping our eyes on her."

"This is Trey Falcon, Detective Rodriquez. Do you have a name for the defense attorney?"

"Elizabeth Wainright."

Trey's eyes widened. "Judge Wainright's daughter. She's outstanding. Watch your P's and Q's around her."

"So I've heard, Mr. Falcon."

When the call was over, Patricia stood and paced the terrace. "Why is Abigail with Hannah?"

"That certainly bears looking into. Unfortunately, the two people who could best answer the question are lawyered up."

"It's quite a coincidence that Abigail has a lawyer with her when the police pick her up."

"It's Hannah's car," Trey replied. "Elizabeth could be in town to see Hannah or, more likely, her dad, Judge Wainright."

Patricia returned to the railing, where Trey now stood. "Did you get the results on the cigarette butt DNA?"

"They had a problem with the equipment. We expect results tomorrow morning. By the way, Chief Patrick told me Preston Somerset took a plea deal and is cooperating with the FBI investigation of Jackson Capital. He claims they started out legitimate and provided outstanding returns for initial investors. Word spread, and soon they had more eager investors than rare automobiles. Apparently, that's when Maywood got greedy."

"So Preston is naming those in on the fraud."

Trey nodded. "Every single one. Or so he claims."

"And Preston gets a get-out-of-jail card."

"Not really. He'll probably be disbarred and have to do some prison time, but not nearly as much time as he was facing otherwise."

"How many people were in on the fraud?"

"According to Preston, just him, Maywood and Cotton McNaly, the CPA."

"What did Preston say about Maywood's murder?"

"He says Maywood was alive when he and Cotton left."

"What were they doing at Maywood's house that

afternoon?"

"Apparently, Maywood had heard the report of the raid on Chao Ping Auto and figured Jackson Capital, a big customer of Chao Ping, would be next. He called his boys over to Jackson Capital's offices and together they cleaned all the computers. Then they went to Maywood's home and cleaned everything there."

"What about Maywood's overseas accounts?"

"Preston says they all had overseas accounts. He's turned information on his over to the feds. And, of course, the journal Abigail gave you was a gold mine for the FBI." Trey picked up his scotch. "In retrospect, it's crazy that Abigail gave you the journal."

"Unless she had an ulterior motive for giving it to me."

"What motive?"

"To distract me from suspecting her." Patricia took a sip of champagne. "Any news on the second journal?"

Trey shook his head. "They still haven't found it."

"Abigail?"

"Her attorney isn't going to let her say a word."

"That's a shame."

Trey shrugged. "That's our justice system."

"Who do you think killed Maywood?"

"Whoever gave him that poison."

Patricia chuckled. "Good one."

"The fact it was the same poison Judy used to kill your mother, Judy's brother and to try to kill Beau and you points to her as the murderer." Trey took a sip of scotch. "And the clumsy attempt to frame you with the stolen gun also suggests Judy. But it's all too neat. Using that poison is like putting a neon sign at the crime scene that Judy did it."

"So let's brainstorm other scenarios, however crazy," Patricia said.

"Go ahead."

"Maybe Maywood's murderer is someone with a grudge against Judy. Someone who killed Maywood and then tried to frame Judy."

Trey swirled his scotch. "Maywood provided a car and a condo to Judy and was probably having an affair with her. Abigail could have found out. Being a jealous wife is a good motive. But how would Abigail get your gun?"

"Maybe Judy told her about it. No. That's too much of a stretch. And why would Abigail want to frame me?" Patricia shook her head. "Nothing fits."

"I'm sure Detective Rodriquez will eventually figure out who murdered Maywood. He's got the resources."

"Is the Cotton Coalition working with him?"

"Chief Patrick hasn't asked us to."

"I appreciate all the help you're giving me," she said.

The penthouse doorbell rang. Trey turned toward the sound. "Dinner time."

Trey and Patricia went into the suite. Trey opened the front door. A white-jacketed waiter accompanied by Simon rolled a service cart into the suite and set the dining room table with linen, crystal and silver. "Would you like dinner to be served now?" he asked.

"Please," Trey replied, looking to Simon.

Simon nodded approval. "The food and drink have been checked, sir."

The waiter poured the champagne they'd ordered, then removed the insulated lids from the plated shrimp and grits and placed the plates on the table. "Would you like the cobbler warm or cold?"

"If you don't mind, put it in the refrigerator."

He did, then he and Simon left.

Patricia and Trey sat at the table across from each other, said grace, and dined.

"I've run out of ideas on Maywood's murder," Patricia

said. "How do you do it when all you have are dead ends?"

"You know, Patsy, I'll support you however this case goes, but maybe you should consider leaving this investigation to the police. Murder investigation is dangerous work. I wouldn't know what to do if I lost you."

"I trust the police, but Judy—"

"Judy will be arrested tonight."

"Even so, I can't drop my investigation, Trey. So what do you do when you're not coming up with answers?"

Trey put his fork down. "I can only liken it to my work with the law, but to live positively as a crime fighter long term, you can't let yourself get distracted by frustration. You learn to set aside dead ends and failures. You learn the lessons from the setbacks, but don't let them define you."

She nodded. "I have no idea if I'm failing or succeeding. I still have no idea who did it."

"One rarely does until the end," Trey said. "But don't back off. Just follow the evidence. You're an impressive sleuth. Amazing. You found me when I was kidnapped, remember?"

"Someone, maybe more than one person, knows what happened to Maywood. Abigail has lawyered up, but maybe the US Marshals can get something out of Judy once they apprehend her tonight."

"Even though Judy is the prime suspect, I think you should expand your list of persons of interest," Trey said. "Ask yourself again, who would benefit from Maywood's death? Big investors who stand to lose a fortune?"

"That's a pretty wide net which would include us and most of our friends."

"You never know, Patsy."

"True," she said, thinking about how wrong she'd been about Judy.

"Preston probably invested and he's cooperating," Trey said. "Even if he didn't kill Maywood, maybe he knows something or has a theory of who killed Maywood. How about Cotton McNaly? He probably invested. Then there's Maywood's father. He disapproved of his son. What does he know or suspect about his son's murder? Or Hannah. She came to you and started this whole thing. Maybe she did it for revenge and to help Abigail. The Jacksons' housekeeper might know something. Likewise, their groundskeeper. And even though Abigail is buttoned up, what about her friends?"

"Yeah. Hopefully, it will be over by the morning. But if Judy won't talk, I'll need to speak with all of them. The sooner the better."

"That's my girl."

"Thank you, Trey, for believing in me."

"Feeling better?"

Patricia nodded. "Are you ready for dessert?"

Trey flashed a bright smile. "Yes indeed."

Patricia retrieved the peach cobbler from the refrigerator. "You still want to binge watch *Game of Thrones*?"

"Maybe just one or two episodes."

As they put their dishes on the service cart, Trey came up behind and gave her a delicious cuddle.

She turned in his strong arms. "I love you so much."

He smiled, pulled her closer and kissed her.

The soft, lingering kiss sent a pleasant jolt of excitement through her. Two bowls of cobbler in hand, she led him to the sofa, where they enjoyed dessert, cuddled and watched TV. After an hour, they went to bed.

HOURS LATER, TREY'S PHONE CHIMED AN INCOMING TEXT. Patricia rolled to her side and watched Trey bring the text up.

"The marshals caught the intruder at our house," he said. "And … oh my gosh. It isn't Judy."

CHAPTER 30

*P*atricia blinked in the hotel bedroom darkness, intruded only by the faint blue light from Trey's phone. *Not Judy.* Had Patricia's sleep-muddled brain heard Trey correctly? Of course, she had. He'd said the intruder the marshals had just arrested *wasn't* Judy.

"Who was it?" she asked.

"Hannah Hunter." Trey's deep voice resonated each syllable.

The bedroom air charged. Patricia's skin tingled. She turned on her bedside light, stood on determined legs and came around to his side of the bed.

Trey, seated on the edge of the bed, looked up at her. "What's going in?"

"I have a murder to solve and a fugitive to track down."

"It's two in the morning." He ran his fingers through his unruly hair.

She gave him a pointed look. "I felt so sure it was Judy. I won't sleep a wink now knowing Judy is still out there, and the answer to where she is might be somewhere in my notes. I'll work in the other room. You go back to sleep."

Trey put his phone on the nightstand, covered her hand and gave a squeeze. "We'll order coffee from room service and work together."

She met his eyes. Throughout their years of marriage, this man had always found little ways of conveying his love. The infatuation of her youth was again sustained.

"Together," she said softly. "Bless your heart."

As Patricia showered, she reviewed the situation. Judy was unaccounted for, but they'd made progress. Preston was cooperating with the FBI, Abigail was being watched by the Chatham police, and Hannah had been arrested by the marshals.

Trey was shaving when she stepped out of the shower. "Will the marshals be able to hold Hannah?" she asked him.

"They'll probably turn her over to the Chatham Police, who will charge her with privacy violations and trespassing." Trey got into the shower while she dried her hair and dressed.

Once coffee was delivered, Patricia sat back in her chair at the dining room table, where they'd set up their laptops. "Do you know if Hannah told the marshals anything yet?"

"I don't know." Trey looked up from his laptop. "But with what Hannah has done by illegally recording our conversations and trespassing, she's going to be sitting in jail for a while and that tends to loosen people's tongues."

"Don't forget she has that high-class defense attorney."

Trey dumped sugar in his cup. "Hannah will need the presence of mind to ask to call Elizabeth and to remain silent until the attorney arrives, which, given the time of day, could be a while. If Hannah doesn't ask for an attorney, she's fair game for the authorities."

Patricia reached for her coffee. "What reason would

Hannah have to bug our house unless she's involved in something we're investigating?"

"I agree." Trey blew across the top of his coffee.

"We're only investigating three things: where Hannah's money went, the rare car fraud, and Maywood's murder. Hannah is clearly a victim in the fraud, so my guess is she's somehow involved in Maywood's murder. Assuming she's going to clam up like Abigail, we need to find irrefutable evidence of Hannah's involvement in Maywood's murder before that attorney gets her released on some technicality." Patricia sipped her coffee. "For starters, I'd like to look over whatever evidence the CSIs took from the murder scene."

"I agree, putting another set of eyes on their evidence couldn't hurt. I can talk to Chief Patrick about that." Trey took a sip of coffee. "But remember, he says his investigators haven't found conclusive evidence yet."

"I'd also like to walk through the crime scene."

"Chief Patrick told me his CSIs were done collecting evidence there. I should be able to get you a walk-through before they release the scene. After all, think of how much help you and your team have been to the police. Shouldn't be a problem." Trey grabbed his phone and sent a text.

Patricia pushed her coffee away. "I hate that I've been so wrong about those people."

"Maybe, maybe not. Let the truth be the judge." Trey's phone chimed. He checked the screen. "We have approval to check the crime scene and examine the evidence."

Patricia rubbed her hands together. "Let's get over to Maywood's home and see if the CSIs missed anything."

"Hold on a second. I'll alert Simon. Judy's still unaccounted for."

. . .

On arrival at Maywood's, they identified themselves to the officer sent to meet them and were let into the house. The officer left, and Simon stood guard on the porch.

Patricia and Trey went directly to Maywood's office. Trey pushed the heavy door open and flinched as the lights came on automatically.

As Patricia expected, the room was still in disarray. Oxidized blood splattered the wall and credenza behind Maywood's desk and stained the highbacked chair. Black fingerprint dust coated many surfaces. There was a ragged hole in the drywall where Patricia guessed the CSIs had dug out the slug. Plaster dust littered the credenza below the hole.

She slipped on surgical gloves and started her look-see at the wall furthest from the desk, slowly pacing from one side to the other, taking in everything on the floor below her, on the furniture in her path, on the wall beside her and even the ceiling above. Nothing jumped out at her. She wasn't surprised. Chief Patrick's CSIs had probably done the same thing.

Then she moved a yard closer to the desk and repeated her wall-to-wall survey. This time focusing on the floor, looking for anything out of place. A button. A piece of jewelry. A thread. A scrap of paper. But she found nothing. She continued this methodical wall-to-wall sweeping until her path crossed Maywood's dust-covered conference table and chairs, which she looked over closely. Still nothing. The next sweep covered the guest chair at Maywood's desk and the desk itself.

The fingerprint dust-covered desk was clear of clutter, just as she recalled from her prior visits. She checked beneath the desk and found nothing.

The gruesome credenza and office chair were her final sweep and revealed nothing beyond the obvious.

Then it hit her; the CSIs had found a bullet, but there had been no mention of a corresponding cartridge. She made a note to check with Detective Rodriquez on that. If the expended cartridge wasn't found, someone had had the presence of mind to pick it up before leaving. But why would they do that if they were staging a crime scene to pin on Patricia? Force of habit? Probably.

Her initial search of the study completed, she turned to Trey, who was standing at the door looking at his phone. "Okay, Trey. Let's check the kitchen."

There was fingerprint dust on the kitchen counters, cabinets and refrigerator. Patricia did the same methodical wall-to-wall survey as she'd done in the study. Just as Patricia finished making her final sweep, her peripheral vision caught a shadowy figure in the kitchen doorway to the darkened laundry room. It couldn't be Trey, he was on the other side of the kitchen, no doubt still looking at his cell phone.

Patricia turned toward the figure just in time to see an arm come up with a pistol in hand. "Gun!" she shouted as she dropped behind the kitchen island and pulled her Kimber 45 from her purse. "Trey, where are you?" she shouted.

"On the floor."

"You okay?" she asked.

"Yeah," he responded. "Where's the shooter?"

"Doorway. Across the kitchen from you."

"No one's there," he said.

Gun forward, she stuck her head up. The figure was gone. "There's someone in this house with us, and they're armed."

"Stay down, Patsy. I'm coming to you." Seconds later, gun in hand, Trey settled by her side behind the kitchen island. "Simon's out front." Trey punched in the speed dial. "I'll let him know and have him call for backup. We'll let the pros take care of whoever is in the house, if they're still here."

When Simon answered, Trey gave him the details, told

him precisely where they were, and asked him to activate a quick-response team.

"Whoever it was had their gun aimed right at me," she said trembling with shock.

"Are you okay? What do you remember?"

"One handed," she rattled off.

Trey scowled "Amateur, then."

"Got to be."

"I hate amateurs," Trey said. "They do crazy things." Trey looked at his watch. "First components of the team should be here in five minutes."

A HEAVY FIVE MINUTES LATER, PATRICIA AND TREY HEARD THE quick-response team enter and make their way to the kitchen. One armor-clad member of the team led the couple to the front of the house and out onto to the porch.

Illuminated by a streetlight, three black SUVs sat at the curb behind Trey's Bentley.

"We'll wait in our car," Trey told the responder. "Patsy, I want you to run to the Bentley when I give you the okay. Go around to the driver's side and keep the car between you and the house."

She nodded.

"Go," he shouted, stepping off the porch with the responder and Simon. All three turned toward the house to provide cover fire if necessary.

Patricia dashed for the Bentley, relieved when she finally crouched behind it.

Moments later, Trey was at her side. "Get in the back seat and stay down. Even though we're out of accuracy range for a pistol, no point in taking any chances."

Patricia followed his instructions.

Trey got in the driver's seat and turned toward her. "We should be safe here."

She like the sound of that.

"What exactly did you see in that doorway?" Trey asked her.

Patricia swiped an errant curl of hair out of her face, then racked her brain to pull up the person's image. No such luck. Just a murky gray picture. "A gun coming up at me."

"Right or left hand?"

"Left."

"Which hand did you shoot Judy in?"

"The right."

"Okay," Trey said. "What was the shooter wearing?"

Patricia concentrated harder, willing her mind to hone in on the details, but it was still gray and murky. If only she had a photo. *A photo!* "Trey. The security system. The shooter should be on Maywood's security system."

He shook his head. "The security system is non-functional after they removed the hard drive for forensic analysis."

"Hmm." Resolutely, she drummed her fingers on her thigh. "Do you still have the geo-fence on Maywood's house?"

A broad smile crossed his face. "Yes. I haven't had time to have it taken down."

Patricia was grateful for that. Normally, Trey, a meticulous man, would have had the geo-fence turned off as soon as it was no longer needed. "If the shooter carried a cell phone into the house, we'll have his number."

Trey took out his phone. "I'll ask for a priority on geo-fence data for the past twelve hours." He tapped in a text message. "With any luck, we'll have the data by this afternoon."

Five armored responders exited from the house. Simon

and one of the responders came to the Bentley. Trey powered down the window.

"No one in the house, sir," the responder said.

"Must have gone out the back," Simon said.

"Okay." Trey extended a hand to the responder. "Thanks for the prompt reaction."

Once the responder left, Simon got into the passenger side.

Patricia leaned forward. "So, we're done here. Let's go down to the station so I can look over the evidence the CSIs picked up."

"It's all electronic now." Trey pulled the Bentley from the curb. "Once Chief Patrick gives us the password, you can use your laptop to review the inventory list and hi-res photos of the evidence. No need to go to the station."

"Okay, then let's get that password and head home." She paused as a thought formed. "Does the Jackson home have a tunnel?" She couldn't believe she didn't think of it sooner. Many of the old mansions in Savannah had one.

"I believe Preston said it did," Trey replied.

The person Patricia had just seen with the gun could have escaped using the tunnel. And if that was the case, the would-be shooter must have known the Jackson house pretty darn well.

ONCE HOME, PATRICIA FED THE CATS, THEN BOOTED UP HER laptop and began to review the digital evidence from Maywood's murder, noting there was no pistol cartridge found, a half-full champagne bottle was recovered from the refrigerator with unidentified fingerprints, and a distinctive cabochon ruby earring was found in a crease in the office guest chair. Patricia was pretty sure she recognized the earring, but to be certain she called Meredith.

Meredith answered on the first ring.

"Did I wake you?" Patricia asked.

"No," Meredith replied. "I've been up since four."

Patricia knew that being up early was normal for Meredith, a habitual insomniac. "Do you recall those ruby earrings Hannah wears?"

"Sure do. She always wears them to bridge club."

"Describe them to me."

"Beautiful deep-red ruby cabochons set in gold."

"Bingo."

CHAPTER 31

After talking with Meredith, Patricia, seated at her kitchen table, called Detective Rodriquez. She blew out a short breath while the phone rang and rang.

"Hello," he said in a groggy voice.

"This is Patricia Falcon. Did I wake you?"

"No. I've been up all night processing Mrs. Hunter. How can I help you, Mrs. Falcon?"

"The ruby earring your CSIs found in Maywood's office belongs to Hannah Hunter." Unable to sit still, Patricia stood and paced the kitchen.

"Are you sure?" he asked in a surprisingly clear tone.

"Absolutely sure. It's a family heirloom. Her favorite pair. She wears them all the time."

"We've been wondering about the earring. We even tried DNA but came up blank. Your identification could be the breakthrough we need to crack this case."

Her pulse sped on the news. "Two more things," Patricia said. "One is motive. Did y'all know Hannah asked me to get her money from Maywood after he refused her request for it? She was extremely upset with the man. And two, have you established how the poison was administered to Maywood?"

"We're keeping that detail to ourselves."

Her chest tightened at his refusal. "This is a two-way street. I can better assist you when I have all the facts."

"Well, you *have* been a big help," he said. "I'll check with the chief to see if we can share that detail with you."

"Regardless. If the poison was administered with the champagne…" Patricia paused, letting Rodriquez in on the fact she was fairly certain on the manner of poisoning. "If it was, I suggest checking Mrs. Hunter's fingerprints against the unidentified ones on the champagne bottle."

"You're right," he said. "The poison was mixed with some champagne he drank. We found traces of the poison in one of the champagne glasses we found in his office. We took Mrs. Hunter's prints last night. Checking the champagne prints is one of the next things we're doing. But it's good to see we're thinking along the same lines."

When Patricia put down the phone, she felt far from elated. But she did feel a small bit of satisfaction that she might have helped find a killer. She looked over at Trey, who was still on his own call.

He hung up and turned to Patricia. "The DNA on the cigarette butt from our backyard matches DNA taken from Hannah Hunter this morning."

"Considering Hannah's recent arrest, I can't say I'm surprised." Irritation again rose at Hannah's deception. "But I sure would like to know where Judy is."

"Connie is working on that fulltime and coming up empty-handed. It's possible that once we started closing in on Judy's little band of thieves, she decided to cut her losses and get out of town."

"If she left, then who was the shooter at Maywood's this morning?"

He gave her a thumbs up. "Good point. If the shooter was Judy, I'm sure she was impressed by the speed and size of our quick-response team. She'd be crazy to stick around after that."

Patricia smiled. "She *is* crazy."

"Crazy, but not stupid. I'd bet she's long gone by now."

Patricia nodded. Having Judy elsewhere would be a relief. "Connie says she has notification requests out for anyone traveling from Savannah using Judy's name."

"She wouldn't have to travel under her own name. In fact, with Judy's kind of connections, she could already have a false ID established. Maybe more than one. All she needs is a valid photo ID and money, and she can travel at will in the US."

A chill shuddered through Patricia. "Then how can we track her?"

"Once Judy leaves Savannah, we don't have sufficient resources to track her, but Connie and the SIV do."

"They haven't been very successful."

"We've seen the SIV at work, Patsy. It may take some time, but they'll find Judy."

Patricia let out a long sigh. "Any idea when we'll get that geo-fence data on Maywood's house?"

"It's only been a few hours." Trey picked up his phone. "Give me a moment to check."

Rodriquez called Patricia back. "The prints on the champagne bottle are Mrs. Hunter's."

Oh, Hannah. What did you get yourself into?

"We have a search warrant for her home," Rodriquez continued, "and are on the way there to execute it. Thanks again, Mrs. Falcon."

"No problem." The robo vacuum came into the kitchen.

She raised her feet as it went under her chair. "Incidentally, I noticed your CSIs recovered a bullet from the crime scene but didn't find a corresponding cartridge."

"Really?"

"Yeah. I thought it was strange for a staged crime scene with an automatic pistol. The only reason I could come up with was that the shooter was a person who habitually cleans up. If Hannah fired that gun, she may have inadvertently picked up the cartridge and taken it home with the poison container."

"I'll let our CSIs know. By the way, the public trash can where we found your gun is in a direct path from Mr. Jackson's home to Mrs. Hunter's. Circumstantial, but still significant to the big picture."

After speaking with Rodriquez, Patricia made a fresh pot of coffee, decaf this time, and sliced some fresh peaches.

Trey looked up as she put a small bowl of the peaches beside his laptop.

"Would you like some decaf?" she asked.

"Perfect," he replied with a broad smile.

She took his cup to the sink, dumped the stale coffee, then filled the cup with fresh brew. Trey was halfway through his peaches when she put the cup on the kitchen table.

He gave a smile. "The peaches are great."

"First of the season."

Trey's computer signaled an incoming message. He put his fork down and tapped his keyboard. "The geo-fence data."

Patricia came around him, looked down at his monitor, and saw five phone numbers with the time of day they were first detected at Maywood's and the time they were last detected there. She recognized three of the numbers. Hers, Trey's and Simon's. A fourth number was identified as assigned to the Savannah Police. The fifth number, presumably the shooter's, was at Maywood's when they arrived and departed shortly before them.

"Who is the fifth number registered to?" Patricia twisted her wedding ring on her finger.

Trey narrowed his dark, deep set eyes and scrolled down the email until a female name Patricia didn't recognize came up. *Laura Pringle.*

"Hannah's in jail. Is Laura an alias Judy or Abigail is using?" she asked.

Trey ran a hand through his hair, then looked up at Patricia. "I don't know. It's a T-Mobile account. The phone is on a two-year contract. I'll have Simon request a copy of the photo ID used to set up the account as soon as we get done here."

"And track the phone?" Patricia yawned. Lack of sleep was finally getting to her. She was well and truly drained, but they still had a ton of work to do. She reasoned Trey was tired too, but he wasn't showing it.

Trey scrolled further down to a data table showing recent ping locations for each phone. The fifth phone was pinged leaving Savannah and heading west on I-16 immediately after departing Maywood's. The last ping in the report was thirty minutes old. "I'll have Simon request ongoing tracking of the number," Trey said.

Patricia arched her eyebrows. "The last time we tracked one of Judy's cell numbers, it was a decoy sent to Jacksonville."

Trey brought up the last portion of the email which showed usage details on each of the phones. The fifth phone had been used several times since heading west.

Patricia pointed to the portion of the screen with call detail for the fifth phone. "That phone was primarily calling numbers in the 678 area code."

Trey nodded. "Atlanta."

Patricia flinched at the mention of the city where Hayley attended school. It didn't matter that Hayley was on a summer vacation internship in Tennessee, soon enough she'd be back in Atlanta. A sick feeling rose in Patricia's stomach. "We need to get this information to Connie and the US Marshals."

Trey keyed his keyboard. "I'll forward it to them now, then have Simon get working on the photo ID."

"How long to get the photo ID?" Patricia looked at Trey expectantly. If Judy was carrying that phone, Patricia wanted her apprehended as soon as possible.

He made a sympathetic face. "Shouldn't take long. No more than an hour."

"Thank you for staying home today and working on this with me."

Trey's eyes lit with determination. "I'd like to get this Judy business off your shoulders as soon as possible."

Patricia leaned down and gave him a kiss on the neck. "Timnit is also a whizz with the cyber stuff if you need an extra set of eyes or hands."

Trey stood and scooped her up into a warm hug.

As delicious as being in Trey's arms was, she was troubled that Judy was getting farther away by the minute. Time was precious. Patricia eased back from Trey and looked up into his handsome face.

"If Judy is headed west on I-16, she's in some sort of vehicle. It could be privately owned, but there's an outside chance she used her alias to rent a car or buy a bus ticket."

Trey sat and banged out a message on his laptop. "I'll have Simon contact bus lines and car rental agencies for any transactions under the alias."

Moments later, Simon came into the kitchen with a smile

on his normally stoic face, handed Trey a piece of paper, then left.

Trey glanced at the paper and smiled as well. "The person who bought the fifth phone is Judy. She set up a T-Mobile account a month ago under the Laura Pringle alias and paid with a credit card issued to the same alias."

"Do you have the credit card number?"

Trey pointed to the sheet of paper.

Patricia grabbed her phone. "I'll ask Meredith to track recent transactions on the card." Before she could dial, Patricia received a text from Detective Rodriquez.

ROD: Found poison container with Hunter's fingerprints in her trash.

Patricia gave a fist pump.

PF: Great. We just got info that Judy Simpson is headed west on I-16.

ROD: Vehicle?

PF: Don't know but checking car rental and bus lines.

ROD: Good work. Keep me updated.

Simon returned to the kitchen. "Judy bought a bus ticket for travel today to Atlanta. Same alias and credit card as on the T-Mobile account. The bus left Savannah at six a.m. and arrives in Atlanta at ten thirty."

Patricia's heart raced at the news. "Any scheduled stops?"

"Macon."

"We need to have local authorities meet the bus at Macon and pick up Judy."

"I'm on it," Simon said. "And I'll let the marshals know as well."

Patricia called Rodriquez and filled him in on the latest news on Judy.

"Thank you for the update," Rodriquez said. "I'll follow up with the marshals. And we have good news on Mrs. Hunter. When she was confronted with the overwhelming evidence of her guilt, she and her attorney decided to cooperate with us in order to avoid the death penalty."

Warmth radiated through Patricia's body, as did gratitude for all those who helped to bring Hannah to justice. "Did Hannah say why she killed Maywood?"

"She said she was furious at him for taking all her money. Abigail Jackson stoked that anger and Judy Simpson provided the poison and the plan to frame you. Apparently, it all came together quickly."

Patricia's cheeks flamed. She'd once again been betrayed by a woman she had thought of as a friend. *Hannah.* Patricia knew very well why Judy wanted to frame her. But Abigail? Why did Abigail conspire against her? Or was Patricia simply collateral damage in Abigail's plan to eliminate Maywood?

Just as Patricia was finishing up the Rodriquez call, the television flashed a breaking news update that substantial assets of Jackson Capital had been seized by the Securities and Exchange Commission.

Patricia sat across from Trey and drummed her fingers on the table.

"It's going to be all right, Patsy."

"Will we get our money back?"

"Some. Hard to tell how much."

Patricia let out a long breath. "How about Judy?"

"We lost Judy once," he said. "We're not going to lose her again."

She nodded. "Meredith is watching Judy's credit card transactions. Simon is monitoring Judy's cell use. And we've alerted authorities to meet the bus in Macon. I know this is the best chance we have to get her. But ..."

Trey frowned. "If something is on your mind, share it."

"Judy's smart. She has contacts. She doesn't make mistakes. This is all too neat. I'm worried we're still missing something."

"What?"

"I don't know."

AT EIGHT A.M. THE BUS PULLED INTO THE MACON GREYHOUND Station. Before anyone got off, a uniformed officer boarded the bus in search of a woman matching Judy Simpson's description.

She wasn't on the bus.

CHAPTER 32

Patricia pulled her Escalade to the curb in front of Summer's Jones Street home.

Summer, wearing her armored vest and tactical gear, came out of the house carrying a large Krispy Kreme box. Patricia's mouth salivated at the thought of a fresh, glazed doughnut.

Meredith reached across the backseat and popped the door for Summer, who handed the box to Meredith.

"For me?" Meredith asked.

"You'll have to share," Summer replied cheerfully.

As soon as Summer buckled up, Patricia eased from the curb.

"What are we up to today?" Summer asked.

"We have a pickup on Wilmington Island," Patricia said. "Danielle Pierce."

Timnit reached back and handed the Pierce case file to Summer. "Not a lot of information on Danielle, but we have good photos of her and her spouse."

Summer thumbed through the case file. "Looks like this is our first contact with her."

"Yeah," Timnit said. "An older couple. No criminal records on her spouse or her. Nothing unusual about her medical records. Owner-occupied home. They've lived there for fifteen years."

"Excellent credit history," Meredith added, licking her lips as she passed the doughnut box to the front seat.

"Children?" Summer asked.

"Two adult children living out of state." Timnit took a doughnut. "Do you want a doughnut, Patricia?"

"Yes. Please."

Timnit handed Patricia a glazed doughnut in a paper napkin, then passed the box back to Meredith.

"I saw they just formally charged Hannah with Maywood's murder," Meredith said. "I'm glad to see that case wrapped up."

"Me too," Patricia said, still disturbed by Hannah's betrayal. "And Abigail got picked up by the FBI. Apparently, she's been helping herself to Maywood's ill-gotten gains. When they arrested her, they also found Maywood's second journal with numbers and passwords for many more overseas accounts."

"That man certainly diversified his deposits," Meredith said.

"Everyone thought he was a lavish spender," Patricia said. "When, in fact, he was as stingy as his father. Lucky for his investors. After the government takes their share, the investors stand to eventually get back much of their investment."

"Do you suppose Abigail knew what Maywood was doing?" Timnit wiped her fingers with a napkin.

"As far as I know, she's only been charged with grand theft for cashing out some of Maywood's international accounts," Patricia said. "But I hear the Chatham Police are considering charging her as a coconspirator in Maywood's murder."

"That poor woman can't get a break," Summer said.

"I'll say." Meredith shook her head. "Her anger corroded her."

Summer reached over and patted Meredith hand. "Well said."

"Unfortunately, we still have Judy on the loose." Patricia tightened her hands on the steering wheel.

"I hope we showed her a strong enough front that she has decided not to mess with us," Timnit said. "Hard to tell, though."

Summer spread her arms. "Don't underestimate what we have going on here. Four talented, passionate women. Each entirely different from the others, yet united by a common purpose: justice. Don't get me wrong. We're each flawed. Vulnerable. We occasionally make bad choices. But together? We're remarkable. And resilient. Truly a force to be reckoned with." Summer raised her doughnut. "To us."

The girls echoed the salutation.

"I'm going to miss Connie," Patricia said.

"Once Judy's trail went cold here, she had no choice but to return to the Vatican," Timnit said. "But she told me if we ever need help to just let her know."

"She's a good soul," Summer said. "Speaking of good, your hair looks terrific, Patricia."

"I just got it done." Patricia twisted her head back and forth. "Ken Li is my hairdresser."

"Lucky you," Summer said as she wiped her hands. "Everyone wants an appointment with him."

"I've been going to Ken for years," Patricia said.

"Did you ever find out why his Barnard Street building had all that security?" Timnit asked.

"I asked yesterday. He said it was like that when he

bought it." The GPS signaled their destination. Patricia turned into a driveway and pulled to the front of a large home on the marsh. "Timnit, deploy the drones. Meredith, wait in the car and keep an eye on what the drones see. Timnit, take the right side of the porch. I'll get the left. Summer, you're on the door today. Okay, girls. Let's go!"

THE END

SAVANNAH
Dragon
VIGILANTES FOR JUSTICE ~ BOOK FOUR
ALAN CHAPUT

SAVANNAH DRAGON

Alan Chaput

Vigilantes for Justice Book Four

ONE

Dr. Rebecca Cortez, dressed in hazmat gear, entered the air-pressurized chamber of the Infectious Disease Laboratory in Athens, Georgia fully prepared to test suspect wild bird and sentinel chicken blood samples sent in from all over the state. Of particular concern to her was a blood sample from a Savannah Sparrow that initially tested positive for the highly lethal bird flu strain H5N1 but didn't completely match the three types of the virus normally tested for. She'd start with a more advanced test that would detect ten distinct strains of H5N1. The test was 100% accurate and would reveal results within a few hours.

Two hours later, Dr. Cortez stood in shock as she reviewed the test results for a second time. The sparrow blood didn't match any known H5N1 sequence. Had the strain further mutated? Was *this* mutation the feared 'Disease X' the highly contagious one that would freely spread lethal bird flu to humans? It had a hemagglutinin sequence that was already known to latch onto human trachea tissue. She called her contact at the Centers for Disease Control in Atlanta, who requested a blood sample, then set about to confirm her findings.

Patricia Falcon left the hotel elevator on the sixth floor and walked the hall to the corner suite where Salon Li did business.

As usual, Patricia would be Ken Li's only client tonight, so she wasn't surprised to see the hairdresser's lobby empty. Sometimes Ken would meet her at the door, but usually he would be in the salon making sure everything was perfect for her.

The lights were on in the back, and through the wall of floor to ceiling windows she could see the last remnants of the orange sun on the horizon.

Patricia strode into salon and froze.

Her stomach clenched with nausea.

Ken Li sat, unmoving, in a salon chair. A knife was plunged deep in his chest.

Despite the tingling danger-warnings coursing up her spine, Patricia rushed to him and felt his neck for a pulse. Nothing. His skin wasn't cold, how long did that take anyway? Had it just happened? No sign of a struggle. How long did it take to bleed out? Why is he just sitting here? Smothered? Then stabbed?

Harsh mercury light from overhead lit up his face and glistened on the engraved golden hilt of the knife. Dragons with ruby eyes.

Hands trembling, she pulled her Kimber 45 from her purse, flipped the safety off and scanned the interior. Nothing. Then she grabbed her phone from her purse, called 911 and Trey, then waited.

What did one do in such situations? Her ears prickled at

every sound causing her to flinch and look. A ping as the window glass contracted. Water passing in the pipes.

Gun in hand, she looked around for any obvious evidence of who had murdered her close friend. The distinctive knife was a clue. She took a photo of that. At the front door, she checked for forced entry and found nothing suspicious. Careful not to disturb anything, she went into the kitchenette. All looked in order.

As she was returning to the salon, the overhead lights went out, casting the room in dimness. Hyper-alert, she dropped to a crouch behind a counter.

Was the killer still here? Adrenaline kicked in. Her fear intensified. She had trained repeatedly to fight and to shoot. But there was no way to train to control fear, other than experience. And she was woefully short on experience with killers.

Was this a spring-loaded trap with the killer about to pounce on her at any moment? He wouldn't know she had a gun. He wouldn't be that stupid. He would run ... or would he pounce.

She listened closely. There were no telltale sounds but her heart thudding in her ears and distant sirens. The police? She hoped so. Nothing behind her but a wall. Two workstations to her right and one to her left that she was tucked tight behind. The chair loomed large between her and the rest of the dim, shadowed room.

The distant elevator chimed. Her chest tightened. The killer leaving, or the police coming? She eased up a bit, searching the room with eyes now adjusted to the darkness. Nothing. She had cover behind the workstation and didn't want to move. But sheltering in place could get her killed by a trigger-happy rookie cop. If it was the police arriving, better that she meet them in a well-lit hall. Gun at the ready, Patricia made her way to the lobby and peered down the hall.

Her close friend Chief Patrick, a competent, cautious man, and two middle-aged men in civilian clothes approached. She didn't recognize the other two, but assumed they were detectives. She put her gun on the reception counter and, arms raised, stepped into the hall.

"You can put your hands down, Patricia," the chief said warmly.

"You don't normally respond to 911 calls," she said to the chief.

"We were meeting with the Saint Patrick's Day parade committee downstairs," the chief said, wariness in his eyes. "The 911 operator said there's been a murder. You have a body in there?"

Her pulse raced. "Ken Li, the owner."

"Where?"

"In a chair in the salon." She wrung her hands. "Through the second door. On the right."

"Anyone else in there?"

"Not as far as I know. Though the lights went out a couple of minutes ago."

The chief made a call and told someone to post men at all exits of the building.

The two detectives pulled their weapons and went in.

"What time did you discover the body?"

"Just moments before I called 911."

"We'll get a statement from you, then you can leave."

Ken had children. Fourteen of them. All grown. And a devoted wife. They'd just celebrated their fiftieth wedding anniversary. She took a deep breath. "I know it's your job, but I'd like to come along and be the person who tells Mrs. Li about her husband's death. We're close friends."

Chief Patrick nodded.

As more and more of his investigative team arrived, the hall became her prison. Though her instincts screamed to get out of there, she couldn't leave until they took her statement.

Not long after Patricia rang the Li's doorbell, the red door opened. Cora Li, in a knee-length mint silk dress, stood in the entrance. As always, her grey hair was arranged in a neat bun.

Though it wasn't the Chinese way, Patricia gave Cora a big hug which Cora returned in kind. Cora had graciously accepted most Western customs years ago.

Patricia and the chief followed Cora into the penthouse foyer. An altar with flowers, fruit and joss sticks stood in one corner. Several ancestral photos were on the wall over a shrine beside the altar. Cora had told Patricia who each person was some time ago. Mostly they were Ken's deceased forbears. Patricia shivered at the thought his picture would soon be on the wall of reverence.

"I thought Ken had an appointment with you tonight," Cora said.

Patricia's throat tightened. She took Cora's hand and stroked it. "I ... I'm afraid I have bad news."

Cora brought her other hand to her mouth.

Patricia took a deep breath. "Cora, Ken is," she tensed, "is dea—"

Cora's wail could have been heard in China. Patricia had expected as much, having been with Cora through the loss of her youngest son.

Patricia drew Cora to her as her friend's anguish continued in convulsions, sobs and moans.

After several painful minutes, Cora wiped her eyes. "Wha ... wha ... what happened?"

"Killed," the chief said. "This evening. At the salon."

"How?"

"Stabbed."

Cora's tear-streaked, flushed face went grim. Lips tight. Eyes fiery. Brow furrowed. Rage personified. "Who would do such a thing?"

"We don't know," the chief said.

"Where is my husband? I need to see him."

"His body is still at the salon."

"I need to see him."

"Not now," the chief said. "The body will be taken to the morgue where it will be autopsied. You can view it there."

Cora seemed to understand.

"Would you like me to contact your children?" Patricia said. Cora's children all lived in Savannah.

"Thank you, Patricia. It's best I call them. Would you mind staying until Luke comes? Being the eldest, he'll know what to do. This is all so sudden. So confusing?"

"Yes. Of course."

Cora sniffled, then pulled out her phone and made a sobbing call, entirely in Chinese. As she returned the phone, she looked at Patricia with bloodshot eyes. "Luke is on his way over. He'll handle everything. He's such a strong, honorable man, just like his father." Cora's tone was firm. Her flushed face had morphed from grim to stoic. The matriarch. The dowager. An outward tower of strength. It was as if she'd set aside her anguish in preparation for that of her children.

"I have tea brewing." Cora wiped her eyes with a tissue. "Would you care for some?"

"Yes." Patricia knew it wasn't about the tea. It was about structure. Strength. Ceremony. Something familiar Cora could anchor on.

Cora took a tray with the teapot and cups to a screened veranda. The chief and Patricia sat on the tropical green silk upholstered sofa while Cora poured fragrant jasmine tea from a cast iron pot into delicate blue willow teacups and offered one to Patricia and another to the chief.

In one corner, a bamboo fountain cascaded water into a basin with goldfish. Orchids filled other corners and several tabletops. Cora was the president of the Savannah Orchid Society. Two of Ken's miniature Penjing trees sat atop an ornate teak chest. He called them 'tray scenery'.

Cora sat motionless, staring into the cityscape. A tear escaped and trickled down her pale, flower petal cheek like a dew drop. Despite appearances, reality hung like a shroud. A great man had died. Husband. Father. Civic leader. Close friend for ... oh my, two decades.

The loss was too much. Everything tonight, all her memories of Ken, their shared families, all bombarded her. Feeling light-headed, Patricia brought her hands to her face, and wept.

Cora draped an arm around Patricia's shoulder. "He loved you like a daughter."

Patricia looked up at Cora. Her face was gentle. Her eyes warm. "Who would do something like this?"

Cora's gentleness withered. "*Tong.*"

"There are no Chinese gangs in Savannah."

Cora sighed. Her teacup rattled. "Not yet."

TWO

*P*atricia guided her car down Jones Street, enjoying the familiar rumble of tires on the old cobblestone roadway. Though she'd gotten over her paranoia about killers stalking her long ago, she remained hyper-vigilant. Sound. Touch. Sight. Awareness was now a way of life for her. She noticed things most others missed. Lighted storefronts that were normally dark. Changes in traffic light cycles. Even headlight design.

The use of LED lights to decorate the front end of cars fascinated Patricia and fed her attention to detail. Because each manufacturer tried to make their light displays unique, she'd learned to identify vehicle models at night by their headlight patterns. Borne of hypervigilance and necessity, it was an extremely useful skill she was proud to have.

There were a lot of variables to the LED lights. The angle of the lights. The spacing between the lights. The height from the roadway. The shape of the running lights, and the positions of the yellow corner lights. Together they were as distinctive to Patricia as a human face. She saw them. She knew them. She tracked them.

Like tonight. An Escalade behind her had made every turn she had taken since leaving Cora's and now trailed two cars behind. There had been ... Patricia counted ... four turns.

Who was that behind here? She glanced at her purse on the seat beside here, thankful she had her gun inside. She'd just left a murder scene and now someone was trailing her. *Oh my goodness.*

She called Simon, her part-time bodyguard. He lived close by. "Are you available for an apprehension in front of your condo?" she asked.

"Sure," he said. "What's up?"

"I'm being followed by a stalker in a black Escalade. I want to ID the driver. I'll jam the car up in the traffic in front of your condo. I just need you on the sidewalk as backup. I'll do the talking."

"I'll be right down. A minute or two. That work?"

"Perfect."

Patricia led the Escalade to Simon's heavily congested street.

Simon, dressed in a black hoodie, black tee-shirt, and distressed jeans, was already in front of his building. The hoodie, no doubt, concealed his pistol and armor.

After taking her Kimber 45 from her purse and clipping the holster on her belt, she slowed in the heavy traffic, then jammed the brakes on. Tires squealed. Hers and those behind her. Horns blared.

She flung her door open, stalked to her trunk, removed her black armored vest, and put it on. She checked to make sure Simon was in place on the sidewalk next to the Cadillac, then she strode back to the Escalade.

As she approached the vehicle, she saw the shocked driver, a tough-looking Asian man, and his petite Asian female passenger staring out the windshield at her.

She went to the back of the car and took a photo of the

license plate. With her hand on her gun, she returned to the driver's door, stopping short of it in case the driver decided to swing it open. When she tapped on the dark-tinted side window, the glass descended.

As the window came down, she quickly scanned the occupants, a woman and a man, then the area under their control, everything she could see in the dark interior. No immediate threats.

Both of the driver's hands rested on the steering wheel. The passenger's hands were equally visible. Two half-empty Sentient Bean coffee cups sat in the console cup holders. An open Byrd Cookie Company bag was also on the console. A six pack of Red Bull lay on the backseat.

"You were following me," she said in a commanding voice, then, keeping an eye on the driver's hands, snapped a photo of him.

"Why'd you do that?" said the pug-nosed, round-faced driver in a New York accent.

"I don't like stalkers." She sent the photos to her secure cloud storage.

The passenger, too far away for a decent photo, stared into the distance.

"It's a public road," the driver said, pressing a palm into the steering wheel.

"I'll tell you what, Sherlock. Stalking is generally done in public places, but it's still stalking. I'll be making a police report of this incident. The second time you follow me—"

As soon as the driver's right hand left the steering wheel, she had her gun out and in his face. "Keep your hands in sight."

"You have a permit for that?"

"Sure do."

"Look, lady. This is official business."

"What kind of official?"

"FBI."

Patricia raised her eyebrows. "Why are you following me?"

"Like I said, official business."

"You got ID?"

"That's what I was going to show you before you went crazy on me."

"Open your coat with your right hand."

He rolled his eyes, then pulled his lapel to the side, revealing his shoulder holster.

"Take your ID out with your left hand."

His passenger snorted, her mouth clearly suppressing a laugh.

"Cut it out, Emma," the driver said with more authority than necessary, but without any apparent impact on Emma.

"You're so screwed, Mike," the passenger said and let loose the laugh she'd been struggling to hold.

The driver, Mike, slowly removed an ID case from his inside jacket pocket and flipped it open to reveal an official-looking badge and a photo ID. Unfortunately, the name was Franklin Chow, not Mike.

"This says, Franklin. Who's Mike?"

"I am," the driver said.

"Who's Franklin?"

"That's me, too."

"I'm confused."

"That's the idea," he said. "It's a photo ID. It says FBI. Are you done with us? If so, put that gun away, get back in your car, and go home. And don't make a police report. You won't be seeing us again."

She holstered her gun and took a picture of Franklin's ID.

"Oh no, lady. You shouldn't do that," the driver said in a growl.

"Why not?" Patricia said. "You're stalking me and

claiming to be FBI. You produce a hunk of metal that says FBI and an ID card you probably bought off the Internet. Now let me reiterate how this is going down—"

The passenger's snorting laughter intensified. Tears ran down her flushed cheeks. She slapped the dash. "Mike, you're so screwed. When the station chief gets wind of this, you're gonna end up freezing your butt off in Anchorage."

Patricia glared at the passenger. "I was talking to Franklin. Understand?"

"Sorry," the passenger said, then pressed her lips together. She looked like he was ready to explode.

"Here's how it's going down, Franklin," Patricia said. "I'm making a police report tonight, and I'm sending a formal complaint to your station chief. If you or anyone else from the FBI follows me again, I'll sue you civilly for stalking, harassment and intimidation. And don't try any of that 'official business' stuff on me. If you want to know where I'm going, just ask."

"So, where are you going?"

"Am I under arrest?"

"No."

"Then where I'm going is none of your business."

He glared. "You don't want to talk with me?"

"Not without a lawyer present. And knowing my lawyer, she'd advise me to remain silent."

"Good lawyer."

"*I* think so," Patricia said. "Now you guys take this car back to the motor pool and start working on your explanation for getting caught stalking."

"Anything else?" the driver said with renewed respect lacing his tone.

"I hope the rest of your evening goes better than this."

"Me too," he said grimly. The window went up.

She gave Simon a broad smile and an okay sign.

He went back inside.

When Patricia returned to her car, a policeman was directing traffic around her car. "What have you been up to tonight, Mrs. Falcon?"

"Nothing much, Charlie." She removed her armor. "Sorry for blocking traffic. Just dealing with a stalker."

"Pictures?"

"Sure 'nuff." She threw the armor in the back of the car.

"The chief's gonna love that."

"So is that dude's boss, the FBI station chief."

The officer gave a huge belly laugh.

Patricia climbed into her car, put her gun back in her purse and started the engine.

Charlie stopped the traffic, then waved her into the interval.

There were plenty of cars on the streets. Locals out for dinner in one of the esteemed restaurants in the historic district or after dinner drinks in one of the quiet bars. Tourists were already arriving for Savannah's Saint Patrick's Day festivities, though the half million crush wouldn't peak until ten days or so.

She thought of Ken Li's senseless murder and hoped the chief would quickly bring his killer to justice. And she thought of Cora Li, and prayed God would grant Cora calm in her emotional storm. As concrete as these thoughts were, something else niggled. The 'why' of Ken Li's murder and, equally important, the 'why' of the FBI following her.

She had confidence the chief would get to the 'why' of Ken Li's murder as part of solving the case. She sighed. It would be up to *her* to render the 'why' of the FBI tailing her. The good news was that she'd known Algenon Melfive, the FBI station chief, for a long time. He'd become a good friend and a person she could trust. He'd be frank with her. She'd visit him first thing in the morning.

She spotted Sheila's flower shop. Just a block to go, and she'd be home. Patricia turned right at the corner. Down the cobblestone roadway on the left lay her home, Falcon House, and to the right, Falcon Square. The statue of Moses Falcon and the walkways glowed in soft yellow lighting. The rest of the square was pitch black except for the perimeter of pink azalea bushes illuminated by her headlights.

She pushed the remote control to open the wrought-iron driveway gate and the door to her side of the garage.

She turned into the driveway, her headlights illuminating the ivy-covered brick wall and the open gate, then the open garage. Trey's Bentley was on the other side, as she knew it would be. Still, the sight of his car gave her comfort. It had been a harrowing night.

And, depending on what Algenon could tell her, it could be the start of a harrowing week ... or not.

She turned off her car, grabbed her purse, and stepped into the house. Quiet. Cool air. The familiar smell of Sheila's fresh flowers. Gardenia's this week. The kitchen lights were on.

Home was the one place she could always relax. The place with the one man she could count on to bring her joy.

Patricia found her husband, Trey, sitting in the study. He was still dressed in a dark blue suit, white shirt and blue stripped tie. The table lamp beside him provided the only light. His head was tilted back, resting on the smooth leather of his high-back chair. A book lay open in his lap. Probably another McDonald thriller. Trey's eyes were closed, his shoes were off, and he was softly snoring. He wouldn't be sleeping if he didn't need rest, but if he stayed asleep much longer in that chair his back would be bothering him in the morning.

The grandfather clock in the foyer chimed nine.

She put her mouth close to his ear. "Trey honey, time to go to bed."

No response.

She touched his shoulder. "Bedtime, Trey."

He blinked, then straightened. "Oh. Sorry. Must have dozed off. Have you been home long?"

"Just got in," Patricia said. "How about you?"

He stood and rubbed his eyes. "About half past eight."

She followed him up the stairs and down the hall to their bedroom.

As they entered the bedroom, he asked, "How's Ken?"

"He died tonight."

Trey blinked as though baffled, then walked over and stared at her. His lips quivered. Shock? Disbelief? Denial? Patricia couldn't fathom what was going on in his mind, and he didn't seem ready to say.

He was clearly troubled by Ken's death. He glanced at his watch, then, looked up at her, frowning. "Too late to extend sympathies to Cora."

Such a thoughtful guy. "I already did that."

He stepped into the bathroom.

She put on her sleep shorts and top, then turned down the bed.

A couple of minutes later, he returned to the bedroom in navy blue pajamas. "Too bad this happened right now. Of course, there's never a good time for murder. But, right now the police are preoccupied with preparations for the Saint Patrick's Day festivities. With 400,000 people looking for fun, our overworked detectives aren't going to have sufficient time to dig deeply into Ken's murder until after the parade." He pulled back the sheets and slipped into bed.

An icy chill went through her as she fluffed her pillow and eased into the other side. Why had someone murdered Ken Li? He was a peaceful man who gave generously to all in need. Why would someone want him dead? Weighed down with anxiety, she turned to Trey, who was lying on his back with his eyes closed. "Trey, are there *tong* in Savannah?"

He turned toward her and opened his eyes. "No. Why?"

"Cora intimated *tong* might be coming to Savannah."

He smiled. "She's wrong. If *tong* were trying to get established here, the Cotton Coalition would know, and we would be taking action against them. Mind you, sooner or later they could try, but right now our intelligence says they're concentrating their resources elsewhere."

"Are you positive?"

"Was Cora positive?"

"I didn't ask, but she seemed genuinely concerned."

"Well, if she's concerned, then I am as well. I'll speak with her tomorrow and see what's up." He touched Patricia's cheek and gave her a light kiss. Then he rolled to his back and closed his eyes.

A warm sensation ran over her skin where he'd touched it.

"Thank you, Trey." She turned off the bedroom lights. "Good night."

Trey didn't reply. She could tell by his breathing he was already asleep. He did that a lot.

Unfortunately, vivid images of Ken's bloody body, and a concerned mind full of unanswered questions kept her awake. There was a killer loose in Savannah. If the police didn't have the resources to find Ken's killer, she supposed it wouldn't hurt to give them a hand.

For the rest of the night, she managed to sleep off and on. Once her mind settled, odd sounds kept awakening her. A distant dog bark or a car backfiring would startle her. Then she'd lie there, waiting for another sound, but none came. She'd doze, only to be awakened again ... and again.

End of preview of *Savannah Dragon*
Coming December 2023

Signup for my New Release Newsletter at <u>www. AlanChaput.com</u> for an email notification when *Savannah Dragon* is available.

ACKNOWLEDGMENTS

First and foremost, I'm grateful to you for reading *Savannah Justice* and hope you enjoyed it. You are the reason I write.

Thank you to the reviewers and bloggers who've so generously spread the word about *Savannah Justice* and who've taken the time to give readers an opinion about it.

Thank you to my marvelous wife who has been at my side at each stage of bringing *Savannah Justice* to you. I'm so fortunate to have her support and unconditional love.

Thank you to my wonderful critique partners, Natasha Boyd and Dave McDonald. Their editing, advice and brainstorming helped me eliminate slow or irrelevant passages and challenged me to further strengthen relevant scenes.

Thank you to my friends Greg Sams, who provided me much advice on financial aspects of this story, and Dave Steven, who guided me on the vintage car business.

Thank you to my beta reader, Amy Coury, who read a final draft and pointed out several errors.

And finally, thank you to my editor, Elizabeth A. White, who not only improved my writing, grammar and punctuation, but also fact-checked everything, from law details to all things Savannah.

As you can see, it takes a team to produce a book, and I'm very grateful to be on this one.

Al

DISCUSSION QUESTIONS

1. How does Patricia change in *Savannah Justice*?
2. What is Patricia's biggest challenge in this book?
3. Discuss the relationship between Patricia and Trey.
4. How does Patricia feel about guns?
5. Why does Patricia investigate crimes?
6. What does Patricia fear?
7. If you could ask Patricia one question, what would it be?
8. What do you think about the plot in *Savannah Justice*?
9. Who was your favorite character in this book?
10. What was your favorite scene?
11. What did you like best about *Savannah Justice*?
12. Would you recommend this mystery series to a friend? Why?

Contact Al at al@alchaput.com to set up a time for him to Skype or FaceTime with your book club.

Alan Chaput writes Southern mysteries. His novels have finaled in the Daphne and the Claymore. Al lives with his wife in Coastal South Carolina. When not writing, Al can be found Shag dancing, pursuing genealogy, or interacting on social media.

BOOKS BY ALAN CHAPUT

THE VIGILANTES FOR JUSTICE SERIES

1. *Savannah Sleuth* (published December 2017)
2. *Savannah Secrets* (published April 2018)
3. *Savannah Justice* (published December 2019)
4. *Savannah Dragon* (coming December 2023)
5. *Savannah Med* (coming 2024)
6. *Savannah Christmas* (coming 2025)

ENDNOTE

Thank you for reading *Savannah Justice*. Please consider leaving a review for this book at Goodreads, BookBub and your favorite retailer.

Your review will help other readers decide if they want to read *Savannah Justice*. It's a fact—reviews make a difference. Along with word of mouth, they are the very substance of how authors and books are discovered

Please stay in touch. I love reading your messages and enjoy hearing what you want in future books.

Warmest regards and happy reading,

Al

LET'S STAY IN TOUCH

If you want to keep in touch with me between books, you can find me on social media at these profiles:
INSTAGRAM
GOODREADS
BOOKBUB
FACEBOOK
PINTEREST
TWITTER

And you can find me on the web at: www.AlanChaput.com